LIFE
AFTER
DEATH

Carol Muske-Dukes

LIFE AFTER DEATH

A NOVEL

RANDOM HOUSE

NEW YORK

Library of Congress Cataloging-in-Publication Data
Muske-Dukes, Carol
Life After Death: a novel / Carol Muske-Dukes.—1st ed.
p.   cm.
ISBN 0-375-50515-6
1. Widows—Fiction. 2. Minnesota—Fiction.
3. Mothers and daughters—Fiction. I. Title.
PS3563.U837 A69 2001
813'.54—dc21   00-046893

Random House website address: www.atrandom.com
Printed in the United States of America on acid-free paper
2 4 6 8 9 7 5 3
First Edition

Book design by Victoria Wong

*FOR DAVID, who gave me constant love
and encouragement in writing this book
since 1994—and whom I lost on October 9, 2000*

Between grief and nothingness, I choose grief.
—WILLIAM FAULKNER, *The Wild Palms*

Let be be finale of seem. The only emperor
is the emperor of ice cream.
—WALLACE STEVENS, "The Emperor of Ice Cream"

Aha, she cried, and shook her wooden leg!
—ELSIE K. MUSKE

THE NIGHT BEFORE HE DIED, Russell Schaeffer came into the bedroom where his wife, Boyd, was getting ready to go to sleep. She'd already put Freddy, their small daughter, to bed and kissed Freddy's frog and the sexless, shapeless, nameless creature who attended the frog. Boyd was sitting in front of the triptych mirror, rubbing lotion into the sunburn she'd gotten that afternoon, deep in thought, hardly seeing herself in the mirror.

It had been a hot August day. Now it was one of those white nights peculiar to Minnesota and other northern states: late-season evenings when the summer dark changed texture and the night sky grew light again. Boyd was thinking about how migrating birds died because of these white nights—they thought it was day again and kept flying long past exhaustion, long past the time of safe landings, instinct urging them onward, till they fell. She had read about these birds in one of Russell's poems; now she was wondering if he had made them up.

Russell was a liar—so relaxed and so appealing a liar that his lying seemed less like deception than a kind of good cheer, a revisionist's optimism: Life *should* be the way I'm telling you it is. Let me make it happen for you.

Boyd noticed a moving light reflected in the glass, floating through the sky beyond the open French doors: a plane soundlessly, steadily descending. Then Russell appeared behind her in the mirror, with the plane hanging like a flashing earring just below his left ear. His eyes always shocked her no matter how many times she looked into them. They were a strange color: yellow green. His gaze looked tender, but Boyd suspected it. She suspected that he'd practiced unknotting his tie to get this precise tousled look—she envisioned him leaning close to the mirror mouthing things as he undid the silk: "Hey. Hey, babe."

He started to speak, then stopped. A noise in the street, a car door slamming. He smiled at her again in the mirror, something dawning.

"Hey, babe—the Pizza Boy," he said.

The Pizza Boy was famous in their neighborhood. He always got lost; he never arrived on time. Because he worked for his father, Mr. Kokendorfer, he also never got fired, but the nights that Kokendorfer, Jr., drove, there were no happy delivery customers.

They had grown used to the Pizza Boy arriving an hour late, then tenderly and shyly handing over the large white, shallow box spotted with grease. He would watch, rapt, cheerful, as they lifted the paper lid and peered at the cold, soggy pie.

"I always forget that Laurel doesn't go through," he would sigh, as if the street were fluid. Each time, Boyd drew a map for him. He nodded over it, pocketed it with his consolation tip.

His name was Kyle. He would mouth the street names along with her as they pored over the map. She would recite them aloud and point to them on the map: Montcalm, Locust, Myrtle. Russell and Boyd lived in a big house on Mississippi River Boulevard. The streets around them sounded like a roll call of summer, that cruelly brief season.

Across the room from her, Russell began to imitate the Pizza Boy, picking up Freddy's Twins baseball cap from a low chair, screwing it down on his head like a bottle cap. It was too small for him, it sat off-kilter. He hunkered down, let his jaw drop, and scratched his scalp, pushing back the cap.

"Pepperoni? Yeah, well, it's a little cooled off. Also cool are olive, mushroom, pineapple, Canadian bacon—oh yeah? You ordered goat cheese, porcini, and lutefisk? So what's the diff, man? They're all cool."

Boyd did not react.

Russell grinned, embarrassed, and bowed, then tossed Freddy's cap back on the chair.

"I could get ice cream," he said. "It's not too late."

"It's eleven."

"It's not too late. Not for me. I'm the fuckin' Emperor of Ice Cream."

A breeze picked up outside, leaves cascading over leaves down the boulevard: oak, ash, sycamore. Russell glanced out the window, tugging off his tie, then he snapped it across the room with his left hand. Boyd jumped. There were faint sounds down the street, a door opening a half block away, audible exclamations: The Pizza Boy had landed.

Russell stood at the window, hunching and unhunching his shoulders.

"I found the perfect way to create interest in poetry," he said, turning around. "I walked down Kellogg Boulevard with a bunch of poems in my hand and virtually everyone I met expressed interest in taking one—and in reading it."

"They did?"

"Sure. And of course it didn't hurt that there was a five-dollar bill attached to each one."

"You *paid* people to take your poems?"

"That would be the cynical way to look at it."

"Russell . . ."

"You don't get it. It's a *delivery* system. The combination of poetry and money is irresistible—it's never occurred before. Money creates interest. People think, *Hey, the least I can do is read this thing,* and then—bingo! They're hooked. They say, 'Excuse me, could you tell me if that giant armadillo in the third line is meant to symbolize God?'"

He hunched his shoulders again, smiling down at his feet, thinking.

"It's marketing," he continued. "Poems printed on lottery tickets. There's another idea. People would snap them up. They'd think they were *clues*—and they are! Clues to the big mystery! Forget the sappy haikus on buses next to hemorrhoid ads and quickie divorce attorneys. Forget anthologies in motels next to Gideon Bibles—how depressing is that? Connect poetry to its spiritual enemy, and—"

"Oh shut up."

"What?"

"Just shut up."

———

He shrugged, then turned to her, his face beseeching, exactly like the Pizza Boy's. He picked up a framed photograph of Freddy taken five minutes after she was born. She looked like a baby rabbit, squint-eyed, bluish. He squinted back at it, set it down. Boyd dropped the lotion bottle in the wastebasket—a hint. But Russell wasn't ready to say good night.

"I work!" he cried. "I work in the business my father made. And it's not for me, Boyd. I'm like the Pizza Boy. I get it all wrong at the job."

Boyd laughed. "What bullshit."

"You know that saying about how it's easier for a camel to thread a needle than a rich person?"

"It's *go through* a needle's eye, not thread a needle."

He came up behind her again and stabbed at the V of his un-buttoned shirt. "I *know* that. Do I feel *hot* to you?"

She glanced mildly at his half-bared chest, rising and falling as he panted. He reminded her of a flight attendant offering her peanuts from a tray. She didn't touch him.

He reached out suddenly, his hand hovering at her shoulder. Then he turned and picked up another photograph from the phone table—the two of them on their belated honeymoon in Tahiti—then let it slide from his hand. It hit the floor with a glassy crash.

"What are you doing?"

He picked up the photograph and set it, in its cracked frame, back on the phone table. His face climbed up in the mirror again behind her frowning one, his hair disheveled, his eyes bright.

"You're mad at me, right?"

Boyd flinched as he placed a hand on her sunburned shoulder. She'd been building a city in the sandbox with Freddy in the late afternoon. The setting sun had printed her sundress straps in stark white on her back and shoulders. Russell's hand felt ice-cold. She brushed it away.

"My God. Have you been curled up in the freezer?"

"You're seeing into my future now."

He held up the hand in the mirror, waving at her.

"The unthawable paw of a dead man. What if I told you that I was going to die? That I'd been told I had an incurable disease? Just today? Poor Russell the camel has to try and pass through—"

"Tell me, how many scotches did you manage to get down tonight?"

"Not even one. Not a whiff. I was keynote speaker at the Drug-Free-Today Foundation dinner."

Boyd snorted. "Yeah. And Alice Toklas and I were just sharing a brownie."

Outside, the Pizza Boy slammed his door, revved his engine, turned the truck on a dime, roared away.

Russell began to whistle softly. "Way to have faith in me, babe."

Boyd whirled around. "You left her in the park, *babe*," she cried. "You left her there all alone, *babe*. You drove off and then you couldn't even remember where she was. Jesus fucking Christ, what's the matter with you?"

"What's the matter with *me*?"

"What could possibly be the matter? You left a four-year-old all alone in a city park—hey, I'm delighted. She'll learn to be independent, right? Today you taught her that her own father could let her wander off, maybe get kidnapped, get lost. Then you walk away and you call me and say that you can't remember where you left her!"

"I didn't walk away."

"Russell, don't do this. Thank God someone from the pre-school saw her there all alone and brought her home."

"I didn't walk away. I was too embarrassed to tell you this before, okay? I was inside Sneezy."

"Pardon?"

"Freddy and I were playing hide-and-seek and it was my turn to hide. While she was counting, I tried to climb inside Sneezy. You know those metal statues of Snow White and the Seven Dwarfs? Sneezy is bigger than the others for some reason, and hollow inside. I had to slide in backwards, and my legs stuck out, but I got in. She came looking for me but couldn't find me. She kept running past, so I put my mouth to the inside of Sneezy's metal lips and I yelled, 'Freddy, Freddy!' but she never heard me because Sneezy had just that ACHOO! shape for a mouth and I had to twist around inside to yell out of it."

Boyd curled her fingers, looked at her nails, counted them.

"I thought I heard her go off toward the swings, still calling me, but I'd pretzeled myself in there: I was really stuck. Which is more humiliating, I thought—to be pulled out by the Jaws of Life or a passerby? I started shouting, 'Help! *Help!*' and some people came by and heard me. A little kid piped up: 'Daddy, Daddy—Sneezy just talked to us!' The kid's father came up close and whispered, kind of scared—'Sneezy? Sneezy? Hello?' It took about twenty minutes for the guy to help extricate me. By the time I'd thanked him and his kid and their dog, by the time I raced down to the swings, Fred was gone. That's when I called you, desperate."

"So you were inside Sneezy the Dwarf and you got stuck. That's your excuse?"

"That's right."

"You're lying."

"Boyd, it really hurts me when you . . ."

"No, it really hurts me when you bullshit me, especially about something like this."

"The truth is, I acted without thinking, okay? Like a camel trying to pass through Sneezy."

Boyd turned back to the mirror and waited. Russell wiped the smile off his face, put his hand over his eyes, his shoulders slumped.

"I'm like a guy with an incurable disease. I *am* a guy with an incurable disease."

Boyd stood up very slowly and faced him.

He stopped speaking and waited.

"You have an incurable disease? Don't get cured."

Russell opened his mouth, but she pushed on.

"I'd prefer you dead. Throw yourself out that window, for God's sake. Swallow some pills! You think I'm joking? You left her in the park? You went off somewhere. You got a goddam drink! I don't want to listen to you anymore. Do me a favor, Russell. Die."

The words did not reverberate. No lightning bolt struck. The Pizza Boy roared by a second time—he was lost again—and down the hall, Freddy cried out in her sleep. Russell smiled at her, a very slow smile. Then he touched her at last, on the cheek, briefly, with his icy hand. And before she could get her breath, he was gone.

PART
ONE

CHAPTER 1

P RISCILLA SOUKPUN COMES IN with Will's mail while he
is on the phone with his mother. Priscilla is beautiful:
heart-shaped face, a solid curtain of jet-black razor-cut
hair down her back—a Laotian girl, Hmong, of the Boat People who arrived in Minnesota in the wake of the Vietnam War.
The church groups that had sponsored them welcomed them—
and the Hmong settled in, opened restaurants and flower
shops, but did not assimilate easily. But Priscilla is different:
young, Americanized, modish in her short skirts and bangles.
Her quick fingers are delicate, each one circled in a thin gold
ring. Will notices this as she sorts envelopes. *She is like the girl
in "The River Merchant's Wife,"* he thinks. He's heard the poem
read recently, read by a Bereaved lover, with a mixture
of depthless sorrow and heroic restraint. Priscilla's hair is cut
straight across her forehead, like the girl's in the poem, and he
can sense in her the timeless passion of the poem's narrator.
If local people resent the Hmong, it is because of their close-

knittedness, Will thinks, or their melodious liquid tongue. He thinks of heavy-breathing Swedes playing hockey and smiles gratefully at Priscilla over the receiver. She has come to him from the Pre-Need department, because his mail often gets mixed up with theirs and vice versa. In a business built on euphemism, "Pre-Need" would stand, more or less, for "still breathing." Priscilla counsels individuals and families on burial versus cremation, purchase of family plots, lawn crypts, or mausoleums, and financing for these various options.

He hangs up, and Priscilla gestures toward the phone. "Your mother."

"My mother. Absolutely right."

He makes a face and Priscilla laughs.

"She wants chamber music played all over, not just at wakes. In the casket-selection rooms, the viewing rooms. It's touchy. Most people don't want too-serious music, you know. They want a little subdued Catholic doo-wop or elderly Lutheran Shepherd with flute."

He stands up, mimes playing a flute, swivels his hips. Priscilla's eyes narrow as she checks out his hips.

"Get some respect. Your mother is right. Waxy flowers on the coffin, creepy organ tunes. People need something better at funerals. They don't need to hear Elton John."

She turns away, busying herself with the mail. *Elton John*, he thinks, and he sits down, chastened. He stares at Priscilla's bent back. He's running four mortuaries now—all offshoots of his father's original Highland Park trunk business, where he keeps his office. The branch mortuaries, scattered across the Twin Cities and suburbs, each boast an executive manager: Not one is a woman. He glances at Priscilla again, abruptly envisions a black camisole.

He imagines Priscilla advising her Pre-Need customers in the black camisole, which shimmers, turns to the smoky embroidered silks of her country, veils that drop one by one, revealing her small, golden breasts. She opens the lid of a black lacquer box and waves away red opium smoke, smiles into the faces of the large-boned, sensible folk who have come to talk about the storage or disposal of their enormous dead bodies. She claps her hands and fields of flickering red petals turn to a blue rain of poppy seeds and diamonds—she dances naked against a backdrop of mountains in Lan-Xang, land of a million elephants. But then she vanishes: Will is back in the diminished atmosphere of Pre-Needs. Here, the living hurry to purchase the pay-by-the-month La-Z-Boy death lounger, the faux-Hellenic vault, the *Star Trek* sepulchre (the lost one is beamed up on a video screen)—padding the threshold to the afterlife.

Much to his dismay, he has just now seen his own future in the death industry right in front of him, on his own desk: a glossy stock brochure and prospectus. Here is a huge conglomerate trying to buy up all the mom-and-pop funeral homes, of which his holdings are an example. How does one repel the advances of these sharks? They blow into town, buy everything up, consolidate the services (no more in-house embalmers), and then raise prices. Astronomically. They're doing it all over the country and Will feels overtaken, feels the heavy breath of the inevitable on his neck. Take the money and run, a hot voice, the voice of the camisole, cries within him. He thinks of his mother again, how she's slowly lost touch since his father died, how she hoards food and talks to herself. *Take the money and run,* he thinks. How much time do any of us have? Let Mega-Death bury the dead.

Priscilla smiles at him again as she leaves. A flower grows up inside him, its perfect blossom her naked body, but it hasn't the same power over him now. His thoughtful assessing gaze wraps about many breasts, many legs, but his heart is not engaged. Will is weeks away from forty, unmarried, though he has come close.

He comes close to people, swerves away. Perhaps it's because of the false intimacy of his job. He's not close to anyone, really, though he has many friends. He doesn't call to mind the spooky cliché of a funeral director—he's tall, athletic-looking, was a hockey player in college. His boyish face has stayed boyish, his longish hair in its gentleman's ponytail is darker now, his blond mustache combed neatly. His slightly unexpected appearance endears him to people. Of course he's been told that he has a haunted look—meaning, he supposes, that no matter how un-threatening his aspect, he could suddenly *turn,* reveal a pair of fangs, red-laser eyes. Will pushes aside the stock brochures im-patiently. *Haunted? Of course I'm haunted, I bury the dead. I sell eternal resting compartments to the dead. The dead come to me to get out of this world with a little dignity. I shake hands with the dead every day.*

People offer their suffering to him and he orchestrates it. "Don't cry," he whispers, and hands them tissues. "Try to for-get," he murmurs, and produces a Memory Book. He signals for his salesmen, never shadowy—attractive, rather, and tran-scendentally attentive, capable of producing everything from monogrammed pillows to musical caskets to audio-video–screen grave markers to Aladdin urns for ashes. Will appears at the right moment to shake the hands of the Bereaved. He knows who has sustained the real injury here (not the dead; never the noncommittal dead!), and when he shakes the hands of the survivors, the left-behinds, he meets their stricken, inquiring eyes head-on.

Loosening his tie, he glances into the mirror over the wet bar. He might be a young husband in a framed portrait, a photo set on a mantel above a fire. He wants, he thinks, nothing less than the love of all time, a River Merchant's Wife kind of love: dust mingled together forever and forever. But his life is Pre-Need: expectation, then nothing.

THE OUTER OFFICE buzzes him. The female head of the Schaeffer family is on the phone. Their youngest son dropped dead very early this morning on the tennis court. Heart attack, forty-two years old. Will had heard it on the car radio, driving to work. He had been expecting this call.

"Mrs. Schaeffer?"

The voice is cultured, controlled. Gerda Schaeffer is a woman in her seventies but very much in charge of the Schaeffer family fortune, which was made in real estate by her late husband. Now the family owns everything from a chicken-and-biscuit chain to property-management companies; they are a mini-conglomerate. Will detects a slight crack in the façade of her voice, but then she recovers. Will has gotten to know Gerda a little over these last years. As a wealthy young bachelor, a desir-able guest, he's often invited now to black-tie fund-raisers and chic dinner parties.

He keeps his tone reserved but concerned as they discuss arrangements to deliver the body, the death certificate, the date and size of the wake, the funeral, who will officiate, problems with the press. Mrs. Schaeffer tells Will that her newly widowed daughter-in-law will visit him soon to go over some "readings" for the funeral ceremony.

"It's not necessary," says Will firmly. "Not at a time like this. I'll send someone to her when you feel it's the right moment."

"It's probably better if Boyd comes to you, if you could help guide her in her selection. Do you know what I mean? Give her a couple of days, and she'll be there."

"Certainly." Will grimaces, glancing at his calendar. "What-ever you think makes sense."

Two days later, Boyd Schaeffer sits across from him in one of the four overstuffed parlor chairs he keeps rearranging, trying to anticipate the seating preferences of his visitors. She is saying nothing at all. She is around his age, maybe younger, or a little older; he can't tell. She wears her dark red hair, the color of cin-namon, pulled back and held by a silver clip, a bird in flight, and she is dressed in a pale summer-weight tailored suit. Will waits for any acknowledgment of his presence, but there is none. She appears lost in thought, her eyes on her feet.

Will decides, staring at her, that she is secretly annoyed, or (he relents, knowing what he knows) she may be just uncom-fortable and awkward, like a root-canal patient in a dentist's waiting room. He has offered her coffee, tea, bottled water—he even indicates the box of tissues placed discreetly on an end table by her chair, though she has shown no sign of tears. He tries again.

"You're sure I can't get you anything?"

She looks up finally. Her eyes are gray and clear but ringed with darkness.

"To tell you the truth, I'd like a drink. I walked a long time before coming here. I'm thirsty. Do you have any scotch?"

Will gets up. "Absolutely."

He comes back with her drink in a cut-glass tumbler. She accepts it without a smile and drinks a little. She stares at him, still saying nothing.

Will is starting to get restless. He glances surreptitiously at his watch: He's due downtown soon for a meeting. He clears his throat.

"You know, I met your . . . late husband a few times. We played handball together at the Athletic Club. Shot some hoop. Really a fine guy and—"

"A fine guy?"

"I beg your pardon?"

She swallows more scotch. "Just your choice of words. A fine guy. I'm always hearing Russell described like that. A fine guy."

She sighs and twirls the ice in her glass. Will, stung, thinks he recognizes the gesture from bad movies. Her obviousness irritates him. Will has observed people react to death and the grief of death in many different ways sitting in the chair opposite him—he knows a phony when he sees one. He believes she probably feels something but needs to hide it. Or, he realizes, stung deeper, she may feel nothing, feel no obligation to even bother faking grief in front of him—a mere undertaker, invisible attendant, hired opinion.

She looks straight at him and, as if he's read her mind, says, "Form's rather important here, isn't it? And I've been sitting here trying to feel something for him, trying to look as if I feel something."

"What I'm thinking is that you're really . . . upset."

"Why? Why do you say I'm upset? Because I implied my dead husband was not a fine guy? Or because I'm not acting upset?"

She laughs. Her laugh reminds Will of something, he can't place it. She puts a hand over her eye and shakes her head. "Jesus."

She finishes the drink and holds out the glass to him. He gets up and gets her another, worried.

"This is weird," she says. "I don't even like scotch. My husband . . . it was *his* drink."

"Why do you want to put together readings for the funeral if you . . . feel like this?"

She crosses and uncrosses her legs. Her hosiery makes a soft sound. Will feels the hairs on his neck stand up.

"I suppose you'd say my mother-in-law is trying to help me make sense of something that doesn't."

"Make sense?"

"Yes. No. *No* death makes sense, I suppose. Though look at all this *stuff*. It's supposed to what—*structure* the experience?"

She takes sweeping aim at Will's carefully designed grieving space with her clinking glass.

"I mean, all these . . . picture books and albums—it's worse than a wedding! Do people come in here and actually *cry* in front of you? And sign Memory Books? It's so ironic, because this is just the kind of weird thing that Russell loved."

"I'm sorry. You lost me."

"My husband, Russell. He loved . . . what nobody else loved."

Will glances slowly around the room at the weird things no one loved.

"The thing is," she says, "I should be feeling guilt. Russell made up a hypothetical death for himself, and I suggested he make it happen. The death."

She leans forward, glaring. "I told him to die, do you see? And he died. He *died*."

Here, at last, is familiar ground. But before Will can launch into his list of Reasons Why We Feel Guilty, she interrupts him.

"I hate him more for *that* than anything."

She's going to tell me that he beat her, Will thinks, or that he cheated on her. But she does not. Instead, she tugs at a strand of hair and smiles oddly at him.

"I'm a doctor," she says. "I'm an M.D., but I've never practiced. Well, except for a year in a women's clinic. In New York, before I graduated."

Will turns his head away, then looks back at her, startled, feeling suddenly like an amnesiac who's just remembered something important, a key clue to his past.

"I used to live in Philadelphia. I was trained as an architect—before I came back here and took over my dad's business."

She stares at him, hiccups very softly.

"I once designed"—he shakes his head and laughs—"a customized kennel. My client, a dog breeder, didn't like it because he thought it was too futuristic. You know, dogs-in-geodesic-domes kind of thing. Beagles in yurts."

She stares at him. "I don't even know what a yurt looks like," she says softly. "I used to know."

She hiccups again. Will sighs, sure she is making fun of him.

"I didn't practice medicine because I got married. You could say it was a whirlwind romance, but it was not a whirlwind romance. It was more like wind shear."

She laughs, a surprisingly sharp-edged laugh, like a bark. The ice in the scotch glass clinks as she lifts it.

Will laughs a little, too—guardedly. He's losing control of the situation, he thinks. He is feeling a strong desire to confide in a Bereaved. He is feeling impulsive toward a Bereaved.

"The thing about the geodesic dome was, the dogs really liked it. Dogs love polygons, did you know that?"

"No."

"Dogs respond to shapes. If you want your dog to go to the bathroom, walk him around in a figure eight."

"I don't have a dog. My mother-in-law has one. I'll pass the information along to her. Listen, I think I'll just read Keats."

Will panics momentarily, thinking that for some reason she wants a book immediately—one that he doesn't happen to have on hand. Then he realizes that she's talking about the funeral.

"Russ, my husband, loved Keats. He read poetry, he even wrote a little—did you know that? Did he mention that during your handball game?"

"No, he didn't."

She straightens up, smiling down at her drink, balancing it on her knee.

"Of course he didn't. Did you know that Keats was a doctor, a surgeon? He diagnosed his own TB by the color of the blood he coughed up. It was arterial. I wonder, have you ever seen the sketch Keats's friend Severn made of him as he lay dying? In that little room on the Spanish Steps? He looks as if he has already entered the other world, except for his skin, the sweat, which is pouring from him."

Will shakes his head, staring at her.

"Well, it's devastating to look at. He looks human—unlike the other portraits of him, which make him look like Barry Manilow."

Will coughs into his hand, a half laugh.

"Russell kept that sketch above his desk. I've been meaning to ask you . . . the girl's photograph on your desk, with the Keats quote . . ."

"My sister," he says without thinking.

"Your sister?"

A sound like wind rises in his ears and he shakes his head.

"My twin. She died when we . . . when I was fourteen, almost fifteen." He pauses. "A sledding accident."

"You're a twin?"

"We *were* fraternal twins. Two different eggs. Brother, sister. We were not exactly alike."

"I *know* the difference. And you're still connected, aren't you?"

She leans forward, bending at the waist, peering at him, then sips her drink again. Her face is growing a little flushed.

"I don't know what you mean." He looks around him, as if the coyly lugubrious setting, the ponderous chairs, the wallpaper, the framed degress, clarified the single incontrovertible fact forever. "She's dead."

He gets to his feet, troubled. She stands, too, facing him. She is very close. He can see the black dots in the clear irises of her eyes, feel her ragged breath. He takes an unsteady step backward. She's shorter by an inch, but her eyes are locked directly on his.

She nods, quoting a little drunkenly, " 'Darkling, I listen and for many a time / I've been half in love with easeful Death.' "

Will points into the air as if he were seeing the words floating there.

"I picked that quote out. For her. For her headstone."

A sense of recklessness overcomes him.

"She was headstrong—a tomboy. A powerful figure."

He laughs, astonished at himself. Has he lost his mind?

"Russell was a powerful figure, too. He was manic, constantly inventing little dramas. It was like being married to Robin Williams. And you know what? I can't *bear* Robin Williams."

They stand, a few feet apart. Phones ring in the outer office. Boyd laughs her bark-like laugh, shaking her head.

"The thing is, Russell was interested in being wonderful. He just couldn't stop being wonderful. It was terrifying. He needed to seem happy all the time. Even being married to *me*, someone who did not share his worldview, didn't faze him."

She hiccups again, nods to herself.

Will looks at his hands, then clasps them behind him, turns away from her, hating himself for showing his stirred emotions. He walks to the big double-glazed windows and looks out at the summer trees.

"Then Keats is the decision? We'll read Keats?"

"Keats," he repeats, his voice steady. "That's a very good idea." Then he says, as if tasting the word, "Wonderful."

He stares out across the green lawn to the apron of concrete driveway in front of the garage, where two of his fleet of five funeral cars are parked. Both of them, black Cadillacs (he also owns a hearse and two customized minivans in dark gray), gleam darkly at the curb. He watches one pull out—slowly, ponderously—and drive off.

Somewhere behind him, he hears her put down the glass. Hears her cough politely over a hiccup. Then she stands beside him and he glances at her. She looks happy now, he thinks. She smiles, as if she'd heard him speak, then throws her arms wide. He knows what she is going to say before she says it—it was something his dead sister, Signe, always said.

"Ah, Nature," she cries. "I hate it."

Will turns and stares at her. She smiles at him again.

"I believe I get *a break* at a time like this, don't I? I am a survivor, whatever that means. Although maybe"—she glances sideways, off-kilter, at him—"*you* do. You know what that means, perhaps, Dr. Death?"

"No," he says, not quite loud enough to be heard. "I don't know. I do not know."

But when he turns, she has picked up her bag. She is gone.

CHAPTER 2

THE DOCTOR HAS GIVEN HER a tranquilizer, but Boyd cannot relax. She sets the clear plastic pill bottle carefully on the marble counter in the bathroom. It's early evening, and her four-and-a-half-year-old daughter, Freddy, has been asleep for a couple of hours, having asked, uncharacteristically, right after dinner, to be put to bed. Since her father's death, she's been sleepy all the time, wanting to curl up in her bed and drift off, away from the unpredictable present.

Boyd crosses the hall to the playroom, presses the light switch, blinks at the lit room's aggressive panorama of color and narrative. A mural of *The Wind in the Willows* blithely travels the walls: Frogs in open motorcars bounce jauntily past animated trees on the way to Toad Hall; mobiles spin from light fixtures, Euclidean shapes and galaxies casting their meaningful shadows. A blue mermaid in a glittering bra, her gaze jaded as a hooker's, stares from a corner. Boyd begins picking up toys. She stacks blocks, tosses balls and furry shapes into the enormous gaping mouth of the bright green hippopotamus toy chest; she lifts two tiny plastic figures, a married couple, from their gold convertible, jackknifed against the hippo's green molded foot. She unbends the stiff plastic legs and returns the couple to the dollhouse, to their bedroom, where they stand, facing each other, dazed, next to the four-poster canopied bed. She, Brenda, wears a tartan plaid miniskirt with fringe; he, Norman, wears a Hugh Hefnerish smoking jacket, and a pipe juts from his thin lips. Boyd parks the convertible on the dollhouse roof, near the satellite dish. Then she retrieves a pot of rainbow Play-Doh that has rolled, spilling, across the floor, and lifts a corner of the Winnie-the-Pooh rug, searching halfheartedly for the pot's missing lid. She feels herself drawn back irresistibly to the dollhouse. She reaches into the bedroom, plucks up Norman, and transfers him to the pink bathroom, where she upends him in the tiny toilet. He is submerged up to his shoulders, but his arms remain flat at his sides, his legs locked together, straight up, feet flat, as if he's standing at attention, smoking his pipe upside down, experiencing a reflective moment in the john. Brenda is deposited in the laundry room, on her back atop the ironing board, her arms lifted as if she were belting out an aria.

The adventures of Brenda and Norman are part of an ongoing dollhouse drama that Boyd has found herself composing with Freddy. The idea of it both frightens and delights her. Something, not exactly a story, unfolds step-by-step as Freddy positions Norman maniacally jockeying a speedboat in the attic or Boyd balances a chandelier on Brenda's head as she kicks up her heels alone, debauched in the den. It's fun, Freddy says, to let them do "tricks."

Has a marriage counselor pointed out the obvious—that these tableaux reflect the drama of a troubled marriage? "Yes," Boyd says aloud to herself. "Yes, you moron." But she won't tell Freddy to stop. Nor will she stop. All her life Boyd has had trouble stopping, except for once.

How many people have screamed "Drop dead," or "Die and get it over with!"? How many husbands and wives have imagined, have hoped for, prayed for, the car crash, the backward, arm-flapping drunken fall down the cellar steps, the chunk of masonry plummeting earthward as the front door slams emphatically shut? But how many who have imagined such things, and even articulated them, have picked up the telephone and heard the words that stop time? How many have turned into the driveway and parked behind the paramedic's van, its blue-and-amber lights flashing, and seen the one so recently commanded to die lying on the ground, dying or already dead in the grass, strange people and machinery attending him? Dead eyes locked on the eyes of the one who shouted, "Die—just die, will you?"

She sits down wearily in a red child-sized chair at a low red table covered with brightly colored palm trees made of Play-Doh: orange fronds, purple trunks. As she nods at the palm trees, slowly bending forward, questions dart around in her head like Freddy's goldfish in the aquarium across the room. She sleeps, bowing to the palms. At a touch on her shoulder she rockets up from the chair, stumbling backward as the chair tips and clatters behind her.

"Boyd—dear Lord," cries Gerda. "I'm so sorry. I was trying to wake you gently."

Boyd blinks rapidly, shakes herself, sets the chair back in place.

"No one can wake me gently. I'm like a goddam bomb ticking."

"How about some tea? I'll go make you some."

"No, Gerda. No thanks, really."

Gerda, dressed in a black cotton sweatshirt and slacks, her thick white hair swept back and regally pinned, waves Boyd back into her chair, then lowers herself carefully into the seat across from her. She wears makeup, which is unusual for her. Boyd notices that despite the gray eye shadow and mascara, her eyes are weary.

"How long have you been up now?"

"I will sleep, Gerda. When I get tired enough."

"You need to stop thinking for a while."

Boyd's arm shoots out, leveling the colored Play-Doh trees. Gerda, startled, jumps back in her chair. Boyd brushes the dough into a container.

"It's okay. Freddy said this was okay. And are *you* taking it easy? Why did you drive all the way over here when you should have been drinking your tea and sleeping?"

Gerda shakes her head. "How's Freddy?"

"Asleep. Oh God—remind me to take Norman out of the toilet and Brenda off the ironing board before she sees them."

Gerda stares at her.

"The dollhouse. I was improvising with the dolls. Does it seem really hot in here to you?"

"Did Janicek give you something?"

"I don't know. Yeah. Something to knock me out."

She leans forward, pursing her lips, blows colored crumbs off the table. She spies the lid at last, upended against a pile of picture books. As she bends to recover it, she shakes herself like a wet dog, then grimaces over her shoulder at Gerda.

"It didn't work."

The lid pops onto the can.

"He left Freddy in the park—did I tell you this? He couldn't remember where he'd left her. He said that—'I can't remember where I left her.' One of the mothers from her preschool recognized her, saw her swinging all by herself, and brought her home. Freddy told me they'd been playing hide-and-seek."

"Was he drinking?"

"Was he *drinking?*"

"He was absentminded in the best of . . ."

"Gerda." Boyd reaches across the table, takes Gerda's hand. "You never gave up on him, did you?"

Gerda blinks once, her face darkens. "Maybe not."

Boyd straightens up. "So. I guess then one of us should break down, right?"

Gerda shakes her head, pulls her hand away. Boyd lets her outstretched palm drop.

"Except we're both so *strong*. We can't, can we? He counted on us never giving up."

Gerda makes a face and Boyd points a finger at herself, at her heart.

"I'm stronger than my own power to destroy. That's my motto now."

She rises unsteadily, kneels before the dollhouse. She fishes Norman up from the plumbing and Brenda from the ironing board and the convertible from the roof. She parks the car in the semidetached garage. In the living room, she stands Brenda and Norman together on a tiny white-tufted bearskin in front of the red-foil crinkle of fire in the fireplace, their extended hands nearly touching.

Boyd sits back on her heels, surveying the miniature rooms.

"Dollhouses terrify me. They always have. Look at those teeny porcelain teacups, that little bitty Steinway with the movable keys. A world that calls out for carnage. Tiny carnage. Tiny, tiny Visigoth vandals."

Gerda does not laugh.

"Boyd . . ."

"Really. Perfect little bananas and grapes in a perfect little silver fruit bowl, perfect red-and-white-striped toothpaste oozing from a perfect little squeezable tube—exact replicas, that's what they say. Don't you hate that expression?"

She gets up slowly, glaring at the dollhouse, then drops down opposite Gerda again. They stare at each other, exhausted. Gerda leans down suddenly, plucks a huge blue stuffed frog wearing spectacles and a derby from the floor near her chair. The frog's head pops up on its spring neck. "Will you be my friend?" a wheedling synthetic voice inquires. "Will you be my friend?"

Boyd jumps. So does Gerda. Then they laugh a little wildly.

"*Shit!*"

"Boyd."

"*Toys.* I was thinking maybe a dollhouse graveyard. Miniature cemetery plots for doll-people to tend, with doll-dead inside them . . ."

"Boyd."

"What?" She rolls sideways off her small chair and lies flat on the Pooh rug, staring up.

"Let it go."

"Gerda, I can't help it. I still feel like he's in the house. You know, like he's going to turn on the light, climb the stairs. Then I'll hear his voice."

There is a silence, broken only by a vaguely digestive sound from the aquarium; then Boyd asks Gerda what she would do if she heard her dead son's voice. Gerda crosses her arms, looks up, blinks slowly, imitates Boyd's roll, and ends up at the edge of the rug. They lie together quietly, in a kind of suspense, but nothing happens, no one appears. They breathe together, waiting.

"I'd believe in God again."

They wait for Russell's voice to sound in the room, but it does not. They wait longer. They hear nothing but the faraway sound of an occasional car.

"The young man, the funeral director—Will Youngren? He told me that you talked about what to read at the funeral."

"He told me about how he used to design wigwams for dogs or something."

"The *funeral* director?"

"I'm reading a bit from Keats."

"He loved Keats, didn't he?"

Boyd closes her eyes. "Once, when I was in med school, he flew to New York to see me. He stood on my doorstep, recited Keats's sonnet 'Bright Star.' He wore a cowboy hat."

Gerda looks over at her and smiles. Boyd turns her head to stare at her.

"Maybe this is a gift, Gerda. I point at whatever: a guppy, the

annoying guy at the gas station, Geraldo Rivera, and—*zap*—
dead. *Hasta la vista.*"

She points her finger straight up at the ceiling, then drops her
hand to her side.

"He wrote some poems for me. I opened the front door and
there were butterflies floating in the foyer—I thought they were
butterflies, but they turned out to be origami, a hundred of
them. He had written one hundred haiku on paper wings. It
sounds so . . . you know—I usually hate that kind of thing, but
it was so neat. He kept blowing on them to get them flying
around. Then we sat down on the steps and read them. Big
setup and god-awful poems."

She shakes her head.

"*Awful.* I mean, like, 'Storm clouds over Mount Fuji. Why
does everyone keep picking on me?' Or one about two frogs
who fall in love with a foghorn? 'Big honker across the river.
What's a frog's serious heart to you?' I started laughing and I
couldn't stop."

"He was so funny."

"He was more than funny. He was, you know, dangerous. I
might find an exploding cigar around here somewhere, a bomb.
Know what I mean? I don't want to find . . . stuff."

Gerda coughs. She lifts herself slowly and a little painfully
to her feet. She straightens, then stoops, rubbing her arthritic
knee.

"Come on, Boyd," she says, and holds out her hand. "You
have to rest now."

Boyd shivers and frowns at the ceiling. Slowly, she rolls over
and gets to her feet.

"Rest," she repeats.

Gerda stands in the doorway.

"Are you staying over?"

At Gerda's nod, she seems relieved and moves quickly, almost hurrying, to her side. She flicks off the aquarium lights, then the overhead light, then shuts the door carefully behind them.

CHAPTER 3

B OYD WAKES UP hours later, wrapped in a quilt, in bed next to Freddy. Something has drawn her up at great velocity out of sleep. She knows what it is. It is not Russell. Or not exactly. She glances at Freddy's Cinderella-glass-slipper clock, the numerals radium blue: 3:17 A.M. There's no likeness of him before her now. Whatever's there keeps blurring into another image—a woman's body in labor. What does a body in labor look like? *Like a camel passing through a needle's eye,* she thinks. Every muscle, all strength, concentrated, intent on bringing the second body out of the first body.

And why would she now see herself trying to draw a body out of a second body? She tries to resist the images forming before her but cannot keep herself, at last, from stealing a look. Here she is, product of her mind's almost-perfect reproduction: a second-year resident in Obstetrics and Gynecology, wearing rumpled blues, her young face tired under the scrub cap, the unsparing lights. Before her, a heavyset woman on her back, legs open on a white table in the giving-birth position, a bloody map between her thighs. Boyd is performing a hospital procedure she's done before: a mid-term to late-term abortion—the woman had not been sure of her conception date. Ultrasound was not so technically accurate then. The fetus was much larger than they'd thought.

There was trouble. They'd injected the saline solution after draining the amniotic fluid out of the womb (which would induce labor contractions and cause the fetus to be expelled), but the woman began to convulse. Unconscious, the woman shouted, moaned; her left arm began to shake violently in its restraints as she went into cardiac arrest. The anesthesiologist shot a look at Boyd across the table, and the nurse shoved the paddles at her, picked up the phone. *Where was the attending?* The surgical nurse sent out a code blue, rang the attending physician's extension. No one answered.

It was her *situation* now. The woman was named Tina Coburn, overweight, chatty, thirty-two years old, mother of three, *Times* crossword puzzle fan, who had decided, rather late, that she did not want a fourth child. She and her husband were divorcing, her income was uncertain, and Tina made up her mind, set on terminating the pregnancy—a decision reinforced when her amniocentesis had come back "compromised," requiring a second test. What had not been detected was that Tina had a heart condition, an undiagnosed cardiomyopathy. The vascular saline interacted with the damaged heart and caused infarction. This would all be revealed in the future. But at the moment, as Boyd watches her younger self, she is raving, talking aloud wildly as the team begins taking steps to pull Tina back—Tina, who is disappearing before their eyes. Boyd's gloved hands press down flat against the rib cage (she sees the five-pointed gold star on the chain around Tina's neck, the star she'd begged to take with her into the O.R. then gave up finally to the nurses; she sees the tan line above her white, lolling breasts), then, after seconds of pressure, she applies the paddles and the wounded, stricken heart is shocked once, twice. Tina's body leaps on the table. Everyone around her is shouting, but a silence envelops Boyd and Tina as the bond between them alters. The energy is going wrong between her hands and Tina's heart, and even electrical interception, jolt after bullying jolt, can't set the rhythm right. Boyd is pleading: Like a key in a skipping ignition, a chain wrenched over clutching, ratcheting gears, she cries out for the heart's engine to catch. Mercilessly exact is her memory, yet now, as she sits up in bed, she cannot quite re-create the finality and brute power of that hopelessness, riding the faltering heart with a fork of voltage. She hears herself addressing the live wires in her hand: *Shock the fuck out of this heart. Go. Now. I can save her.*

Down the hall, Gerda, asleep in the guest room, coughs. *I can save her,* Boyd hears in her head as she gets up and stumbles on the quilt's hem. She was a doctor. And she'd been very good at what she did.

But she hadn't saved her. The week after Tina Coburn's death, they held an "M-and-M"—a morbidity-and-mortality conference—at the hospital. They were required to do so. Her peers and the faculty convened, asked her questions, deliberated, decided that she had done all she could have done in the circumstances, and closed the books. But someone—she'd never found out who—called the *Post* and the *News* and for three days she was the subject of headlines: BOTCHED ABORTION KILLS MOTHER OF THREE; YOUNG ABORTIONIST BROUGHT BEFORE BOARD; RIGHT-TO-LIFE GROUPS RALLY ON HOSPITAL GROUNDS, CALL FOR DOCTOR'S DISMISSAL.

She was not dismissed. She had followed procedures exactly. Better technology might have found the damaged heart muscle, but she could not possibly have found it in the routine presurgical workup, though she'd written into the chart a couple of nearly rhetorical questions addressed to no one but as general reference—a query about respiration rate, another about blood gases. The M-and-M review came to the conclusion that she'd done all that was in her power—the report noted that the attending was not available, the attending had been overseeing a complicated delivery and hadn't gotten there in time. She was a resident, but she was a good doctor; she'd tried everything she knew to save a human life and she had failed.

Now Boyd pauses in front of the curtained windows. She pulls the quilt tighter around her as she sweeps the flowered fabric aside, peers down at the dark yard. She'd known so many things back then. What was it she once knew? Back then, she knew the shiny doughnut look of a dilated cervix, she knew how many centimeters of dilation meant it was time to mobilize, she knew how to perform a hysterectomy, how to scoop the uterus out of the abdomen or suck it into a tube inserted into the vagina, how to slice the bloody sac open to retrieve a kicking or still infant, how to spray an abdomen with Betadine (as a nurse slipped a Chieftains tape into the O.R. player), then cut through the rectus fascia, fat, and muscle to the organs, to the womb, cervix, tubes, and ovaries (those heavy-headed pods nodding in their suburb of blood). She knew her way around the Garden: the flora of the cavity, the gleaming opacity of the walls; she knew, by intuitive, educated touch, how late a woman was and nearly to the day when the baby was due. She had a gift.

Back then, she could palpate breast tissue and unerringly isolate a lump—she had an instinctive feel for a possible malignancy. It adhered, it was discrete, it was not painful. Her fingers would nimbly isolate a cyst or blocked mammary tissue, infected milk ducts—she knew how normal changes in breast tissue presented. What was hidden or encrypted revealed itself, rose to her fingertips like smooth, readable welts of Braille.

In fact, the reason for her choice of specialty had had to do with discovering what appeared to be a lump in her own breast. She'd just begun med school and she'd shied away from the Columbia community of doctors for her examination: She didn't know anyone yet. Her roommate's mother had taken her to their Park Avenue ob/gyn, who snorted when he heard Boyd's mild *Our Bodies, Ourselves* introduction.

"You young women," he roared as he roughly kneaded her right breast. "You're all rushing in here hysterical, convinced that you have breast cancer because of those damn self-examination books!"

He twisted her breast one more time, like a dial. Boyd could feel his unthinking fingers touching and missing the round mass of tissue, marble-sized.

"There's no lump here—there's nothing here!"

He scowled at her over his glasses and held up his large, blotchy hands, waving them like a Pentecostal convert. His face was smooth-shaven as a pumice stone but extremely ruddy—

Boyd saw him squinting into the sun above a sand trap, furious, his jowls shaking like a basset hound's.

"See these hands? These are *trained* hands! They're sensitive!"

At first Boyd had been intimidated by Park Avenue's scorn—maybe what she'd felt wasn't anything to worry about after all. But when the non-lump kept growing larger, she'd had it aspirated with a needle, then biopsied by a university surgeon, who asked her why she'd waited so long. The mass had turned out to be benign.

She'd sent Dr. Park Avenue a succinct note requesting that he stop sending her bills and that he stop lecturing women about their bodies (and their selves). She thought of making gender analogies—how would he have felt if there'd been a growth on his dick? His left testicle? But she'd gone for subtler points in her letter to him:

> My *hands are so sensitive that they tremble as I write the word* malpractice, *or the word* negligence—*but somehow I still manage to get them on the page!!*

The letter served its purpose. The bills stopped. And Boyd had made her decision about what kind of doctor she wanted to be. Like obstetricians before her, and like midwives long before them, she could ease delivery or end a fetus's growth. There were things she could do to change fate, whatever fate was. "Fate is a woman" was a line in a popular song. She listened to women in the clinic; she *identified*. She had grown tired of men talking about women's bodies, waving away women's complaints. But then she, who had wanted to help women, who had wanted to help them take control of their bodies, had lost control.

Boyd drops the curtain, lifts her quilt, and turns back to her pacing. She'd done all she could for her patient but could do nothing for herself.

One day—after the headlines had disappeared and the screaming faces with placards had vanished—she stopped. She remembers clearly stripping off her gloves and soaping her hands at the O.R. sink the day she stopped. She'd just completed an episiotomy, just snipped off the last vicryl threads suturing a mediolateral incision, and the delivery room nurses were helping clean the woman up. The woman shouted, "Where's my baby? You stole my baby!" in a postpartum haze exacerbated by a few cc's of Versed, given by IV, to relax her during the suturing. She fought free of the nurse's arms and pointed at Boyd. "You stole my baby!" she shouted, her face dark. Boyd looked at her own face, still masked like a robber's in the wavy metal mirror above the sink. *I stole her baby,* she thought. It seemed plausible. What had she done with the baby? "Tell her again that her husband took her kid," an intern called to the nurses restraining her. "Tell her he went with the team for the baby's Apgar test." This was the truth, yet Boyd suddenly felt certain that she *had* somehow conspired against the woman. Should she tell the woman's obstetrician, who'd stayed only for the first twenty hours of labor, then raced to a family wedding, that she'd somehow lost a baby? "You let my *husband* take my baby?" The woman was going for broke. "That sonna-bitch is a *drunk!* Are you all crazy?" Boyd pulled off her mask and her cap, and waved, pushing through the swinging doors of the O.R.

———

She continued her residency on automatic pilot, graduating, then passing her boards and getting licensed, but she'd refrained from applying to any hospitals or private practices for work. Then she'd married Russell, just like *that*.

She snaps her fingers, then jumps, startled at the sound. They'd moved back to Minnesota and she'd never practiced.

She stops pacing and stares at the curtained windows again. *How many ways are there to take a life?* Here's Russell, standing on her doorstep, his arms crossed, staring up at the poems swirling, floating up to her skylight. *What's a frog's serious heart to you?*

They'd met at the U of Minnesota, but she had had no time for him then. She'd already planned her escape route: New York, a white coat, and a stethoscope. When he tracked her down, he showed up with flowers and gifts. In Minnesota, he worked hard at impersonating a business executive. Then one night in New York he asked her to marry him.

"I know you don't love me, exactly, but we are two Minnesotans," he pointed out as they sat across from each other in a restaurant, "Minnesotans, who are by nature more poetic than any other people on earth. We're meant to be together."

She nibbled on a breadstick and considered him. He was wearing a burgundy leather jacket and a Twins necktie. He was quite drunk, and one of his eyes crossed slightly. He picked up two red plastic swizzle sticks and inserted them in his nostrils.

"It's the winters," he whispered, and as the swizzle sticks quivered, his nostrils flared. "You either become a poet or you turn to torsk. Which, you recall, is cod. What you're looking at is my imitation of a cod proposing marriage."

When she answered, finally, throwing up her hands, he stood up, a cod who had successfully proposed marriage, and shook hands with every other patron in the restaurant, a bistro near Bloomingdale's with a smoked-mirror decor. The maître d' followed him, begging him to sit down, as Russell congratulated the room on his good luck, the swizzle sticks still in his nose, shuddering as he breathed, a cod who had been accepted: torsk in ecstasy.

"But you *are* a Minnesotan," Boyd said later, making tea in her apartment kitchen. "You're supposed to be repressed. You're supposed to be Scandinavian. Minnesotans would rather die than be embarrassed, and look at you."

"I was embarrassed," he said. "That's what I do when I'm embarrassed."

"God forbid you should feel confident."

"Look," he said. "If a Minnesotan gets too poetic, you see what happens: Robert Bly. But look at the alternative Hubert Humphrey. Naturally, I lean to the Bly end of the spectrum."

He was leaning down to pet Mumrath, her immense, mean-spirited yellow cat, and he smirked up at her, his hair in his eyes. He had changed into a Hawaiian shirt and cutoffs.

"Don't worry. I'm not going to run off with strange men to the woods to chant and shake my butt. I'll reserve those special moments just for you." He looked back down at Mumrath. "You know one of the questions they ask out there in the woods? *When did you lose your grandeur?* What do you think of *that?*"

Mumrath reached up suddenly, fast, and clawed at his chin and when Russell grabbed his chin, she swiped open his knee for good measure, then padded off, her tail held high.

Boyd lets the quilt slide softly to the floor, smiling at the sight of Russell clutching his knee, falling to the floor, then struggling to his feet to limp heavily, Frankenstein-like, after the cat. She'd always known that it pleased him that he had money, that he was capable of making illusions seem true—and that she had no money and no illusions. He loved that he had purely material gifts to give her. She was the perfect receiver.

Stopped. Bad-luck baby doctor. Botched.

She glances at the rumpled bed. Freddy sleeps restlessly, dreaming, mumbling, her arm flung over her head, two stuffed animals standing mute guard at her pillow. And she and Russell had had their own baby, their own fragile testimony to faith in something. Or to his. *His* faith in something. She stares at Freddy.

There are nothing but gifts on this poor, poor Earth. He'd loved that line of poetry. She touches Freddy's face, watches her eyes begin to flutter, her lips puff out, as if she anticipates a kiss. Boyd waits till Freddy sinks back into dreams, then shrugs back into her quilt, goes on walking till dawn rises in the window.

CHAPTER 4

BOYD WAKES TO A QUICK steady breath on her face. She opens her eyes and there is Freddy, looking worried, her reddish hair in wild disarray, a chocolate-milk mustache on her upper lip. The room has filled with moving brightness. Birds chatter in the trees outside the window.

Boyd glances toward the randomly lit, quizzical faces of stuffed monkeys and rabbits shouldering each other on the deep-set chintz-covered window seat. The light pours from one end: a large window shade lopsidedly drawn up. Freddy has been at work, bringing in the day.

"You were snoring, Mom. Really loud. It shaked the house." She smiles suddenly, distracted. "Grandma is making bacon."

Boyd pulls herself up in bed, leaning on her elbow. "I can smell it. You know what, Fred?"

"What."

"I wasn't snoring, really. I was calling swans. It's a noise like this." She half chortles, half snores. "Was that the noise you heard?"

"Maybe. But where *are* the swans, Mom?"

"They're a little slow—it's their webbed feet. They can't waddle very fast."

Freddy shrugs, losing interest. "Grandma fixed my trike."

"She did? Grandma is a genius!"

Freddy raises an eyebrow and looks shyly down at her feet, signaling the use of a word or expression she does not know.

"I mean that Grandma is very smart."

"I know. And, Mom?"

"Yes?"

"I saw Daddy. But he went by so fast, before I could catch him."

"Where was Daddy, honey?"

"Outside the window. But he went by very fast. Like the wind."

"Dad is gone now, honey. Remember? We talked about it? We'll see him at the special place tomorrow—but just his body. His soul . . ."

"Daddy waved to me."

Boyd sits all the way up, brushing back her hair. "No, Freddy," she says softly. "No, honey. Daddy is gone."

Freddy, grown more serious, pats her hand. "It's all right, Mom. Don't worry. Grandma said I could talk to him when I see him."

"I'm not worried," Boyd says in a different voice, and Freddy glances up at her sharp tone. Clutched in her right fist is a dust ball she has extracted from under the bed.

"This can go in the dollhouse. Okay, Mom?"

Before Boyd can open her mouth, she turns and pads away down the hall to the playroom. Boyd swings her feet to the floor, shakes out her hair. She hears Gerda downstairs in the kitchen, clanging pans, clinking china as she sets the table. She sniffs the bacon-scented air. Then she crosses to the window, lifts the undrawn shade, straightens the other, stares out at the backyard below, the tennis court bordered by sycamore trees. A procession of ghastly images starts to quicken and flicker before her eyes. She blinks and there are only trees, sunlight, garden walls, a shadow moving along the rose-lined walkway, preceding Gerda, who is shaking out a dishcloth and singing softly, off-key, to herself.

Boyd fastens her hair with a pink Hello Kitty scrunchie lifted from Freddy's dresser, bends to check her face in Freddy's crescent-shaped bureau mirror. Still wrapped in the quilt, she moves purposefully down the hall to the master bedroom. The room jitters with flying angles of radiance: sunshine; ordinary morning.

She opens her oak desk and takes out a manila pocket folder. Inside are papers—a typed page bearing the letterhead of a local college, another with a physician's letterhead. The quilt drops to the floor as she reads then refolds the letters.

Gerda's voice fills the stairwell—"Breakfast!"—and scents float upward, bacon and coffee and cinnamon toast. Her voice is too loud. She has the kitchen radio turned up: canned laughter. Listeners out in WCCO land tune in to get pork-belly futures and a little humor as they fry their eggs and drink their watery coffee. Radio high jinks: Scandinavians laughing at themselves, a mildly uncomfortable enterprise. An old joke flashes its wares like an old man in a trenchcoat. Boyd recognizes the up-and-down jokey-rhythmic accent immediately.

Sven says to Ole: "Say, Ole, you better vise up and close them living room window curtains at night. I drove by last night and I saw you and Lena really goin' at it on the couch there." And Ol' Ole, he looks real cagey, y'know, and he says, "Ya know, Sven, I'd say the yoke's on you. I vasn't even home last night!"

There is a rustle in the playroom, the huge padded mouth of the hippo toy chest thumping shut.

"Okay, Grandma, okay!"

Freddy is on her knees before the dollhouse. Norman teeters on the roof, looking as if he's going to jump, his pipe clenched between his teeth. Brenda and the children look up.

Freddy frowns at Boyd as she enters the room. "He's trying to fly, Mom. But he can't go up in the air. He's afraid."

Boyd kneels beside Freddy, drags the quilt over both of them. In the shut gold light, under the stars and hexagons, she touches her daughter's face. "Let's go down and eat breakfast with Grandma, okay? Norman can solve his own problems while we're gone."

Freddy reaches outside the quilt for her shapeless stuffed animal. She holds the creature to her heart. Then slowly, growing taller, like the Alice looming over a height-measuring chart ruled on the wall, she rises to her feet. The soft tent, their protection, slides to the floor.

Boyd pushes up the sleeve of her nightgown and takes Freddy's free hand. Freddy pulls her hand away.

"I'm sorry, Mom," she says. "Right now I got to walk and think."

Boyd does not turn back to lift Norman from the roof. She follows Freddy, leaving Norman alone on the widow's walk, pipe between his teeth, arms stretched outward, trying to fly, while they walk and think in tandem on their way downstairs.

CHAPTER 5

D OWNSTAIRS THAT SAME MORNING, Will walks in on
a distraught group in the casket-display room. Ted
McCullum, one of his salesmen, a prim, prematurely
balding man, is trying to calm a young couple who have lost
their infant daughter. They have not slept much in the last desperate hours. Their faces attempt human expressions, which are
immediately erased by sudden animal looks of uncomprehend-
ing pain. Like all the Bereaved who stand in this room choosing,
they want to make sense of what has happened to them in some
material way. They glance every now and then at the caskets as
if they are explanations. Word had come up to Will's office that
this couple had selected the most expensive infant casket in the
showroom and that it was obvious they could not afford it.
They would never be able to handle even the most creatively
arranged payments. They are renters, they own nothing, have
no insurance. Will silences Ted, who had begun introducing

him, with a look. He walks over to the baby casket, Dreaming Cherubim, bends down (caskets are usually kept at heart level, a sales technique, but Ted has, at some point in the negotiations, managed to lower Dreaming Cherubim to about hip height in an attempt to distract them), sighs.

He touches the casket tentatively, then draws his hand away. The couple stare at him distrustfully. They have already claimed it—it is theirs. Will glances up at them and smiles. Here before him is the living personification of his conflicts with the death business. The young husband ("I'd like you to meet Ellman Rutuski, Will," Ted puts in quickly) is dressed in work clothes, an oil-stained gas-station-mechanic's suit. He smiles back, then hangs his head. She does not smile. ("And Mrs. Rutuski, Mary Kay . . .") She is dramatically overweight, her orange-blond hair coal black at the roots. She wears a shapeless miniskirt with a pink terry-cloth top, appliquéd with teddy bears and embroidered patchwork letters: ASHLEY'S MOM.

Ellman begins to weep unabashedly. He makes terrible noises, gasping. Tears fall on his shoes, and Ted hurries toward him with tissues and a Dixie cup with water. Mary Kay remains stone-faced. She is the one who found Ashley, just four months old, staring open-eyed, unmoving, in her crib. She is the one who dialed 911, screaming, holding the limp then stiff body to her heart. In the preceding hours, it had never occurred to her that she would be here, or somewhere like this, now, in daylight, selecting a vessel so specifically designed to assume the shape of her loss.

Will understands that she is far beyond shock. He sees her pure despair—a place from which there will be no real return.

She turns slowly to him as if she has overheard his thoughts. "This guy wants to know if we got any insurance policies took out on our baby!"

Will shrugs, shakes his head. "Let's not worry about that right now."

He turns his attention to Dreaming Cherubim. They follow his eyes, Ellman snuffling. It is absolutely what it is—nothing could be more defined. It is, for them, more than a primitive symbol, object of terror and awe. It is both reminder and refutation of all they have so unjustly endured, yet the closest thing they have found to a compensatory gesture: a little bed, a crèche, a baby's boat—built to hold the precious one, the heartbreakingly small body, forever and forever, in the cool, placid embrace of satin. Its high-white mahogany gloss, brushed with angel wings, fine-line gold engraving, with gold inlay and gold putti handles, costs $2,700. Next to it, the other infant caskets (Heaven Sent and Littlest Angel) look diminished, uncaring.

"Let's go to the Arrangement Room," Will says.

Mary Kay turns her eyes away from the casket. "No," she says. "Let's straighten this here out right now. We got money and we're sayin' we can pay. What are you sayin'?"

Ellman, still sniffling, reaches into his back pocket, pulls out a plaid-covered checkbook. He watches Mary Kay for a sign.

"See," Ted puts in. "It's not just the casket. There are other . . . expenses involved in arranging for Ashley's interment and burial." He begins scribbling with a ballpoint on a YOUNGREN MORTUARY: WE CARE notepad.

Ellman shakes his head but watches out of one eye. Mary Kay looks away.

"This very easily could end up somewhere in the area of four

thousand dollars or more. Even with our minimum services—
by which I mean dispensing with chapel, viewing, ceremony,
but retaining embalming, interment, vault, burial, understated
monument—most likely no limousines, no flowers, no program, no cards—you would still be investing nearly . . ."

"Of course," Will interrupts, "this casket is on sale." He feels
rather than sees Ted flinch.

"You can have this one . . . for the baby, for Ashley. I'm
putting it on special."

After they have signed documents and a check has changed
hands, after Ted has escorted them back upstairs and out the
front door, Will lingers on in the casket-display room. He leans
against Dreaming Cherubim, arms folded, thinking. Then he
walks upstairs to the front portico, Youngren's colonnaded entrance, and stands gazing at traffic in the distance. Ted comes
around the corner from the parking lot, hurries up the steps,
stops beside him. Ted says he feels like a cigarette. He is trying to quit, but he still wants one badly. He wears a tiny staple
in his ear that he touches again and again, like a charm. He
fishes in his pocket for chewing gum, offers a stick to Will, who
shakes his head. Ted nervously unwraps the foil and folds the
gum into his mouth.

They stand in silence as he chews. After a minute, he half
turns to Will, attempting a casual tone. "Not good business, I
suppose, to randomly reduce a top-line item. At least that's my
opinion."

"Well, it wasn't mine."

Ted shrugs, pointedly chewing. He moves cheerfully to another subject. "We got an AIDS client in today—Sechman and
Robideaux won't work on him."

"They're pulling this again?"

"Well, Will, we've only had that one other case a year ago. St. Paul ain't exactly what you'd call a gay town."

"Then who's doing the guy?'

Ted shrugs. "Dunno." He unwraps another stick of gum. "Most likely Griggs."

There is another long pause. Will turns away, walks slowly down the steps. "I'll be back later," he says. "There's the Schaeffer funeral coming up, and I've got to think about it."

•

CHAPTER 6

AT RUSSELL'S FUNERAL, Boyd watches Gerda. The older woman stares straight ahead, her jaw strong, sapphires at her ears. A crescent-shaped black hat, pinned with a circlet of fringed jet beads, appears stylish, unintentionally rakish, set on her thick white hair. She frowns slightly. Everyone seated near her, including Boyd, thinks that she is looking at the jutting profile of her son, framed in a white satin ruff, in the coffin on its flower-covered stand directly before her. But Gerda is looking through what she thinks of as a symbol of her son on display among the subdued explosions of mortuarial blossoms (*How I loathe gladioli!* she thinks) and is staring hard into a summer day thirty-six years ago. Like a ghost, she enters the heat and damp of that day, running her hand lovingly over the glossy leaves of the privet hedge, over the oxidized-copper face of the sundial on its mottled pedestal. She smells orange blossoms, pool chlorine, Coppertone. Before her is a child of six, a little boy, glaring at her. She has warned him again and again not to swim immediately after eating lunch. They stare at each other across the pool. A bird releases a long, complicated series of love notes from its perch high in the sycamore tree.

The boy sits on the edge, one brown leg dangling, casually stirring the clear blue surface with his foot. Every few seconds he inches forward, slides a bit more of himself into the water, all the while holding her gaze, defying her. His back is slightly arched now, his hips in the red-and-white-striped trunks straining forward. It must hurt him, she thinks, to suspend himself like that. She sees herself, a young, dark-haired woman in a jade-green bathing suit and green-jeweled sunglasses, reclining uneasily on a chaise longue. *How alike the two of us are,* she thinks—jaws set, brows pulled together: furious!

"If you go in that pool," says her young voice, threatening, "I will spank you."

At this, Russell smiles radiantly, waves, and shoves off, propelling himself into the deep end. She leaps up, stands at the edge of the pool, staring down at the small figure now curled into a tight ball on the bottom, a stream of bubbles rising from his mouth. He clings to an iron rung embedded in the cement. Seconds pass. She curses.

She curses again and, flinging off her sunglasses, dives. Eight feet down, she reaches for him, but he wriggles away and she flutter-kicks after him. He jabs mightily, ineffectually, at her with his right foot. She puts her arms around him. He pushes away, striking at her, his furious gestures of repudiation and her frantic grasping both softened into an underwater ballet. They move over and under each other, embracing, flying away. Finally, she pins his arms behind him and hauls him kicking to the surface, where they thrash together and sputter.

"You are such a bad boy!" she shouts when she gets her breath at last. "Why would you do a thing like that? You could have killed us both."

"You are bad!" he cries, sputtering, shaking her hand from his shoulder as she tries to steer them to shallower water. Then, abruptly, the struggle is over and they bob quietly up and down, facing each other. His enormous clear green eyes stare into hers. She has seen this look before—the contained, unperturbed gaze of a creature sure of its absolute will and mischief.

"I will be drown-ded," he says calmly, staring into her eyes, "but I will not do as you say, Mama."

Gerda snorts, remembering, startling Boyd on one side and Freddy on the other. Boyd places her hand on Gerda's arm. She has heard Gerda's outburst as a sob. Gerda bows her head so that Boyd will not see the look of amusement on her face.

Will, watching surreptitiously from a side pew, cannot guess Gerda's thoughts. He has not grasped that she is a woman who hates ceremony of any kind. There had been no opportunity for him to know. She appears a calm matriarch, knowing, like any mother, how families rely on these theater events to protect their all-important illusion of unity. Gerda—repelled by the momentous pulpit, the waxen flowers, the absentmindedly melodramatic organ, the daft liturgy, and the little stink of piousness and pent breath, the girdled and necktied and perfumed living bodies with eyes downcast, stealing peeks at the prominent, embalmed Russell—could not admit to Will her aversion to religion.

Gerda asks herself what she believes, and when she does, she sees the face of that six-year-old boy, defiant. She believes that face. That is what she believes. She will never let that face go.

The magnitude of her love for her dead son washes over her now, and for a heartbeat she falters, her strong hands grip the pew in front of her, and Boyd brushes her arm. She shakes her head: I'm fine. She believes that, too—that she is fine, that her heart is good, and that love is eternal, love is transcendent. There is no heaven, she thinks, but there is that face each of us sees, the face that love gives us to recognize forever. She feels Russell here, not prone in that rococo casket but in the air, circling her body as he orbited her, flying under water that summer morning so many years ago—beside her, around her, touching her, pulling away. *"I will be drown-ded. But I will not do as you say, Mama."* Abruptly, surprising her, tears leap to her eyes, spill over. She fishes for her handkerchief and, holding her breath, stops the tears, takes Boyd's arm, stands straight and tall, nodding to the minister as he comes forward now to officially greet the mourners.

A few minutes later Boyd gets up, book in hand, and walks to the front of the chapel, turns quickly on her heel, and faces the crowd. She has had to stop herself from muttering aloud, she realizes. She believes, irrationally, that Gerda's memories of Russell, secret images never shared with another, have somehow bled into her brain. She can see nothing for a moment but Russell as a little boy, standing in the sun, near water. Then, with an enormous act of will, she clears her mind, concentrates on the task at hand. A microphone has been set up near a bank of flowers, and she pauses as if lost in thought before speaking into it. Will watches her warily, though with helpless interest. She looks pale but quite beautiful, wearing a charcoal-colored suit, pearls, her hair pulled back. There are dark circles under her eyes, but when she looks up at last, he sees that her eyes are bright, accusing, scanning the faces before her.

There is some shifting among the mourners, a cough or two. And still she waits, appearing not to notice their discomfort. At last she opens the book, then snaps it shut abruptly and begins to recite "Bright Star" from memory. Will closes his eyes and lets the beautiful sounds of the words touch him. Boyd thinks of Russell on her doorstep in New York City, a pale, creased cowboy hat with a red braided band sitting on his head, his arms held out to her, declaiming:

> Bright star! Would I were as steadfast as thou art—
>   Not in lone splendour hung aloft the night
> And watching, with eternal lids apart,
>   Like nature's patient, sleepless Eremite,
> The moving waters at their priestlike task
>   Of pure ablution round earth's human shores,
> Or gazing on the new soft fallen mask
>   Of snow upon the mountains and the moors;
> No—yet still steadfast, still unchangeable,
>   Pillowed upon my fair love's ripening breast,
> To feel forever its soft fall and swell,
>   Awake forever in a sweet unrest,
> Still, still to hear her tender-taken breath,
>   And so live ever—or else swoon to death.

When she sits down, Boyd smiles gingerly at Gerda and puts her head down, relieved. It is not a terribly hot day, but she has been feeling overheated, feverish, and now she is grateful for a sudden breeze through the side chapel door. She glances across Gerda at Freddy, who's been sitting stiffly, her mouth slightly open, clutching her teddy bear and her other shapeless creature throughout the ceremony, her eyes fixed on the coffin. Boyd wonders, terrified, if allowing her to come was a mistake. But Freddy had begged her, Freddy had insisted. She looks over and smiles wanly at her.

She allows herself, finally, a close look at Russell. The expression of humor on his face is so familiar that she almost laughs aloud. She feels the famous fear of the Bereaved—that the corpse will sit up suddenly, laugh, wave, then point to her, his face changing. How was it possible that he was dead? How could he, of all people, have fallen down, his racket clattering beside him as he fell heavily to one knee on the tennis court, his right hand tearing at his chest, the other gesturing to Nicholas across the net? Who kept laughing at him, thinking he was horsing around: "Hey, Russ, get up! Come on, you bullshit artist!" Nick kept repeating this account of the heart attack to anyone who would listen, as if it proved something beyond doubt. "I was all set to serve," he kept saying. As she came up the driveway that morning, she'd opened her window to listen to the birds, singing so violently in the sycamore trees. Then she'd noticed it: the paramedics' van, parked at an angle in front of the house.

The breeze through the chapel's side door grows stronger, ruffles her hair. The chapel is quietly air-conditioned—why then is the side door open? Boyd wonders. She notices a few people—mothers with babies, restless mourners coming and going, milling around outside the door. She returns her gaze to Russell. As she watches, a little wind moves a dark curl across his brow. The breeze strengthens and Boyd waits, appalled, for him to brush the hair from his eyes. She is conscious of her pearls, white weight at her neck, and she thinks of her long-postponed honeymoon—three years after Freddy was born—in Tahiti. Thinks of her head between his legs, thinks of him moving beneath her, above her—metal fan-blades flashing above, deep gardenia scents, a long intense ecstatic struggle in pale sheets. She puts her hand to her lips, suddenly shy as she remembers his body and hers simplified in lust.

"Dear heart," he says. She almost answers him, deep in the moment, till he whispers, *"Jolie, jolie coeur."*

She nearly laughs aloud, remembering. His French is terrible, his French is appalling—plus it's just so *froggy* of him to speak French—but he wants to be like Paul Gauguin, one of his heroes. Russell has, for the moment it takes the Tahitian trade winds to worry his hair, given up writing poems for painting. He has set up an easel on the terrace, a canvas splashed with yellow and dark blue and chestnut and peach. A misshapen Polynesian girl is emerging from the colors. He quotes Mallarmé to her: " 'Paint not the thing but the effect it produces!' " "Paint the thing!" she yells back cheerfully, "and shut up about it!" The painting is pretty terrible, like many of Russell's attempts at art—clumsy but cheerful, vivid, embarrassing.

"How bad is it?" he asks.

She sighs. "It's pretty terrible," she says, and his face sags.

"But not," she says, "you know, *hopelessly* terrible. Anyone can see there's potential."

Quelle horreur. Or as he would say, *Quel horror.* His French is rotten, but he charms everyone with it—concierge, waiters, maids, people on the street in Papeete. Everywhere he sees Gauguin's faces, totemic, profound—the same ones he painted over a century ago. Russell speaks French to everybody, hilariously. He is convinced that he recognizes the inherited face of Tehemana, Gauguin's child-mistress, maybe a great-great-granddaughter. She knows when he makes love to her that he calls up Tehemana in his mind—or the teenage maid who cleans their rooms: long, thick black hair, flower-face. She doesn't care. *Anyone can see there's potential* in a rich, hard-drinking, dangerously funny fellow.

Potential, she thinks, the soul's potential insisting on itself suddenly, peering out of the present's bad painting, then disappearing again, back into the unexpressed reservoir—the blue and chestnut, the peach-colored skin, the thin liquifilm over the eye as it opens and shuts on images of what one will never, in this life, be.

Every morning she sleeps in a cabana chair on the sand, in her print bikini, a transparent purple visor over her eyes. She wakes up to catch Russell surfacing suddenly in the bay near the broken coral reef, in a snorkel and mask. He pulls off this headgear and strides through the breakers, silent, holding her gaze with his. Pearls, a string of them, flashing, threaded through his tanned fingers.

"Look what I found."

Strung pearl necklaces in the coral, swollen orchids on pillows, an emerald ring in a champagne glass. Honeymoon. One dawn: a lei of pale-green luna moths on a garden path to the sea—rising up, slowly coming apart, scattering upward. Ghost-eyes on the wings, separating.

One morning on the beach she presses her fingers against his brown back, slick with tanning oil. His hair has lightened; his whole body is chestnut-colored. His back muscles ripple at her touch. (He had asked her seriously before falling asleep, "Gauguin wore a brown cowboy hat when he arrived here—do you think it would work for me?")

"I miss Freddy," she murmurs.

She watches a tiny bright-green lizard run up a banana-tree root at her eye level. Russell rolls over and looks at her. His eyes are the exact shade of the lizard.

"She changes in an eyeblink at this age, you know."

Holding her gaze, he puts his hand inside her bikini top. His fingers, curiously cool in the heat, feel shocking against the flesh of her nipple, which instantly contracts.

"I change," he says. "I change in an eyeblink."

The lizard's red tongue flicks in and out.

"Russell . . ."

He guides her hand inside his trunks to his erect penis. His cold fingers tighten on her nipple, painfully. The lizard stretches out its sticky toes, then darts halfway up the trunk, peers back at them.

He blinks once, twice. His fingers twist and tighten. Before she can protest, his mouth covers hers.

Boyd stares at Russell's pale profile, the hair at his brow stilled now. She is conscious of Gerda beside her.

Why did I stay with him? Because of something so obvious as the stupid hope that passion—that eternal awkward *potential*—represents? A rush of disgust. She touches her mouth again. Death's implacable presentation of the body has brought back the limitations of her own capacity for . . . hope? Potential:

a kind of terrible smooth erotic mechanism, then shame. *Did you come, baby?* That she could grasp her own suffering only through the intellect, only through a steady refusal of the flesh, of its possibilities of healing, has been clear to her for some time. The phrase *rich boy's body* sidles into her mind and she hears it as both terrifying and erotic, then is filled with self-disgust.

After they made love that afternoon in Tahiti, she reintroduced the subject of missing Freddy and he reached across her abruptly, lifted the phone jingling from the bedside table, and punched in the familiar numbers. Gerda, cheerful in her vacation baby-sitter capacity, answered briskly, then put Freddy on. Boyd could hear her tiny voice screaming in delight as he held the phone away from his ear. Freddy wanted to talk to Daddy, Freddy shouted that she loved Daddy. Later, she asked for Boyd. Her voice was much lower, calm now. She told Boyd she could "wait some more time" to see them both.

She looks wonderingly at Russell's body. *I am in shock,* she thinks. She's seen it in the clinic and in the emergency room. The teenager who had lost an arm carefully massaging with her remaining hand the thin air where the limb had been; the woman whose baby slid from between her legs choked by the umbilical cord, the dead mouth she insisted on holding to her breast. Boyd had diagnosed it tens of times—the stricken eyes, the clammy skin, the dropped blood pressure. A trained part of her mind steps back, observes, writes in a chart. She feels Gerda's eyes on her suddenly and turns to her a face emptied of all emotion. The congregation stands up all at once; the minister prays. Across the aisle Boyd notices Will Youngren, the funeral director, staring at her.

There is the burial, she thinks, *the interment to get through, then the reception afterward. I will make it through. Freddy will get through this, too.* Gerda takes her hand. Nicholas had said: *He just fell down, that was it.* Green eyes, his hand on her breast. "Rest in peace," she murmurs, touching the pearls at her neck.

Will stands alone at the grave after the mourners have driven off. Everything has happened as he'd planned it. The pallbearers carried the casket to the grave, slid it across the rollers set above the vault already sunk into the grave. The casket stood, gleaming mutely (Blessed Threshold; $6,000), during the interment ceremony and the graveside reading of psalms. Now the first man from the cemetery crew starts the hydraulic lowering. The casket shudders, jerks, then hums, sinking into the earth. Soon the rest of the cemetery crew will arrive; the vault man will put the top on the concrete box, then seal it. Then the landscapers will unroll strips of sod over the new grave. Weeks later, the monument will be delivered—a marble marker, a cross, an angel with a sword or a stone scroll—inscribed with the indelible name and dates.

He watches as the crew works, thinking of Gerda Schaeffer. The funeral service had not pleased her. He saw how she flinched at the music, the minister's banalities. The chapel, which holds three hundred and fifty, had overflowed; there was another crowd of fifty or so beyond the doors. The funeral location should not have gotten into the papers. But it had. Russell Schaeffer was well known and well loved. It seems to Will that everyone Russell had ever known grieved for him: his family, his friends, his business associates, recipients of his philanthropy, foundation heads, family lawyers, basketball and tennis partners, literary acquaintances—even literary-magazine editors had sent flowers. Strangers stepped forward to tell tales of Russell's generosity—a little business assistance, checks written on the spot for ill ex-employees whose insurance had run out, money for scholarships, a disabled boy's university tuition paid, a widow's pension supplemented, an operation paid for, an ailing arts project and a drug rehab program bailed out. Funds for public television, for the Guthrie. Flowers sent, an encouraging letter, a fraternal handshake, a palmed check, a high sign, an unforgettable boyish grin as he turned, waving.

Only Boyd had seemed somehow apart from the public drama. And, he had to admit it—Gerda, too. Gerda had refused an enormous church ceremony. Now he saw why.

The Keats had worked, he thinks, watching the vault man do his job. Boyd had understood what he had not. He sees her reading the poem, how her face altered, how she stood. She frightens him, but he dreams suddenly of touching her hair. Then stops himself. He looks out over the rows of angels with swords, the infant gods with raised hands, the messages for the living carved into the ornate stones. *Why don't we keep the dead better company?* he asks the air, the angels. The vault man whistles as he mixes cement to seal Russell Schaeffer forever in the earth. Birds sing.

CHAPTER 7

THE DAY AFTER THE FUNERAL, at Gerda's suggestion, Boyd and Freddy went shopping. It was a beautiful summer day, but the display windows of the stores were already filled with mannequins dressed in autumn fashions. As they entered Dayton's department store, Boyd stopped suddenly and held her head in her hands, leaning against a counter, Freddy reached up and brushed a finger against the moving sheen of her silk jacket. Boyd jumped. Freddy stared at her accusingly. She'd been trotting in Boyd's wake for five minutes, her patent-leather purse strap snapped and snaking behind. Her hair had sprung out of her pigtails and the brim of her small felt hat was askew. Now her tongue hung out the side of her mouth like that of a small winded dog.

"I hafta throw up, Mom."

Cosmetics loomed: a salesperson in a white uniform painting cream on a faceless seated figure under a turban. Boyd murmured to her and she pointed discreetly.

Freddy tugged at her. "I feel okay. I don't hafta throw up."
Boyd slowed and looked down.

"I want French fries."

They ascended, solemnly riding a series of escalators to the top floor, where there was a ladies' tearoom. They were seated in the River Room—in wicker chairs under a chain of skylights. The sky above them had clouded slightly; the light that fell on them was diamond-edged, refracted. Boyd blinked. Across the table from her, Freddy seemed outlined in an infrared glow. When she noticed Boyd watching her, she disappeared behind a huge fabric-covered menu. Illiterate, she sighed and spelled aloud, making clucking noises. Boyd reached across the table to smooth her hair and she pulled away.

"Do you want me to help you read?"

"I am reading, Mom."

The waitress arrived and Boyd ordered coffee. Freddy asked for French fries, a glass of milk, and chicken noodle soup, the menu still propped before her.

"I'm sorry, sweetheart," said the waitress. "We don't have any chicken noodle soup."

Freddy refused to lower the menu. "I readed it right here."

Boyd smiled the requisite winking smile at the waitress. Behind the menu, Freddy began to cry.

"Listen," Boyd whispered. "How about cream of tomato soup instead? With toast?"

Freddy sniffled. After a long pause, she lowered the menu. "Toast with just one butter?"

After the waitress left, she locked eyes with Boyd and kicked halfheartedly at the table legs.

"You look very mean today, Mom."

"Do I? I wonder why."

"Because my purse broke and you didn't even *see*."

"I'm sorry your purse broke, Freddy. I'm going to try and fix it at home."

"They put Daddy in the ground."

Boyd waited, ready for anything.

"Is Daddy in a place like a hotel room under the ground?"

Boyd considered the unsatisfactory options—heaven, angels, spirits, and stars—but at this moment she could summon nothing, no symbol, no reassuring word or phrase. She heard her voice speaking. "I don't really know. Maybe there are rooms. There might be rivers and parks. The thing is, honey, I don't know. I don't know where he is."

There was a silence. Freddy stared back at her. Then Boyd forced a smile, recovering. "Daddy's gone away, honey. But you can still remember him however you want."

The waitress placed coffee and milk before them. Boyd focused on glass and cup, skylit. She drank her coffee.

After Boyd paid the bill, Freddy tugged at her sleeve. "Maybe Daddy can dig a way out. He could blow up the dirt with a bomb!"

Boyd nodded. "Maybe."

They drifted down on the escalators and left without buying Freddy's school clothes. As Boyd pushed on the glass pane of the revolving door, herding Freddy before her, she noticed Will at the very second he saw her, looking up from his wristwatch. They began to mime greetings, then fell silent, stolidly urging their glass cages in opposite directions. Behind them, people pushed them into their separate afternoons: Will to buy a tryst gift for Priscilla, a box of watercolors, and Boyd home to the house where she had lived with her late husband. Where, after driving up the drive, parking, noticing that Gerda's car was gone, opening the door, she discovered late mail scattered on the slate tiles before the front door under the brass mail slot. She bent and picked up the letters, then glanced at a larger stack of mail on the foyer table. There were neat square white envelopes, a few days' accumulation of condolence notes, sympathy cards, and one envelope that caught her eye. She picked up it up, glancing at the postmark—the day of his death. She stared a long time at the handwriting—sharp wings, predator swoops. It was a letter from Russell.

Boydie,

You will think this is a suicide note. It is not. It is a love note, which a suicide letter can't be. Anyway, is there an etiquette book published somewhere that includes the proper way to write a suicide note? Thank your survivors sincerely for putting up with you, but mention an urgent engagement of some long standing (since birth?) and that you do not want to presume further on their hospitality. Leave the bathroom in order even if you do dirty the razor and sink—and if you hang yourself, do not be thoughtless: there are few things less pleasant for an innocent survivor than bumping face-first into a pair of swinging loafers upon entering a room. The same rule applies if you decide to plunge from a great height: do not spread yourself on a sidewalk in front of a restaurant. Think how you would feel stepping on somebody's knuckles after a tasty lunch of sweetbreads. Be considerate, be quick about it—and as tasteful as one can be, given the circumstances.

The doctor called me a Dead Man. I found this rather presumptuous of a guy who looks like a botched embalming job himself. Yes, I saw the doctor earlier today and now here is the Dead Man writing to you, blundering a path through proper etiquette to you. Trying to find a way to say, not melodramatically: I'm done for and I need you.

What other reason is there for the Dead Man to live? I'm scared shitless to walk through that door into our bedroom. Why? They flee from me, that one time did me seek. *I love you without reason, so not without faith.*

And I love Freddy. It may be impossible to do these things, as I think of you both. But I plan to issue a travelers' advisory: don't follow where I go; only I know the way. *I got lost today when we played hide-and-seek—that's all she knows.*

They'll be weeping and tearing their garments in the streets. Like Auden's elegy for Yeats, "He became his admirers." When more is revealed, just remember this: I was stuck inside Sneezy, Boyd, as stuck as if I'd tried to go through the eye of a camel. Stuck in the punch line, that's me. Did you hear the one about the guy who became more invisible with each joke? I can't remember the rest, because my body's disappearing.

And this letter, with apologies to Rilke—I stare at it fading in my faster-fading hand.

Russell

CHAPTER 8

T HE DAY AFTER BOYD opened Russell's letter, Gerda
stood in the driveway of her great Tudor house on the
shores of Lake Minnetonka, an oddly military figure in
her dark-blue jogging suit. Towser, her chocolate Labrador, exploded from the dog door behind her as if shot from a cannon.
He paused near her, sniffing the raked, crushed gravel as she adjusted her running shoe. Then, as she bent down again, retying
her laces, his ears went up and he ran forward, barking, as
Boyd's car pulled up. Gerda pushed back her hair and started to
raise her hand in greeting, then saw Boyd's face behind the
wheel and retracted her hand.

Boyd got out of her car and the two women faced each other.
Towser sniffed Boyd's legs, his tail wagging, till Gerda made a
sign for him to stop. Boyd held out the letter. Gerda took it,
read it. When she finished, she handed it back to Boyd without
a word.

———

"Gerda. I had a talk last night with that guy, the funeral director at Youngren's. He mentioned that you were eager not to have an autopsy."

Gerda looked down the long drive, the march of summer-green trees, a natural track. Even at her age, she was a fair runner. Now she was seeing the driveway in winter. Before her eyes, the snow flattened, sprayed back against the trees by the wind, the powerful wind from the north—battering, bright.

"There was no need for an autopsy. He'd been seeing a doctor, and that doctor signed the death certificate."

"Do you mind if I ask how long he'd been seeing this guy?"

Gerda continued to stare down the drive. She lifted her hand to shield her eyes—a jewel on her left hand caught the light. "When Russell was drinking less, he decided to go get a checkup. He didn't want to see a family doctor—he wanted a fresh start. He went to an internist at the university, who sent him to a cardiologist. Maybe three weeks ago."

The dog looked at each of them quizzically, then barked twice, sniffed his privates.

"Boyd. Come inside."

"No, no. You're going jogging."

"Please come in."

"I can't, Gerda. I can't."

"It happened so fast, Boyd."

Boyd tried to interrupt, but Gerda continued.

"When the first doctor ran a routine echocardiogram, he saw severe deterioration in the arteries. The cardiologist he sent him to was recommending a bypass."

Towser began to whine softly, eager for his run. Gerda

put her hand on his smooth head. He licked her hand, then dropped like a stone at her feet.

"The doctor told him to avoid too-strenuous exercise, didn't he?"

"Yes."

"Especially tennis, right?"

"Boyd . . ."

"It would have been highly dangerous. Like tempting fate, wouldn't you say?"

"Do you really think he wanted to kill himself?"

"You must have. Otherwise why fear an autopsy?"

Gerda put out her hand, and Boyd pulled away from her. "What would have been the point of an autopsy? His body violated like that—for what purpose?"

"To confirm the cardiologist's findings about his heart. To see if he took something to . . . exacerbate his condition. Any number of things."

"He's dead, honey. Nothing will . . ."

The gardener's motorized cart came putt-putting along behind the stately row of trees.

"I wouldn't mind being aware of some . . . *inevitability* to blame. Something besides myself."

The motorized cart accelerated, then stopped. Down the hill, a dog barked. Towser, who'd curled dejectedly on the gravel, perked up, his ears high, and began pacing back and forth.

"You had this special relationship with him. I was always on the outside. Or does it just seem like that now?"

"Tear up the letter, burn it, sweep away the ashes! We both know how his mind could work. Sweep it all away!"

Gerda waved her hands in the air, flicking away the floating, imaginary ashes. Another bark. Towser took off running. Gerda looked after him, tried to speak, could not. She raised her arm, shielding her gaze from the sun.

"I was going to tell you. But I decided to wait." She shrugged, then her face sagged. "He was my son."

"Yes he was. Your son."

Boyd tossed the letter onto the gravel, got into her car. Instead of turning around the wide semicircle, she threw the engine into reverse, her arm over the seat, her profile set, looking backward as she shot down the drive. Gerda stood staring after her, then reached down and picked up the envelope at her feet.

She opened it, read it again, then folded it and put it in the pocket of her sweat suit. She took a deep breath, waited. Then she began to run.

After a mile or so, she was out on the road that circled the enclave of estates fronting the lake, the warm glossy macadam under her feet, and she slowed to a walk. A few cars hummed by her. A neighbor honked and waved.

She walked with a loping gait, talking a little to herself, commanding herself to go faster, then slower.

"Slow down, slow down, old goat!" she cried at one point. She was telling herself that she was strong, from strong stock. She had been born in Stillwater, where the enormous gray wall of the maximum-security prison rose like a glacier outside the pretty little town. Her parents were both immigrants, he German, she Norwegian. Her father was a baker, a quiet man. He and her mother were passionate readers. When Gerda, pregnant, married Thaddeus Schaeffer in her second year of college, they disapproved but nevertheless baked a splendid wedding cake for the reception. Only Gerda noticed that her father had sculpted a miniature spun-sugar diploma and set it in the bride's tiny sugar fist. Tad Schaeffer was from a rich Minneapolis milling family, and during his lifetime he would triple the family fortune, mainly through shrewd investments. They had three children, and by the time she was carrying the fourth, Russell, she was tired of being a full-time mother. She hadn't wanted Russell. She had drunk gin and quinine when she'd first discovered her condition, in an attempt to bring on bleeding. After Russell was born, she had gone back to college, taking courses in history and literature. She had begun a very brief, very awkward dalliance with her history professor. She took Russell, a toddler, along the two or three times she met the professor in a hotel. Russell had been her excuse to leave the house—a ride, a play group. Nothing much happened except some heated yet ultimately chaste embraces on a hotel bed and boring soul-searching. But Russell was left alone, left to his own devices.

The shame of these memories brought her to a complete stop. She stood at the side of the road, murmuring. She stared, horrified, at an image of herself driving frantically through a rainstorm, her sick four-year-old on the seat beside her, head lolling. His temperature had risen to 108 degrees by the time she'd stormed into the emergency room at St. Joseph's Hospital, carrying him like an offering. Tad was waiting for her in the lobby. He refused to ask her where she'd been when she had phoned him, crying, Russell convulsing. The fever had come on so suddenly, but she had been holding the professor's hand. The baby was whimpering on the hotel daybed. It took her a long time to walk over, put her hand on that white-hot brow. Too long. If there was anything wrong with Russell, it began

there. It began with Gerda's wretched, desperate prayer, one of
the billion bargains struck with God by mothers in extremity:
Let him live and I will accept your punishment. As the little body
convulsed and convulsed, the small bruised arms held rigid,
strapped to the gurney, as the doctors shook their heads, God
did not turn away. God turned Gerda's head to her own child
and forced her to look closely at him for the first time as he was
given back to her, smelling of the other world. She held him as
consciousness returned, the first choking cries, the thin mattress
soaked with death-sweat: saved. But Gerda knew God was waiting for his due. This blessing, undeserved, would gradually reveal itself as judgment. She would not see right away how the
miracle and the punishment were one—how could she? She was
looking into the face of her innocent child, bartered-for and re-
claimed from death: the inimitable Russell.

It took Gerda a while to realize that Towser had found her and
was nuzzling the back of her leg. She brushed him aside distractedly, then patted his head. After a while, they set out together, running slowly, taking the wide loop back home.

PART TWO

CHAPTER 9

ARTON EUGENE GRIGGS, resplendent in a starched madras plaid shirt and kelly-green tie, bought Will a drink. The bright oxblood hue of his still-thick hair asserted itself even in the dim light of Tollson's Lounge. But it was his voice that gave him immediate authority. As his lips moved, the mellifluous broadcast tones of an FM radio announcer, resonant and avuncular, swelled cello-like from his chest.

Griggs enjoyed legendary stature at Youngren's. He was an embalmer extraordinaire ("Give me Liza Minnelli *stiff*—I tell ya, breathing takes something *big* from that gal"), and he'd been around ever since Will could remember. He was the first person Will's father had hired, over thirty years ago. His much-admired "interpretations" of the deceased (ostensibly for the benefit of the Bereaved) included research into the deceased's eccentricities of dress and toilette, close examination of the deceased's favorite photos of himself, and long periods of "listening hard," as he put it, to the desires of "our silent clientele."

Griggs loved the dead, and did not fear them. He was deeply committed to their beautification—it was the living with whom he had trouble. He unnerved healthy companions by abruptly fixing them with a speculative professional gaze, "measuring" the air about their ears and brows with his long, spatulate fingers, crooning a little Cole Porter under his breath ("like the beat-beat-beat of a tom-tom . . .") and jotting comments with exclamation points in a tiny notepad he kept in his breast pocket. He had a certain expression that had become notorious, nicknamed the Death Ray. Gossip had it that if he fixed you too long with this look, you'd end up for certain on his embalming table.

Tonight Griggs signaled Roy the bartender for refills, and Roy yelled back: "Hey, Youngren! He's lookin' at me in that way again!"

When Will looked over, Roy, who was fat and bald, made a guillotine gesture under his chin and pretended to shudder. Will shrugged good-naturedly and Griggs turned around and smiled very slowly and sweetly at Roy, who made a cross of swizzle sticks and held it up in their direction.

Griggs turned back to Will, shook his head and snorted. He had not noticed that Will was unnaturally silent. Griggs was used to unnatural silence; in fact, he had found unnatural silence to be the norm for most of his partners in conversation. Griggs's subtler social instincts were consigned to the dead. In the case of the living, he required very specific prompting.

Will glanced at his watch. He was tired; he had a headache. Griggs had cornered him at his office door and Will had found himself unable to come up with an excuse for not having a drink. Now he longed for home, three aspirins, pillows under his head. The smoke and canned music hurt his brain. *Why was he in this business?* What would Boyd think of Griggs's oddly animated face, the occasional semi-alarmed expression that meant he was about to say something of import? Griggs chewed meditatively on a beer nut, which he'd extracted from a pile he'd stacked neatly on a bar napkin.

"Your dad," he began, leaning closer to Will, his eyebrows leaping, his breath insistently fresh, redolent of pocket peppermints. "He understood the business like nobody before or since. He was a prince of a man, a gent, Willy. He knew how to talk to people, y'see. He would come up with, oh boy, all those Greek and Latin quotes, and he knew his way in and out of a book. But the man also knew how to tend a ledger."

Will looked into the eerie, unfocused eyes, the same shade as the piled nuts. He sipped his second glass of beer and checked his watch again—surreptitiously, though discretion was not necessary. Griggs's gaze was now fixed on the ceiling as he prepared to launch himself into his story.

"Stop me if I told you this one," Griggs did not wait for a response; he chuckled to himself, scooped up another beer nut, and cracked it with his large false teeth. "Now I'm goin' back a few years here. Oh, maybe fifteen, twenty. And how the hell old were you? Let me think now."

He paused, calculating on his fingers, then waved his hand impatiently in Will's face. "Anyway, forget it. You were little, you get it, Willy? And your dad had to go in the hospital for some routine thing, I forget what . . ."

Will looked about in despair and caught Roy's eye again. Roy had been staring at Griggs and shaking his head. Now he high-signed to Will that he'd gotten his order, and turned away to fill new glasses. Too late for Will to cry out that he'd wanted the check instead.

"Now, your dad was in the hospital, I got that far, and they had him in one of them ridiculous nightgowns with no back where your goddam hinder sticks out, and they left him to wait in a little partitioned cubicle? Well, lo and behold, he hears some talking coming from behind the curtain next to him and pretty soon then they're cryin'—he hears 'em—and then he hears a voice sayin', 'Now, just who do we call here, now that Grandpa's gone?' You see, Willy, their grandpa or whoever had up and died in the cubicle next to your dad and they needed to make funeral arrangements—"

"I got it, Jarton, thanks."

Griggs stopped himself at this point and began to laugh. His laugh was a long hiss of expelled air, like pressure bled from a tire. The waitress Will usually flirted with arrived and quickly set down their drinks before Griggs could notice her. She threw Will a look of terror, then was gone. Griggs patted his mouth with a paper napkin and gargled some scotch.

"So damned if your dad didn't stick his head through the curtains and introduce himself to the Bereaved! All these poor souls see is this head pokin' out of nowhere. Your dad says, " 'Please excuse me, please. I know that this is a very sensitive and private moment and I don't mean to intrude . . .' "

Griggs paused to let out another gasp. He nodded, choking, at Will, who smiled and shook his head in wonder, though he knew the story by heart.

"Then your dad says, 'I'm sorry to say that I'm not dressed at present, and I don't wish to offend you in this moment of terrible loss, but allow me to present my card.' So he holds out his hand with the card in it and the curtains open up, so they see him in his gown. He tells them why he's there—can't remember, was it a hernia?—and then, as he says good-bye, he forgets about the gown having no back and he turns around! He *moons* 'em, Willy!"

Griggs held on tight to the sides of the table and whistled like a teapot. Will sipped his third beer and waited, trying to smile.

"Damned if they didn't bring their sweet little old gramps right over the next day. I remember now, that old guy had an interesting jaw structure—"

"My God, Jarton, look at the time! I'll pick this one up—hey, really, I insist."

Will caught himself up. His head was in a vise, but he remembered something he needed to know. "Jarton, could I ask you a question? A professional question? What would you say—I mean, if someone just asked out of the blue—is the first rule of your . . . profession?"

"Let's see . . . you mean besides *Don't date?* Oh, okay. I see you're serious, then. Okay, that's easy—it's dignity to the dead. That the dead be cared for with respect. Not abandoned or neglected, y'know. You know, Willy, I had that car crash come in last night? Four people dead—a whole damn family wiped out out there by 494. Two went through the windshield. I owe it to each of them to see who each one was. They're on the bridge, y'see, Willy. Between the two worlds, the bridge, and they need an escort to the other side."

"Well, what if a body carries plague, or HIV?"

"No different."

"If there are blood-borne pathogens, what then?"

"No different." Griggs cocked his head. "Are you thinking, by any chance, of Mr. Sechman and Mr. Robideaux?"

"I am. I never fired anyone before, Jarton, and I want to be fair here."

"The living—*us*, you see—we're given time to fill our needs. The dead have but one urgent need and must rely on us, the living, to accomplish it in time. If the dead are forgot by the living, well, how can we call ourselves civilized, Willy?"

Will studied the unearthly smile on Griggs's lips.

"Besides. We're suited up when we work. You know, Willy, we're encountering more germs here among the breathing than you'd ever get at the sink." He looked suspiciously into his scotch glass.

"What if a fairly young guy, say in his forties, dropped dead unexpectedly but the family said no autopsy? Would you—listen, never mind."

Griggs opened and closed his eyes, lizard-like. "You wouldn't be talkin' about the young Schaeffer fellow?"

"Amazing," said Will. "Do you forget any of them? Just checking."

Will stood up, a little unsteadily, dots gathering before his eyes.

Griggs gripped his hand suddenly. "Willy. You're lookin' more like your dad every day. You work upstairs so much, I hardly see you."

"I'm often there late."

"I work late too, Willy, as you know. You can always count on me for a late drink. Is that a deal, son?"

He released Will's hand, which had grown numb.

"It is, Jarton. And thanks for your advice."

Will waved and turned, realizing suddenly that if Mega-Death Services took over his business, Griggs, past retirement age, would be the first to go. The thought astonished and preoccupied him, even as he felt The Look: Griggs's strange eyes boring into his back as he made his way out the door and into the night.

CHAPTER 10

I'M READY to go to work."

Boyd faced Dr. Dagmar Remington, Obstetrics and Gynecology, a Corporation, across her gleaming expanse of desk on the fourth floor of the Medical Arts Building. Dr. Remington was actually half a corporation. Dr. Remington's partner was Dr. Irene Resnikoff, also a gynecologist. In back of Dr. Remington's desk was a floor-to-ceiling window looking down into a tree-filled courtyard with a fountain. Perhaps it was due to lack of sleep, but Boyd felt exhilarated, almost giddy, rather than intimidated by the situation at hand: She was a doctor who'd been out of the profession for more than a few years and was now applying for a job.

As she waited for Dr. Remington's response, a human head wearing an orange hard hat appeared in the bottom corner of the window to the left of Dr. Remington's chair. The head hung there briefly, winking shyly at her. Then, in a series of vertical lurches, the head acquired a neck, then the torso of a workman

in a bright orange suit and grasping a chain saw. He was belted
into a cherry picker, which he steered to a shuddering stop, hovering near a dead branching oak bough a few feet from the window. He waved his chain saw at Boyd in a courtly manner, and
she smiled back at him.

Dr. Remington looked up at last, smiling also, but a little confused.

"How strange," she said, "to go all the way through medical
school, boards, licenses, then *not* practice."

Boyd sat forward in her chair. "I got married. I had a child."

Through the window glass, the workman cocked his head at
the withered bough, placed the saw's chained blade tentatively
against its forked base. With his other hand, he reached out for
a waist-level hydraulic switch and the cherry picker lurched
again, bumping closer to the tree.

Dr. Remington smiled and took off her tortoiseshell glasses.
She was petite and brunette, dressed in a navy suit beneath her
white coat. She resembled a wizened schoolgirl as she smiled
again, nodding at Boyd's résumé and board certification, a pile
of official papers on the desk before her.

"My husband died recently." A voice inside her protested,
Recently? How about a week ago? She ignored it.

Dr. Remington opened her mouth to speak. At that instant,
the workman snapped the saw's starter cord. Dr. Remington's
mouth stayed open, and the guttural scream that seemed to
flow outward from it was all-pervasive, a stream of intensifying
sound that could not be talked away or through. In vain they
tried to outmaneuver the onslaught, miming and signing at
each other, Dr. Remington finally indicating the doorway. As

they left the room, Boyd glanced back at the workman. He was intent, the bladed links flashed, limbs fell.

They faced each other in a small, airless room off the reception area, filled with an enormous Xerox machine, which lit up with sudden green passionate flashes of instruction about how it should be treated. It stood next to floor-to-ceiling stacked boxes, a file cabinet, and an antiquated adding machine, out of fashion, unable to comment on itself. There were also stacks of patient files, boxes of thin latex examination gloves, boxes and boxes of pharmaceutical samples of a spermicidal jelly, and low-dosage birth control pills.

"I'm so sorry," murmured Dr. Remington. "I forgot that the arborists were coming today."

The word *arborist* triggered something reckless in Boyd.

"Dr. Remington. May I speak frankly? I made a mistake by not practicing right away. I thought I didn't need medicine, but I was wrong." She laughed. "I need medicine. I need a lot of medicine. I need to work."

Dr. Remington leaned against a trestle table stacked with pamphlets entitled *BREAST-FEEDING BABY* and folded her arms across her chest. She looked thoughtful, assessing even, perhaps a little shocked. "Well, I'm sure that your husband's death must have precipitated—"

"Oh well. My husband. He wasn't a fan of the profession." Boyd struggled to regain her equilibrium. *He's here,* she thought. *I can* sense *him.*

Dr. Remington said nothing; her smile remained, steadfast—quizzical, but steadfast. She watched Boyd carefully.

"I'm a good doctor. When you check my recommendations—and my E.R. and clinic records, my residency, I don't think

you'll disagree. And beyond what's on paper, I'm good with patients. I'm a clinician; I observe. I take careful histories and I
know how to talk to patients. There was an *incident,* which may
or may not still be on my record. I lost a patient in a saline-
injection abortion—she had a cardiomyopathy, undiagnosed. I
was exonerated in the M-and-M. And I will never perform another abortion—that, I know."

Dr. Remington nodded thoughtfully. "This is why we don't
train our staff here to do these procedures. You should never
have been put in that position during your training. You should
not have been put in that position at all. My partner and I will
talk it over in any case. And I can't resist saying I find it refresh-
ing to hear someone talk about taking good histories in this day
and age! Irene is committed to the five-to-seven-minutes-per-
patient rule. The profit margin rule, you know, like a taxi meter
dropping."

"Do you abide by that rule?"

"No, Dr. Schaeffer, I do not."

Boyd started at the appellation, then smiled. Dr. Remington
looked up at hearing her name on the intercom, then indicated
an examination room across the hall that had just been freed up.
A nurse waved them toward the open doorway. White sheets,
the smell of disinfectant, the stirrups, Grave's speculum everywhere displayed like an icon, symbol of female power. Russell
could not stand between her and this, her once-chosen profession. Female power, the speculum. It was all coming back.

CHAPTER 11

THOUGH HIS MIND WAS STILL on Boyd, when Priscilla
painted, Will watched. The idea of painting as a hobby
had never occurred to her. Priscilla was serious. Will
could sense, as she worked, her quick eye reorganizing the
world. Her watercolors never skimmed the paper, suggesting
the mysterious nature of composition or color. They were firmly
rendered; they made sense. Her blunt-cut hair swung over her
cheek as she bowed to the palette. She straightened up and her
half-smiling profile rose, firm and ascendant; she pressed the
wet brush to the thirsty surface.

Since Russell Schaeffer's funeral, Will had sunk, abstracted,
into the gentle pull of her gravity. Where Boyd had confused
and frightened him, Priscilla simplified everything, narrowing
his sense of himself in the most logical and soothing manner:
She would reach up as he spoke, gently press her fingertips
against his eyes, then his mouth, and he was silenced, grateful. Whatever he'd been talking about, protesting in agitation,

didn't matter anymore, hadn't mattered ever. He stared, startled, at her. She shook her head in mock exasperation.

It was Saturday morning, about ten o'clock, just over a week after the Schaeffer funeral. Will sat cross-legged on the floor behind Priscilla. She was naked except for a pair of flowered cotton panties and sat on a bright red stool, working at her art-supply-store easel. Light poured in through the window on a wave of traffic sounds, calling up old car dreams, heat and license. Will yawned and stretched his long legs. He watched Priscilla turn to the window, her left breast swaying under her arm, lifted high, as she held the brush: measuring the depth of brightness. She could alter the quality of light by her self-possession; he'd seen it. Sometimes this self-possession disturbed him and for a second his sense of her was undermined. She seemed heartless, as if she'd lived her whole life in this expository light, recording everything, forgiving nothing. He sighed. But her naked back was so beautiful, the color of gold tea in a clear hourglass.

"Do you like this?"

She moved aside slightly and he looked at the picture. A boat at sea, a pastel sky, bright ruptures. Priscilla bowed, holding her face close to the surface of the stretched paper, waiting. Will had seen this look on the faces of children enlisted as page-turners at funeral services: solemn pride lighting the profile, a half-smile.

"Well. It has a certain quiet tumultuousness."

She sat up and smiled at him, pleased, unsure. "You think so?"

He waited. "Priscilla. It was a joke." He paused again.

She looked away, staring out the window, not listening. "I

want to paint like Hokusai. I want to paint something like the fishermen in the boat, the second before the wave crashes down on them."

Will smiled at her face, rapt, eager, above her small, dark-nippled breasts. She stretched languidly, rolling her shoulders, and lay the wet brush on the lip of the easel. He moved toward her. She was smiling back at him. He almost laughed aloud at the scene before him—the table next to the easel carelessly strewn with still lifes: overripe pears, dark grapes in a cracked clay bowl near a tipped red-and-white-striped aerosol can of shaving cream, the flung silver of his car keys, her lovely body backlit. The whole world to be painted and healed. He lifted his hand and placed it on her sun-warmed breast. What did he need with Boyd Schaeffer? She bent her head, kissing his fingers.

AFTER A LONG, languorous afternoon and an early supper of fresh peaches and fried chicken in a bucket and a bottle of beer or two, Will left Priscilla and went to visit his mother, as he'd promised. She met him in the doorway of the house he'd grown up in. It was early evening, past dusk, but there were no porch lights burning. He breathed in the deep, sweet fragrance of the enormous white and pink peony bushes blossoming on either side of the stone steps, closed his eyes, then slapped at a mosquito. He'd had a long, erotic afternoon. Now he felt unpleasantly exposed, as if he had forgotten his clothes. He watched his mother as she peered nervously down at the pair of worn-down entry steps, uneven between the wrought-iron handrails. She had crippling arthritis and had fallen twice on these front steps—once in icy winter and earlier this summer, when she swore the concrete had jerked underfoot. Now she walked with an aluminum cane. She stood bristling before him in her senior citizen's uniform of sweat suit and sneakers.

"Get in here," she whispered, peering around him at the street, "before they see what I've got."

Will tried to embrace her, but she stepped back, urging him around the door and into the dark hallway.

"Mom. Turn a light on."

"You think I'm rich?"

She had taken all the high-watt bulbs out of the lamps and screwed in dimmer ones. Only one small lamp was on in the cavernous living room. Will felt around a corner for the overhead light switch, but when he clicked it on, nothing happened.

His mother was moving very quickly toward the kitchen, twisting her cane into the carpet, muttering.

Will raised his voice. "Mom, you have money. Dad left you enough to take care of yourself."

There was silence, then clattering, water running.

"Mom, what are you doing? I don't want anything to eat!"

The kitchen was a little less dim than the living room. The yellow fluorescent light illuminated the overstuffed cupboards spilling out booty like shipwrecked cargo: rows of cereal boxes, stacked fast-food packets of salt, pepper, catsup, barbeque sauce, and relish.

She was fixing tea. The stainless steel kettle rumbled on the stove, and she'd set out two flowered china cups on the old oval table. He watched her, knowing she would refuse all offers of help. She used her cane like an extra limb, poking at clutter, lifting the hot kettle off the stove, striking at furniture in her path. Her face under the careful gray coiffure was pale and tidy but

furious. Since her husband's death, she'd discovered she was en-
raged. The cause of this rage was sometimes specific but more
often unclear to her. A lifetime's worth of anger shook the cane
and rattled the spoons in the teacups.

She sat down stiffly, sniffed at her teabag, then dipped it into the
cup. He poured the hot water, then set the pot on an ancient
wrought-iron trivet.

Her eyes met his and narrowed. "We're not going to talk
about sending me out to pasture again."

She banged her hand on the table, rattling the cups. He
didn't jump—he'd expected this. They sat in silence. When she
looked away from him and drank, gulping a little, he studied
her. She was in her seventies and her face was dramatically aged,
but she'd spun a cocoon of refusal around herself, which tight-
ened daily.

Then, amazingly, she smiled, and he saw her young again for
an instant—a bright-haired musician, jangling bracelets, smoking a Lucky Strike. He remembered her standing outside in the
yard, her hair blowing gently across her forehead, her head
cocked as she smoked. She was listening to piano music, someone playing inside the house. Signe playing: a little Brahms,
from the navy-blue book. His mother had taught them both.
He'd come up behind his mother and stood next to her, listening to the insistent downward flight of notes, then an explosion
of rippling keys, jarred jangling chords, the keyboard cover
thrown down, laughter. Signe was very talented, as she had
been told, but she refused to practice. "How can you refuse
such a gift?" he'd heard his mother cry out to his sister's vanishing back. Will practiced daily, but he could read the strained,

excessively patient look on his mother's face as she sat stiffly next to him on the piano bench. He had no gift at all.

"What are you thinking about?"

He jumped guiltily. "Signe."

She put down her teacup.

"I was thinking about her playing—how good she was and how she would never practice."

She put her hands on the table, gnarled and veined, the knuckles like walnuts. "I taught both you kids to play. And they call me a dumb Squarehead."

She nodded at her hands. "Well, dammit," she shouted. "I'd rather have a beer."

She launched herself, furious, on her cane, and flung open the refrigerator, yanked out two Hamm's, and returned to the table. Will twisted off the wet tops.

She raised the bottle to her lips, eyeing him. "She was good, but she tried not to show it. She wanted to impress you."

"Impress me? Signe?" He started to laugh, then stopped, looking at her face. The overhead light flickered. She looked cunning. "So what are you saying to me? That she didn't succeed at music because of me?"

"You miss the point a lot, honey. Did you ever notice?"

He drank down the last of his tea and stood up, ignoring the beer. He was irritated with himself for getting angry. She was just an old woman—she hardly resembled his mother anymore. She seemed to think that she was close to death and that this proximity to the End gave her a kind of *final* authority. She was trying to get him to remember something, her way of making him co-conspirator in her fantasies, her way of enlisting his hapless but steadfast loyalty to her changing versions of the past.

He couldn't help it now. This angling for his intimidated attention upset him—it was so much like playing her straight man. *Straight man to the dead,* he thought, then laughed aloud.

"You don't know what it's like to get old," she murmured, blinking. "I've noticed that everybody has started sticking their tongues out at me. Can you imagine how that feels? I hope you see that serious music is played at the services."

"I'm doing my best."

"The cello, the oboe. Then they stick their tongues out."

"Right." He pushed back his chair.

"Do you have to go, Will?"

"Yeah I do, Mom."

When the time came, she walked slowly beside him to the door, relying less on the cane, he noticed. She seemed to want to keep talking, but there was no way he could do this. At the door, she lifted up her cheek to be kissed.

"The cello. I don't think there's another instrument comes close for teaching the ear about sadness."

"What's wrong with these porch lights? You've got bulbs in here, but no light. Did somebody do something to the wiring?"

But she'd turned away from him, shuffled back into the dark house. He thought he heard her say good-bye, but he wasn't sure.

CHAPTER 12

FREDDY WAS NAPPING. Boyd wandered from room to room, absentmindedly picking up toys, Popsicle sticks, murmuring to herself. She surveyed the hall rugs, trying to remember when she'd last noticed them. She employed a regular cleaning lady, and people had been coming in, helping her with touching up, but she couldn't remember who had been in her house and what they'd done. She'd looked up now and then and noticed flower arrangements in all the rooms and thought, *Why do people do this?* Flowers in the emergency room, flowers in the crypt. Flowers everywhere in the monolithic presence of death: stargazer lilies, iris, freesia, lily of the valley, each floral tribute stabbed by a clear plastic trident offering an inscribed white commemorative card.

She selected one at random, perched in a tree of cymbidium orchids. "Dear Boyd. There are no words to say what we feel in our hearts for you. The Kramers."

There are no words to say what I feel. Dazed, she moved unsteadily into the living room, brushed against a low side table. A book of poems called *Dark Sonnets*—she caught the title as it fell—skittered to the floor. She picked it up, frightened. She knew he underlined and wrote in the margins of poetry books. She did not want to see his sloping hand, and yet there it was as she flipped through the pages, filling the white spaces: *Exactly! Sez who? You must be kidding! Jesuit horniness??* And bouquets of exclamation points and parentheses and bouquets of botanically accurate flowers.

She sniffed the book, the pages, smelling of his smell. Then the phone rang. It occurred to her that the phone had been ringing for days—she remembered discreet voices intercepting these rings and the answering machine's quick commandeering—but this had all been background, a stream of smooth circumventions upon which she floated. She pulled herself up and moved, robot-like, toward the ringing. After she said hello, there was a quick, audible intake of breath on the other end.

"Boyd? Boyd? This is Cherry Ikaml."

Boyd said nothing. She sniffed the air. She smelled Russell, she smelled the beautiful flowers, dying.

"I just called to see how you are!"

"I'm fine."

"Boyd, you don't have to please other people. Remember that. You're suffering, remember? Your pain can be a source of empowerment."

"Cherry, I'm not in pain. If I were, I probably wouldn't talk to you about it."

"That's right. Get angry! Let it out, Boyd!"

There was a silence.

"Everyone is so worried about you. Everyone keeps asking,

'How's Boyd? It's been almost two weeks since the funeral,' and I don't know what to say. They think because I was Russell's right hand, his private secretary, that I know. And I say, 'Just because Russell told me everything doesn't mean that—' "

"Cherry, tell them that I'm in touch with Satan hourly. He wants to send Russell back, but I'm not negotiating. A deal's a deal—you know what I mean? But then Hell's not what it used to be, as far as I can tell. Where's the rigor, that old spirit of fire and brimstone? I'm afraid what I'm dealing with here is Hell Lite."

"Boyd? I'm a little confused as to—"

"I have to go now. I smell brimstone and chardonnay, Cherry."

She hung up, and almost immediately the phone rang again.

"Boyd? Is that you? This is Alphonse Jaglern. I hope I'm not calling at an inconvenient moment. I actually did not expect to get you. I had planned to leave a message. Please forgive my intrusion . . . at such a time, but I felt compelled to express to you personally how deeply I . . ."

"Hi, Alph. How much did he promise you?"

"I beg your pardon?"

"I've been getting letters, discreet little notes? I was just glancing at a few. It seems that you're one in a long line of grief-stricken yet entitled mourners. The vultures are turning the sky black, Alphonse. How much?"

"Well, that's a little *direct*. I would be devastated if you misunderstood my intentions in making this call. It is not about money or questions of money or matters of financial support. I called only to—"

"Well, great. That makes it easy then. I'll just cross your name

off the list of individuals to whom Russell promised something . . ."

"Well. Another time, when you're not feeling . . . so upset,
we can perhaps discuss the terms of Russell's commitment to
me, to the magazine and press. We can discuss the future, in
fact, that Russell so generously foresaw for *Hapax Legomenon.*"

Boyd said nothing. She stared at *Dark Sonnets,* left open on
the table, the printed text crowded by margins crisscrossed with
Yes! and flowers and *x*'s. Tina Coburn appeared before her suddenly, her head rolling side to side as the anesthetic took hold,
the saline dripping into her through the clear plastic tube.

"But you are upset. Obviously. So I will call back—"

"I can't tell you, Alph, how many times I've heard myself described lately as upset when I am not in the least upset. I'm
probably more clearheaded than I've been in years. Anyway, listen. Don't worry. You'll get your money. Everybody's going to
get their money. I'll make sure of it. Just don't ever call me
again, okay?"

"I understand, Boyd. I know that this is a time of—"

"Tell me, by the way. What do you like most about Russell's
poetry?"

"Is that a hostile question? Is that supposed to be hostile? Are
you implying that his poetry was—"

"Crap? Are you?"

"Of course not. I don't understand what—"

"Just tell me. What moved you, what made his poems special
to you?"

"Well. He was . . . unlike anyone else I can think of . . . re-
lentless in his appropriation of certain imageries."

"I hope you don't mind my candor, Alphonse. Russell's dick

fell off during his long though undetected illness. He wrote a series of poems called 'My Penis Is an Autumn Wanderer,' followed by 'The Weasel Wonders Why'—poems that relentlessly appropriate certain imageries of a missing winky—and I was wondering if you could possibly publish—"

The dial tone filled her ear.

"Bye, Alph."

Boyd replaced the receiver and closed the book, coaxed it gently back into a line of poetry collections in the bookcase. Then she turned in a circle, slid to the floor, her back against the flowered sofa, and fell almost immediately into a deep sleep.

T WO HOURS LATER, when Gerda rang the doorbell, Boyd startled awake. Her neck hurt—she'd somehow twisted it as she slept—and her right foot refused to wake up. She limped to the front door. Gerda was dressed to go shopping, in a smart beige suit, but there were circles under her eyes. She looked unwell, Boyd thought, and then turned away, still limping. "You have a key, right?"

"Yes, of course. But I didn't know if I was welcome. Is something wrong with your foot?"

Boyd said nothing. In the living room, she limped about, opened windows, commenting on the cloying scent of the flowers.

Gerda looked around appreciatively, sat down on the sofa. "So many people cared about him. His life was not for nothing."

Boyd cleared her throat, waving her hand impatiently toward the kitchen. "Would you like coffee?"

"Boyd, please. Sit for just a minute."

Boyd stayed on her feet. "Gerda, I don't need any more surprises. Surprises make me mean. The fact is, being mean takes a lot out of me right now."

"Boyd, I just want to say that I'm sorry that I didn't tell you about his heart."

Boyd raised her hand and Gerda fell silent. Then Boyd sat down at last, wearily, at the far end of the sofa, her head bowed and her shoulders bent.

"I'm sorry," whispered Gerda.

Gerda looked around at the silver-framed photos, the dear faces on the polished piano top. She reached over, letting her hand hover, shaking, in the air just above the back of Boyd's bent neck. It trembled there, above the head bowed as if for an execution. Then she withdrew it slowly, straightening her collar at the last second. She closed her eyes. "Just because he's dead," she began, "it doesn't mean that I can't go on loving him."

Boyd looked up at her and laughed bitterly. "Just because he's dead doesn't mean he isn't still driving me crazy. Like all these people calling, asking for . . ."

"Russell helped them."

"You give people money and they love you. What I want to know is how you think loving him meant keeping secrets from me."

"You spent a lot of time looking away, Boyd."

"Looking away? From what? You ought to know."

Gerda stood up, unsteadily, bracing herself against a chair arm. Boyd thought again that she did not look well, but she turned her back on her, leading her to the front door. As she opened it, she heard Freddy stirring upstairs, then a cry. Gerda's face lit up. "I'll just run up quickly and say—"

"No." Boyd opened the door wider. "No, I'd rather you didn't see her, really."

Another shout. Then, "Mama? Is somebody here?"

"Boyd—"

"Good-bye, Gerda. Leave us now. I just need some time."

The door stood open. Gerda looked at her, her expression unbelieving. Looking for a crack, thought Boyd, a crack in my resolve.

"Your grief has made you—"

There were quick, light footsteps above them, then Freddy appeared at the top of the stairs. "Grandma?"

Boyd reached out her hand suddenly and touched Gerda's arm. There were tears in her eyes.

"Shit," she said. "Too late now. You might as well go up."

L ATER, after Gerda had left, the phone rang again. It was Dr. Remington calling to tell Boyd that she'd met with her partner, Dr. Resnikoff, and they were considering hiring Boyd to back them up in the practice. They needed her to come in two days a week at first, eventually becoming full-time, maybe even a full partner. How did that sound?

Boyd held the receiver away from her mouth as she gasped. She told Dr. Remington how very much she hoped that it would work out. The M-and-M and its sorrowful narrative—Remington threw this in before she hung up—was no longer in her records.

———

Boyd replaced the receiver and immediately saw a line of hand-lettered signs bobbing: her name printed large in black and red marker, next to the drawings of dripping knives and skulls and crossbones. Then she saw the pinched face of the woman who had spit on her as she left the hospital. The saliva landed on her jacket sleeve, and she stared down at it as she hurried past the protestors. The woman's voice followed her.

"Got two with one stone, didn't you?" the voice said. "Mother and baby. One stone."

The fetus had been larger than they'd expected, but it was still small, dull blue, curled like a lobster, with claw hands. She could see it with absolute clarity: its pale, distinct eyelashes, its fingernails, the down on its head. Blood clots scattered: olive-colored, red veins. And Tina Coburn's open eyes. Russell's unblinking gaze. One stone.

CHAPTER 13

WHERE IS THE UNDERWORLD? Will knows where it is, exactly: in the basement of the mortuary, where the embalmers work in their thoughtful chambers in deep intimacy with the dead, reversing the powerful magnetism of life in the body, undamming and draining the venous blood yet restoring something of living resemblance. Downstairs dwell death's cosmeticians—eccentric, pale, sometimes a little unkempt, but with clean, very clean, hands.

"I would like to know," said Will, pulling up an assistant's typewritten report and placing it in front of him, "why you refused to prepare for burial the bodies of . . ." He glanced at the paper, though he knew the names by heart. ". . . Kent Albertson last January and Mark Torgaard this last week."

Peter Sechman, sitting uncomfortably in one of the large chairs facing his desk, was a denizen of the underworld, the below-floors, a trollish young man with chopped white-blond hair, white eyelashes, and a collapsed nose.

Peter whistled a long held note, then shook his head emphatically, then nodded, confusing Will.

"Why wouldn't you . . . work on them? You know the bodies themselves were not contagious. AIDS is in the blood, but you handle the blood without touching it."

Peter stared back at him stubbornly.

Will watched his pale complexion redden, violent color pumping into his face and neck. "I am going to have to ask you to do your job, for all our customers. No distinctions made."

Peter Sechman, beet-red, made a snorting noise, then began whistling, off-key.

Will noted how shiny his pressed navy suit was, how frayed the cuffs. He'd dressed up for this interview. Maybe he'd expected a raise. Will's heart sank. It was clear to him that if Mega-Death took over, they would quickly reduce the number of his employees. Sechman, most recently hired, would probably be one of the first to go. Will felt his resolve weakening.

The door opened and Ron Robideaux came in.

"Hello, Ron. Sorry, Peter, I didn't hear you."

"I said I quit, okay?"

Will took a breath. "Pete—"

Pete began whistling again. Will wondered if he whistled into the ears of the dead prior to embalming them. Did they whistle back? Robideaux, a French-Canadian—a short, squat man with a sizable bosom—sat down next to Sechman, who began speaking again.

"I got two kids. I got a wife four months pregnant."

"Then give us both a break. Just tell me you'll do your job."

Pete pointed a finger at Will's heart. "You're the boss's son. And I say, to you: big deal."

Will stood up behind the desk. "Listen, I have some things for you to read."

He held out a sheaf of photocopied articles, bulletins from the government, OSHA, and the Centers for Disease Control.

Peter whistled at the papers, then stood up. He pointed at Will again, then turned to the door.

The door slammed. After a second, Peter stuck his head back in and whistled again, a piercing heads-up blast. The door shut.

"Jesus," said Will. "The guy's like Harpo Marx."

"Will," said Robideaux, leaning forward. "We get a little odd downstairs. Look at it from our point of view."

Robideaux had been a grad student in biology at the University of Minnesota, but he'd dropped out of the program. He and Will had gotten their embalming certificates at the university at the same time, just after Will's return from the East. They'd gone out drinking together now and then, they'd taken in a hockey game or two, but had never been close.

Robideaux had grown irritable, *raggy*—it seemed to Will— and had certainly succumbed to one of the hazards of massaging dead bodies with large quantities of estrogen: He had breasts. Robideaux tried to hide his condition with blousy Hawaiian shirts and tops, but he poked out cheerily through the cheap rayon beneath the blue palm trees and orange crocodiles. He bounced as he backed up a little and, like Pete, raised his arm to point at Will.

"Think about it, okay? Your dad wouldn't have done it, Will. Fired Sechman flat-out like that."

"You sat right here and witnessed what happened. He quit."

"Like you gave him a choice: Work on AIDS bodies or you're out of here."

"No. I asked him to do his job."

Robideaux snorted. His worried eyes fell on the OSHA and other government pamphlets on Will's desk.

"You see, this stuff kills me," he said. "These guys don't know what the hell they're talking about. Look at all the risks we take. I have these . . . *jugs* because nobody knew the long-term effects of these hormones we use. Look at me—I look like Dolly Parton."

"Don't flatter yourself."

"All I need's a platinum wig. And forgive me if I say this, but you're not a scientist. Ain't no scientist alive who knows for sure about AIDS. They don't know the long-term effects of estrogen and they don't know dick about AIDS. Hey, you come downstairs where the real fun is—where you could gather your information firsthand, putting your hands on the posthumous."

"Tell me why morticians all over the country handle these bodies with no problem. Can you tell me that?"

"They've been lucky. You can get blood splashes, loose vacuum hoses, bloody fluid in cavities and, you know, orifices. A perforation in a glove and a blood splash from, say, a nosebleed: I'm dead as my customer."

"The only time of risk, and it's minimal, is when blood is removed from the body."

"You're tellin' me about my own job?"

"I'm sorry. I won't turn away certain of our clients just because you're afraid of a loose hose."

Robideaux patted the lumpy shirt pocket over his left breast and pulled out a cigarette and lit it. "You really have changed since we used to hang out. It's interesting."

He looked at his cigarette, made a face, then stubbed it out in Will's standing ashtray. He smiled a kind of Mona Lisa smile and put a hand on his bosom. He sighed melodramatically, then he drew closer and whispered conspiratorially. "I got a *hunchback* on my table right now. Wanna see him?"

"That is so lame, Ron." Will glanced at a funeral directors' magazine open on his desk: SELLING THE SHADY GREEN: WHAT MOM & POP WANT IN A PLOT. He felt something sliding away from him. "I don't want you to quit. But I have no choice finally . . ."

"Your dad must be spinning right now. He would never have asked his staff to put themselves in jeopardy like this."

"My father did his job. Period." Will walked around the desk and held out his hand.

This time Robideaux took it immediately. "Is this the 'you're fired' handshake?"

"No, this is the 'why don't you think about this before jumping off the bridge' handshake."

"Sorry, I already jumped." Robideaux pulled his hand free and stood back from Will, his chest bouncing a little. He pulled a handwritten letter from his back pocket and waved it. "My resignation. Hey, Will, find someone else to drain the hunchback!"

WILL SLUMPED IN THE SEAT, driving with one hand. He'd left work a little early, just after his interviews with Sechman and Robideaux. Work was upsetting him; work was depressing him. He pulled into a filling station and, while his gas was being pumped, called Roger Leland, a friend who also ran a funeral home, on his cell phone. He asked Roger if he could come by, but Roger had a big wake to supervise—not the evening Will had had in mind. A couple, the mother and father of three young children, had died in a car accident. Roger sounded subdued, but Will could hear voices rising and falling behind him, the grimly buoyant chords of the organ.

"Do you want to come by?" asked Roger. "You'll see how they all are planning to get through this. The children are going to greet the mourners at the door—the twelve-year-old is going to sing gospel. She wants to sing."

Will thanked him but declined. He looked up, startled, as the nozzle popped out of his gas line. "I'm going to go home, thanks."

After he hung up, paid the attendant, and started his car, he was sorry. He was sorry about everything: about Sechman and Robideaux, about Mega-Death, sorry that he was in the wrong job, sorry that everybody had gotten to him. He thought, also feeling sorry for himself, of Boyd. The phrase *she wants to sing* ran through his mind. He thought of getting a drink at Tollson's Lounge, but the fear of seeing Griggs stopped him. Out of nowhere, he thought of Griggs putting the last expression on his sister's face deep in his underground chamber. Thought of Griggs closing her eyes, carefully composing her smart-ass teenage mouth, the lift of her chin. But then, as he watched, Griggs's pale hands drew away, fluttering like a magician's. Her eyes opened again. She turned toward Will, smirking, blinking, and Griggs's bent, solicitous figure, his cautionary look, faded—along with the brightly lit embalming chambers.

She lived again, she was back in her body again—she was running down a path ahead of him, looking back over her shoulder, sticking out her tongue. Then he remembered: Carver's Cave, how she'd found it by what seemed like intuition. How had she known what lay beneath the Bluff? They'd pedaled hard all the way to Mounds Park, throwing their bikes down at the curb, hollering at the top of their lungs, chasing each other in and out of the sacred burial mounds, where the great chiefs lay.

"Can't catch me! Can't catch me!" she sang, taunting, prancing. She wore fringed suede Indian moccasin-boots, rolled up blue jeans, and a ponytail. Girl brave. Will chased her along the edge of the Bluff, and as he watched, she slid over the side, skidding, half falling down, screaming with laughter. He raced down another path, thinking he'd cut across, catch her by surprise. When he climbed over the boulder separating them, she was gone. He looked down at the river, then up the face of the Bluff. Nothing.

Then he scanned the field again, did a double take: An arm waved to him out of the solid earth of the bluff side.

"Hey, Lightning!"

He ran, clattering across and down. The disembodied arm waved and beckoned him, like a dancing girl's, then vanished. He climbed to the spot where he'd seen the arm and noticed a nearly invisible seam in the rock, hidden by brush and nettle. Then she popped her head out of the wall, stuck out her tongue, and crossed her eyes. She was covered with dirt, upside down.

"Simple trick if you want to pull a fast one and disappear," she laughed. "You can slide in head or feet first. If you go headfirst, you can see where you're going. And once you're in—you're invisible!"

Her head disappeared again, but her expression remained in the air, taunting him.

"Come on!" He heard her voice inside the earth. "Come in! I've got matches—don't be afraid. Count backwards, shut your eyes. Follow me!"

He'd followed her into the cool, damp darkness, into the tunnel leading to the main body of the cave. Every so often she lit a match, the flaring light revealed the sweating rock on all sides, ancient graffiti.

"Be careful," he whispered hoarsely. "You'll change the temperature inside here and start a rock slide!"

She laughed and her laugh echoed. She was far ahead.

"Will!" she shouted, and his name ricocheted off the walls.

He pulled into the underground garage beneath a lit bank of condominiums, his home, incapable of any more underworld connections, fending off coincidence, exhausted. He slid his car into the designated space and sat with the engine running, his hands still on the wheel. At last he turned off the engine and got out of the car. He rode the elevator to the fourth floor, trudged to his apartment door, and stood juggling his briefcase, fishing in his pocket for his key. Suddenly, the door flew open. He jumped back, banging his briefcase against his leg. Priscilla stood before him, beaming, awash in air-conditioned air and the syncopated bass of Dire Straits. She wore tight purple jeans, a purple tank top, a black beret, and magenta lipstick.

"Surprise, surprise!" she cried. "You worked late tonight! I got some wine chilling. Okay, I confess, I dipped into it. Hon, I want you to look at my painting. I redid the whole thing!"

CHAPTER 14

FREDDY CAME INTO THE ROOM, walking backward.
When she bumped into a hassock, she whirled around
and shouted, "I said to stop!"

"Are you talking to me, Freddy?"

Freddy sat down comfortably on Boyd's foot, smiling up.
"There's these people who go backwards when we go ahead. I
want them to stop so I can touch them."

Boyd slid her foot gently out from under Freddy's weight.
"Fred, is it Daddy who's moving backwards away from us?"

"Daddy cries every night. I *hear* him. He comes into my
room and he cries and cries, Mom. He wants me to come and
get him."

"He says this to you?"

"Yeah. And now I know how to go get him."

"Tell me."

"Grandma showed me about flowers. I'm gonna plant a

flower Dad can climb up. It'll go down under the ground, like this, and he'll see it."

"Like a beanstalk?"

"Only going down. Backwards. Not up in the sky."

"Did you tell Grandma about this beanstalk?"

Freddy smiled conspiratorially and rolled herself back on top of Boyd's foot. Upside down, she looked crafty, her smile elongating, her long lashes fluttering.

"Nuh-uh. I only told you, Mom."

"Hold on one minute, Bunny," she whispered to Freddy, and lifted her gently, setting her down on the hassock. "I'll be right back."

She walked to the wall phone in the kitchen, picked it up. On the fifth ring, Will answered warily.

"It's me. It's Boyd Schaeffer."

He started to speak, but she cut him off.

"I'd like to have dinner Friday night. Is that possible for you?"

"Friday? Friday? Yeah! Well, sure, it's—"

"Good. I'll call you that morning and we'll decide on a restaurant, okay?"

"Okay. Real good, and . . ."

She hung up and went back to Freddy, who was trying, unsuccessfully, to stand on her head near the hassock.

Will hung up the phone and shook himself like a spaniel, dazed, muttering. Then he noticed, on the floor, still faceup, where it had been flung in anger, Priscilla's painting. He reached down and picked it up. It was a watercolor, taped to a charcoal-colored matte frame. He thought about Priscilla's face as she'd showed it to him.

"Look." Her voice had been low, reverent, her breath fruity with wine. He looked.

The boat floated on a shimmer of light. The figures in the boat seemed to grow directly out of this luminescence rather than from the sharp-cornered skiff. The figures in the boat whom Priscilla had labored to clarify were three: a father, a mother, and a child, seated in a row in the rectangular craft, their expressions uniform, circumspect. The mother was stretching out a hand over the water as if to dispense a blessing. The father stared behind him at the creased white wake. The child looked directly into the eyes of the viewer. Where was the tsunami? Where was death?

"The wake," whispered Priscilla at his shoulder. Then she cried out exultantly, "Do you see? You can tell they're being pulled downstream toward the rapids. And they have no oars."

Will had stared, but he could not see it: the urgent pull of the water, the quiet desperation in the boat. The people looked static to him, the river lit up but sluggish.

Then he'd made the unforgivable mistake. He'd told her exactly what he thought. She'd stared at him for a long second, narrowing her eyes, then hurled the painting to the floor, stalked out. She'd called in sick Tuesday—yesterday. He'd made no effort to reach her. He'd been exhausted that night and he was sorry he'd been too blunt and hurt her feelings, but he couldn't pretend. Now he ran his fingers over the little paint rills, the different thicknesses of color. He just didn't get it. Then he turned the painting over. He saw her initials first, scribbled gaily—"P.S." for Priscilla Soukpun—then above, in her quick hand, "Dear William, you, like no other, understand this moment. I love you."

Will sat down near the telephone table, the painting still in his hand. He stared at it, then at the telephone. He sat for a long time staring, then said, "Shit," very softly and placed the painting carefully, faceup, on the table.

Boyd tucked Freddy in, turned on the small jumping-frog night lamp on the bureau, and stood at the window, watching the darkness move in stages across the lawn. The trees below in the backyard began to hiss and murmur, twisting, the wind picking up. A rupture of heat lightning spilled light along the horizon. The air had turned suddenly cool, rushing through the corridors of trees.

From a distance, the low-talking thunder unwound, followed by faraway light clamor on the horizon: a jagged arc across the sky, a closer boom. Freddy breathed regularly in her bed. Boyd lowered the window as the first drops came down hesitantly, then faster and faster. She moved dreamily to the doorway, then froze at the sound of someone in the house, footsteps, windows being shut, one by one.

She clutched the doorjamb for support, heard her shocked voice carry into the dim light of the stairwell: "Who is it?" Then, in abject terror, against her own will: "Russell?"

There were more footsteps, then a concerned face looking up at her. A woman in a shiny red slicker. "Mrs. Schaeffer, did you forget that I come in tonight? Your mother-in-law, y'know, sent me over tonight to stay here. She thought you might need a little help. She said you weren't sleeping too good."

Boyd tried to make herself laugh. "Mrs. Nelson."

The red slicker gestured at her. "Honey, we got a storm here. I'm gonna close up the house and pick up a little here. You go to sleep now."

"I will," said Boyd, and stumbled a little. "Right now."

She waved feebly and started toward the master bedroom, then turned around. As she'd done every night since the funeral, she slipped off her jeans and crawled into bed with Freddy.

❦

CHAPTER 15

ON FRIDAY NIGHT, they met at Rolvaag's, a restaurant in a restored Victorian house in the Selby-Dale neighborhood, which was being slowly and haphazardly gentrified. Across the street from the restaurant was a shop that sold fresh pasta and crème fraîche and cappuccino with cinnamon sprinkles. Next to it was a fledgling art gallery filled with unabashed and very bad Albers imitations. On its left was an abandoned body shop and a slightly seedy laundromat. A few streets away, Will knew, was Leland Mortuary, the funeral home run by his friend Roger, with whom he'd gone to school. He considered telling Boyd about Roger, but she seemed completely absorbed in her mushroom risotto. She hadn't said a word to him since they'd been seated. She'd ordered with her head in the menu and had concentrated on her food when it arrived.

Will took a sip of his wine. He'd managed to order an expensive white, too expensive for his taste, but Boyd had not seemed impressed. She'd sniffed at the cork when the bottle was presented, then shrugged when he asked her what she thought. He'd nodded to the waiter, then looked at her with some resentment. She'd gone on stolidly eating her appetizer.

Puligny-Montrachet, he said to himself. *A goddam Puligny-Montrachet.*

Boyd looked up suddenly.

"You have a weird look on your face," she said. "You look as if you're irritated with me."

Will glanced around the room, then leaned forward, a supplicant's posture. "I don't get you. I'm a simple guy."

She smiled sweetly. "You're a simple undertaker, Dr. Death. A plain old"—she smiled self-deprecatingly—"down-to-earth funeral director. Just the person I need to talk to."

"Mrs. Schaeffer, when you say you want to talk to me, I suspect it has to do with . . ."

"It's Boyd. And it does have to do with my . . . with Russell. I have reason to believe that there's more that I might be told about his death."

"You have a legal right to know just about anything you want to know here. But since I don't think I can answer any questions, especially in the absence of an autopsy, it would be unethical of me to sit here and—"

"I'm certainly not interested in compromising your ethical standards."

She smiled sweetly again and he shrugged, stung. Her low voice thrilled him even as she humiliated him.

"Okay. I saw him not long after he came in, and his skin had a darkish tinge, which is not inconsistent with . . . let's say alcohol or drug use. But it's also not inconsistent with oxygen deprivation—something that tends to happen when you die. And blood, when it stops circulating, settles, turns blue. Without an autopsy report, it would be wrong to describe any physical symptom as a cause."

He picked up his fork and resumed eating, watching her out of partially lowered eyes. She looked attractive but tired. Certainly far less assured than she'd seemed in his office three weeks earlier. Her hair, pulled back into a ponytail, looked damp. She hadn't particularly wanted to come to dinner with him, he realized unhappily. She'd forced herself to be here. When she looked up, he saw that she was angry.

"I guess you forgot that I'm a physician. I *know* what oxygen deprivation looks like. You're worried that I'm after some scandalous revelation. I'm not. My mother-in-law told me about his heart problem, the one *he* didn't mention to me while he was alive. He had a bad heart and he died of a heart attack. I've got that straight now. But my mother-in-law is the one who didn't want an autopsy. You see, I wouldn't mind hearing an opinion or two. What the experts have to say, yes—but frankly, I just wanted to talk to the last person who . . . touched him." She'd paused carefully before the verb.

"Are you talking about . . . yeah. Our most experienced person worked on him."

"I'd like to talk to him."

Will had an abrupt vision of Boyd sitting across from Griggs at his gurney and sink as he fixed her with his famous gaze.

"I don't think he'll want to talk to you—in that kind of official capacity."

"Can you at least ask him if he'd see me off the record? On his own?"

Will took another large sip.

Boyd looked at him, then lifted her own glass to her lips. "This wine is not bad at all."

"Griggs doesn't talk to the living much."

She stared at him. To her mortification, she felt tears rising up from somewhere. She ducked her head and lifted a shoulder up like a bird lifting its wing against rain. The tears disappeared. "Well, that's that."

"I'm sorry."

Her left hand lay on the tablecloth. He touched it awkwardly. She pulled it away.

They ate in silence for a few minutes. Then Boyd looked up. "I wanted to ask about your sister. The one who died?"

Will put down his fork and patted his mouth with his napkin.

"Thought I'd pour more wine," he said. "And I suggest that you have another glass. Or two. Somebody has to tell you this: You really need to take a rest."

He lifted the wine bottle by the neck. It dripped from the bucket as he nodded at her.

She sat back in her chair and laughed. She laughed long and hard, and he had to glance at her twice to make sure she wasn't crying again.

He half stood, his napkin in his hand. "Are you okay?"

Boyd pinched the bridge of her nose and waved him back down in his chair. At last she caught her breath.

"No. Jesus Christ, no. I'm a mess. I haven't slept in days. I'm seeing things. It just struck me funny—you know, you tempting me with wine. Like I'd sip a little and forget. I mean, why didn't I think of that? Wine!"

Will swallowed and stared at the tablecloth. "Maybe I don't want to talk about my sister. Did that ever occur to you?"

He raised his eyes to stare at her defiantly, but he'd lost her, she wasn't listening anymore. Her eyes had gone vacant, focused on her meal. She was eating again, mechanically. "At least tell me her name."

Will sighed. "Signe."

"So Scandinavian. My people are mostly Polish and German, a little Norwegian."

"You grew up in St. Paul?"

"Close to downtown. Cathedral area. Till I was seven. Then we moved to Roseville. You?"

"Highland Park."

"Where the sledding accident took place?"

Will turned his head away. For a while they listened to the other diners, the clink of glass and cutlery.

Boyd smiled and shook her head. "I'm getting drunk."

"Great!" cried Will passionately. "Stop torturing yourself. You haven't given yourself a second to rest, a second to take in what has happened."

"I suppose that's because I don't know exactly what happened. Wouldn't you say?"

His face fell. Boyd smiled, mildly amused at his reactions. He seemed to take any countering of his views, any variance of opinion, as a personal slight. Pretty face. Maybe nothing upstairs, she thought. Arguments would be a torment of explaining— *No, this is not about you; this is about radio waves.* He couldn't seem to get past himself and open to a little repartee.

The waiter carefully placed a dessert menu by each of their

plates and stood at attention, waiting to recite the long litany of sweets.

"Please," said Boyd. "How about if you just bring us some coffee?"

After the waiter turned on his heel and disappeared, wounded, Will sat forward, a determined look on his face. "You grew up around Cathedral? Tough area."

"It was. We left when my dad got a better job."

"I keep wondering how you got to be Boyd."

"When my mother was carrying me, my father decided that I was a boy—no chance of error. He had the name already written in on the birth certificate. The doctors weren't sure then if she could have other kids, so when he got a girl, he named a boy."

She laughed. "It turned out that the doctors were wrong. I was followed, almost yearly, by their three sons. But I got stuck with the name."

She smiled at the waiter as he set down the coffee cups, then held her head between her hands. "I'm wrecked."

"I know what," cried Will. "Let's have some brandy! Trim the loose ends, so to speak."

The brandy came in teardrop-shaped crystal snifters, thin-skinned. The waiter stood by, pushed his spectacles up his nose, and risked a sardonic smile. "Cigars?"

"Maybe later."

Boyd felt slightly relaxed. She knew she was getting drunk but also knew her sorrow would outdistance alcohol. She ran her index finger back and forth across her numb lips, smiling.

"When we moved to Roseville, we got bumped up a little on the social scale. We had a bigger backyard and a rec room. Wood-paneled, but it still smelled like a basement. That smell epitomizes the Midwest sometimes for me—the smell of knotty-pine paneling and basement, cold and dank, bleeding through. The smell of cheap improvement."

"You're a snob."

"No. I'm just good at describing things that terrify me. Knotty-pine paneling and the Minnesota Undead—I mean the Vulcans. The Winter Carnival Vulcans? Grown-up males in devil suits riding around on fire engines? Sneaking up behind women and kissing them, rubbing soot on their faces? I find that terrifying."

At his look, she sighed. "We both left."

"And we're both back."

She seemed not to have heard him. She was smiling to herself. "I won scholarships. God, I was lucky. All the way through college, then medical school in New York. I did well. I mean, even as I struggled to make ends meet. I loved it."

"But then you married money."

"Yes." She turned a level gaze on him. He couldn't tell if he'd offended her. "I married money."

She looked down, swirling her brandy again. "I became a doc. But it was kind of a false start. I got married. To money, as you said. Anyway, how boring."

"Why would it be boring?"

"I don't know. I feel like I'm getting my life back and I'm at the stage where my own history excites me. How pathetic is that?"

"Not very. I want to know more about you."

She looked at him and then, for the first time that evening, she smiled. "No you don't, pal. Look what happened to my husband."

Will laughed, not sure what to say.

She raised her snifter and toasted him.

"Who was he?"

"Russell? Russell was someone who knew exactly how much everything cost. He was so good at business because he understood trade, deals, what makes the wheels turn between two people or among ten people, or himself and ten thousand stockholders. And he understood life as trade: You give me this; I'll give you that. But it *seemed* like he didn't give a damn about any of that, because he was so . . ."

Will shook his head, wondering on what the transaction between Boyd and Russell had been based.

"Sex!" she cried suddenly. Then: "You should see your face, Dr. Death."

Will, embarrassed, jerked his head away

"Your face makes your mind so easy to read. I was just thinking about Russell, his hands, which were cold all the time. He said it was because he had had a dangerously high fever and convulsions as a child and that his thermostat was off ever since. His hands were cold, but he always seemed *warm*."

She shivered and sipped her brandy. A lock of hair had fallen over her eyes. She gazed accusingly at him. Then, as if in response to some internal command, she sat up, blinked. "Jesus. What am I talking about?"

He started to say something polite, but she interrupted him.

"Let me tell you something: I talked to the doctor who signed the death certificate—a physician who knows my mother-in-law—and he won't say anything. He's stonewalling. I tried approaching him professional to professional, just to get a little information, and he treated me like a subhuman—that is to say, a patient."

She tossed back the dregs of her brandy.

"Doctors want you to believe that death is inevitable. But doctors screw up all the time. All the time. Like your own work with the dead. Don't you ever get the feeling once in a while that some deaths just shouldn't have happened? That they weren't meant to be?"

Will saw snow blowing on a slope. He watched the trees rising up before him, their black branches beckoning. "No."

Her mascara had smudged a little. She looked like a tough, querulous kid. Will smiled at her and shook his head again, feigning preoccupation as some self-possessed, accommodating robot of his unconscious accepted the check from the long-suffering waiter, figured the tip, signed the credit card slip. All the tables around them were empty. He sat up, smiled at her. She nodded. Time to go. He cleared his throat.

"There is one thing I'm sure of. Each person who dies becomes a mystery to the living. Suddenly they realize they knew so little about this person. Even if the person was loved dearly, even if the death was expected, the survivors feel like they never knew whoever it is lying in the coffin."

Boyd stared at him for a long second, then glanced abruptly at her watch, exclaimed. It was late.

"Wait," said Will. "Wait."

Listening to her, he'd felt overcome by a vague possessiveness. He didn't want to leave her yet. He wanted the night to go on. He stood up, shaking his head to clear it, and held out his hand. "There's somewhere, a place I want to show you."

"Right now?"

She ignored his extended hand and rose briskly, brushing off her skirt.

"It's a sacred place. A place that might *make sense* to you."

Boyd glanced at him, expecting him to smile, but he looked completely serious. She checked her watch again. "If I go somewhere else, I have to let the baby-sitter know."

T HEY DROVE TOGETHER in Will's car, subdued now that they had gone out into the night together, settled into the front seat of Will's dark compact sedan, in a date-like intimacy that made them edgy. Boyd's head had begun to ache. A glimmer of Russell-thinking moved in her mind: a trade.

"I've forgotten the name of the person who . . . attended to Russell. What did you say his name was?"

"I didn't."

He looked smug in the streaking light from passing headlamps. Then he began to flinch under her gaze. He faltered.

"Griggs," he said. "His name is Griggs. But like I said, he won't talk to you."

"Why not?"

"There's an unspoken policy among embalmers. Plus, there's the fact that Griggs—Griggs is . . ."

"Is what?"

Will made a right turn onto Mounds Parkway. "A standard unto himself."

F REDDY POINTED TO a sketch in *The Colonial Flower Book*. " 'Hollyhock,' " Gerda read. " 'In medieval times, it was called Holy Mallow'—they think maybe it was brought from the Holy Land, a land across the sea. Althea rosea. Althea means to cure," she added primly. *It means to make you feel better.*

"Read to me about the root, Grandma."

Gerda ran her finger down the column of flower names and characteristics. " 'It has a long thick root,' this says. And that root has been used for medicines since the days of ancient Egypt."

Freddy looked at her.

"Since the days of the pyramids." Gerda drew a triangle in the air, knocking her glasses down her nose. "Remember the pyramids?"

Freddy nodded, then reached out and turned a page or two. "What about this one?"

Gerda pushed her glasses back up and frowned. "Rue. Now, this is an interesting story. It was said that it kept nightmares away if you crushed its seeds and mixed them with vinegar and smeared them on the forehead of the sleeper."

She stopped to rub Freddy's forehead.

"And it would help people see into the future. Plus, it helped when mad dogs bit you or bees stung you or snakes got after you. The witches in France used to yell, 'By harrow and rue— and my red cap too! Hie! Over to England!' when they climbed on their broomsticks. Oh well, let's see. Oil of rue used to, hmmm, bring on the monthly cycle."

She turned the page hurriedly.

"Okay, let's go backwards. Here's peony. Peony has thick roots and it's another healing plant. Plus, the flowers are beautiful, honey."

She read on a little as Freddy hung suspiciously over the page, watching her lips move.

"And it says that in the Middle Ages, people dug its roots by the light of the moon so that they wouldn't be seen by woodpeckers."

Freddy shrieked with laughter. "Woodpeckers?"

Gerda peered over her glasses at Freddy's delighted face. "They thought that if woodpeckers looked at somebody digging or planting peonies, that person would be struck by blindness. They wouldn't be able to see anymore." She squinted at the page. "But it doesn't say why here. Why would woodpeckers make a person go blind, for Pete's sake!"

Freddy lost interest as Mrs. Nelson came into the room. "Your daughter-in-law called. She said she's gonna be just a little late, y'know, comin' home." Mrs. Nelson waited, her plump hands clutched in front of her.

Gerda smiled encouragingly at Freddy, who was turning cartwheels, talking to herself. "Well, I'm going to leave now, Eleanor. I don't want to bother Boyd."

Gerda sat straight in Russell's chair, smiling at her granddaughter. "Which flower would you like to plant, Freddy?"

Freddy stopped and stood absolutely still, looking past her grandmother. "Sunflowers," she whispered. "I want sunflowers."

CHAPTER 16

WILL REALIZED, pulling the car into a space in the Mounds Park lot next to a dumpster shimmering in the moonlight with phosphorescent NO DUMP-ING strips, that he'd made a mistake. This dark certainty grew as he excused himself, reached across Boyd, flipped open the glove compartment, and, though the moon was full, pulled out a flashlight. A moment later, they stood staring at the smooth cemetery mounds. The wind flattened Boyd's skirt against her legs, and she pulled her thin suit jacket close around her. She shot him an ironic glance.

"Look," Will said. "It's too cold. Let's go back."

"Oh no." Her voice was light. "We've come this far, we can't turn back now." She shrugged, looking around. "I've never been here before."

"You grew up around Cathedral and you've never been to Mounds Park?"

She ignored him, moving toward the park. The six large pre-historic burial mounds housed several Sioux chiefs and their tribesmen. They were set into a rise gradually ascending to the bluff over the river. These were the only remaining graves of the original thirty-seven, Will reported to Boyd in a wind-loud, self-conscious voice. He knew these odd grassy humps well, clustered like wounded buffalo; he'd come here ever since he was small. He nodded at each dark, matted swell of earth as he moved down the paved walkway, which curved around the sacred dead in their domed beds facing the Mississippi, built as the Great Spirit had commanded them to be built.

The effects of the alcohol had worn off, and Will's mind searched for distraction—anything to diminish his anxiety. The trees shuddered and leaned toward Dayton's Bluff. He set off and looked back once or twice, to be sure that Boyd was following him. She loitered in the moonlight, reading the plaques, staring at the grave configurations, her lips moving. Once again, Will felt annoyed with her. He was feeling, rather suddenly, in a hurry. Now that they were here, now that they'd committed themselves to the place, he wanted it all to happen quickly. He was unsure about what he was doing. He hadn't been to the Bluff in many years. He didn't even know if what he was looking for was still there.

The moon lit up his path overdramatically, and a large crow landed on an oak branch to his left, then on a branch to his right, as if leading him. Will stole glances at Boyd; her lips were pressed together, and when her hair blew across her profile, she brushed it away impatiently. He felt they'd somehow acquired a common sense of purpose, even in this completely impulsive, dazed effort. But then what had possessed him to climb Dayton's Bluff in the middle of the night with a strange woman?

The path ended abruptly, and they stood at the edge of the Bluff. Below, the Mississippi flowed pale and clear, ghost-colored under the moon, bordered by the craggy bluffs. A solitary tugboat drifted with the current. The river bent in such a way that it created an optical illusion; the city, though it was on the same side of the river, appeared across from them. In the foreground were the old railroad yards, a fish hatchery. But these were in darkness—the skyline of St. Paul rose spot-lit, imperial: its seven mild hills, its gold Capitol dome, the spires and turrets of its Renaissance cathedral built of pure St. Cloud granite. Will felt embarrassed suddenly, realizing that Boyd would probably think this romantic imagery was the point of their climb. He glanced at her again, but she was preoccupied, staring down at the water. He touched her elbow.

"Come on. There's more. And I'm afraid this next part is the hardest." He stretched out his hand.

She looked down and laughed. "You're not saying that you want to climb down that thing?"

"Not too far down. If I remember right, it's just a little way down here."

Her eyes flicked over him. "Remember what? Can you give me a hint what we're doing here?"

He heard the threat but shook his hand impatiently. She took it at last, and they half slid, half stumbled down the loose dirt and rock, dislodging stones that skittered and flashed, one clattering all the way down. The wind had died, or they were protected from it by the overhanging brow of the Bluff.

Will hesitated on a plateau about a third of the way down. He remembered the flashlight and fished it out of his pocket. Just behind him, Boyd stumbled on something sunk in the earth—metal, a twist of old railroad siding. She cursed softly. Will bent, feeling around the rusted tie, then dropped to his hands and knees. He let himself skid a little down the side of the Bluff. Boyd stood on one foot, then the other, on the plateau above him.

"I'd like to go back now."

He looked up at her. "Wait," he said again. "I know it's around here."

The moon rose higher. For a second, everything became a reflecting surface: stones, tree roots, railroad ties, the sheer rushing water below. Boyd, gazing down at the river, blinked her eyes, an odd somnolence pouring down her spine from her skull. She felt for a second as if she could sleepwalk, stone to stone, all the way down to the platinum river, then out across the moon's path to the city. A desire to sleep made her sway in her shoes. She felt something stirring in the landscape. Would the great chiefs above her rise and walk tonight? Where did the dead go? Where was her husband? She shook herself awake as Will spoke.

"There used to be a marker here," he called up to her. "We used to always leave a marker."

He felt sweat wobble down his back, heard his own sawing breath. He knew how ridiculous he must look, and he kept his head down as he scrabbled in the dirt, the flashlight held in his teeth, its beam jumping from stone to stone. He moved, crawling, away from her, mumbling to himself. Twenty, thirty feet. Five minutes passed.

"You know, this sounded like a swell idea about two hours ago."

There was no response. Boyd pulled at her sleeves, checked her left heel.

"Is this an example of a funeral director's Fun Night Out? Because—"

"Please, just wait. Two more minutes."

Boyd hummed a little, stopped, checked her watch, then turned to climb back up the Bluff.

"Wait, wait! I think this is it." He stumbled back to her, covered with dirt, frantic.

She turned slowly, regarding him coolly from above. "You know we don't really know each other that well. So you probably haven't guessed that I'm really incredibly annoyed right now."

"Listen, please. I found it."

He took her arm, half pulling her down, then along a rock- and debris-filled path, to a sunken mound of sandy dirt, which resembled, oddly, the rounded graves above them. He knelt down, waving the flashlight again, the dry, sandy Bluff wall disintegrating as he probed it. "I found it."

As she watched in astonishment, he lay flat on his back at her feet, staring up at her, then flipped over and slithered into the face of the Bluff. He began, incrementally, to disappear.

"My God."

His body was vanishing before her eyes, sliding into the dirt wall. His cordovans kicked, then disappeared.

A second passed. His head reappeared, then his shoulders. He pulled himself out. He sat up, shook himself, coughed, spat a little dirt self-consciously behind him. He ran his hands rapidly over his scalp and a sprinkling of grit fell from his hair.

"Signe always knew where it was. She could always find it."

"I hate to be a spoilsport, but I'm really not that interested in watching you bury yourself alive."

He nodded at her pleasantly as if he hadn't heard her.

"Lie down," he said. "And slide in on your back. Or you can crawl in on your stomach. Either way, you go in headfirst. It's dirty, but it's one of the most amazing sights you'll ever see, so it's worth it." He paused dramatically. "This is the entrance to Carver's Cave."

It had been Signe's secret hideout. Though the natural entrance to the cave had been sheared off in the twenties by the railroad, Signe had found the buried lip by herself and then revealed it to him, showed him how to inch through the terrifyingly narrow opening. Over the years, the city had tried resealing the cave mouth—and the one or two secret entrances in the rock—to keep kids and transients out, but this had never curtailed Signe's visits.

"How can I get this across, pal? I'm not keen to do this."

He turned to look at her. "Why," he asked suddenly, "do you keep saying things that sound like my sister?"

She shrugged and looked away from him, irritated. He ran his hand across his damp, dirty brow. What was he doing? he asked himself suddenly. Maybe he was still a little drunk, not thinking clearly. Once through the opening, it was a dangerous, precipitous climb down through the dark, rock to rock, into the huge cavern, its walls covered with defaced petroglyphs, graffiti of explorers. There was no way she could do it, even with his help—

he could see that now. He was acutely aware suddenly of her flimsy skirt and shoes.

He stood up slowly. They faced each other a little sheepishly.

"Let's reschedule this."

"It's the most amazing cave in Minnesota, and, believe me, this whole city, the county, is built on a honeycomb of caves. But this one is unique. It was called the House of Spirits by the Lakota. An explorer named Carver visited it in the eighteenth century. Underneath here is a huge cavern that leads to the shore of an underground lake, with a white sand beach so big that the Indians lit torches and canoed on it. There are blind things, crayfish, in the lake. I'm not kidding. Nobody is supposed to know the way in anymore."

Will looked at his muddied hands. He was shocked at how much information he'd kept in his head about Carver's Cave.

"But *you* know. So you're just lucky? Or amazing yourself? Which is it?"

"You haven't picked up yet on how amazing I am? Look, I can shine the flashlight on the walls, then you can just slide a little way in. Take a peek."

She inhaled sharply and looked at him as if he'd just suggested she throw herself into the Mississippi. They stared at each other. Then she shook her head and sat down, leaned back, finally flattening, inching along on her back. Her face kept its cynical look as it disappeared, little by little, from Will's view.

As Will aimed the shaking beam above her head, she slid farther in, then twisted around and down to look backward at the striated walls. As soon as her head entered, she felt her scalp contract and the hairs on her neck rise as she bent back into the void. It wasn't just that the temperature had dropped—she sensed something else in the held expiration of dank air. Like being inside a living body. A cold embrace, she thought wildly, out of nowhere, then heard it distinctly: the sound of dripping water. Other water sounds. She held still. It was true—there was a lake down there. *Maybe there are parks,* she thought giddily. *Maybe a reverse beanstalk.*

Abruptly, she panicked. Will, who'd been staring at the sinuous twisting movement of her legs, encased in gleaming hose, jumped at her muffled shout.

"Get me out now!" Her legs flailed, kicking wildly.

Will grabbed her waist and pulled, nearly dropping the flashlight into the cave. "I just wanted you to get a sense . . ."

"Just get me out."

He helped her stand, brush off her suit, shining the beam on it. It was hopelessly smeared with dirt, torn in a few places. She faced him, composing herself, embarrassed by her outburst. He touched her shoulder, trying to comfort her, but she flinched and pulled away from him.

"It was Signe's secret place," he repeated apologetically.

"Yes." She bent down and shook a stone from her shoe. She flung it in the direction of the river. There was no sound when it struck.

"Look," she murmured after a long pause. "It's just not my kind of thing."

"Forget it. It was a mistake to come here. I should have known better."

They stood apart on the bright path as the moon slipped under a cloud and the world went black. Will snapped on the flashlight. When the beam jumped to her face, he saw her gleaming tears. He kept the light moving, training it on the return path as she turned her back on him, starting the steep climb back up the bluff. As they crested the rise, Boyd stopped short. He nearly collided with her from behind, then stepped back down as she turned to face him.

"Listen. I'm not your dead sister, okay? And you may believe you're distracting me from . . . thinking about what I need to think about. But you're not."

Without waiting for a response, she whirled and climbed over the top, disappearing into the dark.

Will's beam bobbed wildly as he stepped over the impassive face of the overhang. Its jittery ray lit up the iron pickets surrounding one of the sacred mounds: They stood in relief, like a row of brandished spears.

MRS. NELSON, framed in the doorway, clutching the folds of a baggy gray wool sweater to her throat, stares.

"I fell." Boyd brushes past her, smelling of rock and damp, smelling of terror. She blinks at the living room, its opal curtains and pale patterned carpet, finding silent rebuke there, too.

"Is she asleep?"

Mrs. Nelson nods, still staring at Boyd's torn hose and stained skirt.

"Y'know, she went right out—she was all petered out from runnin' around tonight. Just a little excitement, y'know."

Boyd drops her purse, raking her dirty fingers through her dirty hair, and considers Mrs. Nelson. Mrs. Nelson, she realizes, will now tell her that Gerda has been here. Gerda seems to be with her granddaughter constantly these days, teaching her gardening, the names of flowers, new words.

Mrs. Nelson stands before her, waiting expectantly for Boyd to talk to her. Boyd becomes aware of the older woman quivering like a custard into which a penny has been dropped, full of self-important agitation. Mrs. Nelson is bent but somehow square-shouldered, stocky but not fat, flushed in the face with bluish-white plaits bobby-pinned to her skull—her face the full, uncontemplative hangdog mug of a Swedish tax collector. Mrs. Nelson's gift for helpfulness is twinned to her capacity for uncharitable judgment. Boyd watches the two inclinations battle before her eyes.

"Your mother-in-law was here, y'know, honey."

Boyd glances at a new storybook, *Butterfly's Journey,* slipped showily over the cover of *The Colonial Flower Book* on the coffee table. She plucks up her dropped purse, pulls out some bills, hands them to the older woman.

"Oh now, thank you, honey. That's way too much, y'know. Next time we'll have to even it out."

Boyd smiles distantly, opens the door. Mrs. Nelson gropes in the hall closet for her flowered windbreaker, her knitting bag, waving vigorously as the door closes on her.

Boyd pauses for a long moment, listening to Mrs. Nelson's car backing out of the driveway. She runs upstairs to check on Freddy, then, after a quick and blazing-hot shower, comes back downstairs wearing her nightgown, her wet hair pinned up. She curls up in the armchair with the storybook that Gerda brought, begins to read about a traveling butterfly.

After a moment she closes the book, gets up, and looks across the room. There, in the stand of photos on the piano top, is a shot of Russell as a Vulcan, his arms around his brother Vulcans, their soot-ringed grins cocky and wide. They stand on a snowy curb, a vintage fire engine parked behind them. One salutes; one holds up a can of Hamm's beer. Russell is looking off into the distance. On the fire engine is draped a banner reading ST. PAUL WINTER CARNIVAL: DOWN WITH KING BOREAS!

She picks up the photo, then replaces it, facedown. The Vulcan had come staggering through the door not long after that photograph was taken—it was nearly midnight. The Vulcan had brought her flowers—irises, her favorite. (Where had he found them at midnight in January?) But a few of the stalks were broken and the purple lion-heads bowed as she slid them into water. Then Bonnie Raitt filled the air, and the Vulcan began dancing.

"Don't wake Freddy," she called to him. He stopped; his shoulders drooped. He walked to the CD player, flicked off the sound. "Don't wake Freddy," he repeated in a high, sharp, mocking voice meant to be hers. "Don't wake *Freddy!*" He wore the ridiculous bloodred tribal outfit—a red-and-black ski cap and a black mask and gloves. Now he pulled off the ski cap and shook out his hair, running his gloved hands through it, then lifted off the Batman-like mask, winking at her. He threw it on the floor, next to the cap. He started to peel his gloves off, then thought better of it, left them on. The Vulcans were local volunteers, recruited to do a job—chase women and kiss them, leave soot smears on their lips and cheeks as the mark of the gods of the underworld, of hellfire. They would bring warm weather back to the realm of King Boreas of the North Wind, hanging out of their fire engines as sirens warbled and keened, offering a gritty, swoony adolescent hint of sex and anarchy to the King's celebrations: to the ice palaces and torch-lit skating rinks where the serious-faced, stocking-capped population dipped and twirled. Everyone loved the Winter Carnival—local executives and politicians were appointed Carnival royalty—and every year Russell was asked to be a Vulcan. He held out his gloved hands to her, drew her into a dance. She felt the cold air of night, the chill of the north wind still about him, though he was meant to be a messenger of heat and light. A gloved hand held hers; a gloved hand pressed against her back. His rough, stubbled cheek brushed hers. They swayed in place as he hummed tunelessly, then she felt his lips on her neck and pulled away.

"What's a little kiss to you? When to a Vulcan it's lifeblood?"

"You smell like Tic Tacs—and cheap perfume."

They stopped dancing and stared at each other. The Vulcan pulled away from her, turned to the bookshelf, and turned back around with a lit cigarette, gazing at her, affronted, his kohl-lined eyes wounded.

He puffed out his cheeks and blew a perfect smoke ring, a pale blue heart, which elongated into a lasso, then faded. "I love you," he said.

She stared at the disappearing heart in the air above her head and sighed.

"You never believe me, Boyd."

"You're drunk."

"And, sweetheart? You're really, really *not* drunk."

She began to turn away.

"How else can I say it? You know I'm a smoke-and-mirrors guy."

She turned back around. "I have an idea. Break the mirror. Put out the fire."

———

" 'The fire,' " he had sung over Bonnie's lyrics, " 'is out.' " She sighs deeply, then shifts her thoughts to Russell's stash of cigarettes. In a drawer below the oak bookshelves she finds them, a crumpled pack. He'd smoke them when he was up late drunk or writing his poems, or both. She hasn't smoked for years, was never really a smoker, but now she wants a cigarette, desperately. There is a silver lighter in the drawer. She holds it to the tobacco, then inhales deeply, looking up at the books. She reaches up for one—Rilke: *The Duino Elegies*. She opens it slowly and a piece of paper flutters out.

She stoops too quickly to retrieve it and feels herself rocked back on a wave of dizziness. The cigarette is too strong. She nearly loses her balance, coughing. Suddenly she notices what she holds in her hands. A poem by Russell, called "Marriage," with an epigraph from Rilke: "Two solitudes that border each other."

The hawk circles high and away from the pair
on horseback, miles above the canyon floor.
The narrow switchback trail to No Name Ridge

just wide enough for two, head to head. Above,
the hawk slowly drops. On the inside path, her horse
cuts left, as if to edge him to the slide. Her horse

trots: precisely to the rhythm of her thoughts.
He knows what she thinks—that's why his horse
nods and shies. What if he let her go, flung hard

against no resistance? Would she fall—or fly?
The uncrowned summit looms, the hawk falls upward
into height. What they once called desire foots the stirrup.

Brinksman: the hawk swoops down on night.

Boyd, looking up from the page, sees the two of them on horseback, high over a rocky pass in Colorado, urging their horses forward, arguing. After a while she stretches her stiff limbs, and slowly the liquid tick of the mantel clock grows audible again. She stands, walks to the window, pulls the curtains back, stares outside.

Russell is standing there. He's in jeans and a navy jacket, hair blowing across his brow, one shoulder lower than the other, a smile pulling at the line of his mouth. He loosens his tie, then quickly brushes back the hair on his forehead with his hand. Intimate gestures, gestures so familiar that she gasps. She stumbles through the living room, through the kitchen, the mudroom. Trembling, she unlocks the jingling back door, crosses the flagstone patio. The grass is cold and wet and her feet are bare, but she feels nothing. She stops on the lawn. He is still standing there, across the yard under the sycamore tree. She opens her mouth to speak, but only shocked whiteness, cold, comes out. She holds her hand out toward him, taking a step in his direction, and like an image in a mirror, he holds out his hand and moves one step toward her. Then they wait, still.

Boyd is aware of a disturbance of air. The wind picks up suddenly and a scattering of leaves float gently from the trees. Some spiral upward. The terrible haikus floating up into the skylight come back to her suddenly, and she laughs aloud, gasping. He bows slightly, and one large leaf, a butterfly shape, tumbles into his outstretched hand. Proffering the leaf, he starts across the lawn to her. She is aware then, in an instant, that he is not smiling, that he is approaching her with intent.

I wished you dead, she thinks. *I wished you dead.*

Their eyes lock. Slowly, slowly, he reaches up his hand, touches his heart. Boyd begins to shake, her whole body shuddering. Fury, fueled by terror, pumps through her. Tripping over the soaked hem of her nightgown, she begins to run toward him, shouting senselessly, waving her arms.

"Get out, get out of here! Go away from here now!"

The wind rises again and he pauses, one leg set forward. He smiles his unforgettable smile, and then he releases the butterfly-shaped leaf from his hand; it blows across the lawn toward her. She feels resistance from the air. Her legs slow to a nightmare gait. The leaf flutters toward her in the grass. She bends down and picks it up, half aware of what she's doing. *It's only a leaf,* she thinks. *It's only a dream—he is dead.*

"Russell?" She hears her own voice, apart from her, calling.

He is no longer there before her—he has vanished—but she feels a presence at her side. A hand touches her nightgown. She whirls around, crying out, arms raised to defend herself.

"Mom," cries Freddy, looking up at her, alarmed, tugging at her sleeve. "What are you doing out here, Mom? Is that a leaf, Mommy? You left the door open—did you know that? Are you having a bad dream?"

PART THREE

CHAPTER 17

THE NEXT MORNING there was a phone call from Dr. Remington. The office was open until noon on Saturday ("We're *that* busy") and Boyd could hear phones ringing in the background. She was all but hired. Remington wanted her to meet her partner and also wanted Boyd to come to the office and observe the practice on Monday. Boyd immediately called St. Catherine's College and found a student babysitter; she didn't want to see Mrs. Nelson anymore. She didn't want to see anything that reminded her of Russell for a while, though that was hopeless. Russell was with her all the time now, she thought as she stood at the kitchen counter drinking her coffee. He was around her. She could feel him thinking, moving, breathing next to her. She looked out at the backyard, then shook herself, put her cup in the sink, turned away. *It was a dream,* she thought. *Everybody dreams.*

———

She had let Freddy lead her inside the house after she'd come out of the cold terror, the trance. Freddy had reached up and taken her hand, pulling her slowly back through the yard, across the flagstones, through the open back door, and into the lit kitchen. Her small face was determined, her red hair stuck straight up in back like a turkey tail. Her pajamas were patterned with grinning, cavorting porpoises.

"It's time for cocoa, Mom," she whispered, her eyes intent on Boyd's face, her manner cheerful and abstracted as a geriatric nurse's.

She stood on a chair and opened a cupboard. Watching her, Boyd snapped awake at last. "Are we having marshmallows?"

"I would like just two, Mom, two. I will get them."

Boyd looked around the kitchen, forbidding herself to glance at the dark windows.

"I had a dream," she said as Freddy handed down the chocolate-and-silver-colored cocoa container and a plastic bag of marshmallows. She helped Freddy down. "A bad dream, but it's all gone now."

She put the cocoa and marshmallows on the counter and hugged Freddy to her heart.

Freddy pulled away and looked up at her. "Dreams come out of boxes. Christmas boxes inside of your head. You can't see inside till you open them."

Boyd had stood thinking about the dream boxes as she stirred hot milk into the cocoa powder in two large spotted-cow mugs. Freddy sat at the table, chattering to her two marshmallows, one in each hand.

The boxes were shiny, gift-wrapped. But as you peeled away the glittering paper, there was another bright surface, then another.

Boyd closed her eyes, then opened them. You kept unwrapping the surfaces, until you realized the bright boxes were mirrors.

Boyd blinked again, shook her head. "Here's your cocoa, honey," she said.

In the mirrors she saw herself hurrying down a corridor to Infant Intensive Care. She'd been to the cafeteria for a sandwich—and now she was returning to the mirrored room, where the doctors and nurses could observe every move, every breath of their tiny patients (all under three years old). Here the computers blipped at their satellite modules, the ventilators and monitors, here the dreadful emergency horn (a long cry like a Minnesota loon) indicated infant trauma—or respiratory or cardiac stress. Here were the patients: the Coma Baby, pale as the linens that swaddled her—a victim of infant botulism, contracted at six months, when she was weaned; the infant born with absolutely no physical capacity to support herself—no ability to breathe, no ability to move her muscles. She lay in a bed in a nest of machines and tubes—and once a day, for twenty minutes each, her parents (a young Orthodox Jewish couple), were allowed to pick her up (her tubes still attached) and hold her in their arms, the way other mothers and fathers held their children. Then there was the two-year-old who was dying of leukemia. Her bed was festooned with balloons and stuffed animals and gold stars and printed signs that proclaimed RUTHIE IS GOING TO WIN!! *As Boyd hurried along, cradling a steaming Styrofoam cup, she noticed that Ruthie's parents were just down the hallway dressed in protective caps and gowns—also on their way to Infant Intensive Care. Boyd considered calling out to them—they were the most optimistic visitors on the ward and she liked them a lot. They loudly cheered Ruthie back toward health—and all the babies around her. They donned clown wigs—*

and they sat up late reading stories to anyone who would listen. They brought a little music into the ward: quiet strings and (once) kazoos. Now, as Boyd drew close behind them, about to tap one of them on the shoulder, she stopped. She noticed that they were literally leaning on each other, staggering a little—and then Boyd heard the sound of sobbing. They were both weeping, their bodies racked. Their grief was huge and yet fiercely contained. They bent into each other as if they were one suffering beast—beaten down by sorrow. Then, gradually, as the entrance to Infant Intensive Care loomed, they pulled apart—they stood up straight, brushed at their clothes, dabbed at their eyes. Boyd watched them take breath after calming breath, shake off the crushing weight, square their shoulders. They reached for each other's hands, they glanced at each other—then they were at the doorway. They pushed in, laughing, calling: "Hi, Ruthie. Hi, sweetheart! Look what we brought you, see? Hi—there's Teddy—hey little Denny . . ." From Boyd's perspective, they were alight, moving—in the mirrors, they were radiant energy at Ruthie's bedside, laughing as she strained to look up, her small, thin face shadowed, her shaved head nodding, reflecting their delight . . .

She smiled at Freddy. "How about one more marshmallow? I think we can find a place for it."

Freddy looked up at her. "It can go in your cup, Mom. Okay?"

ON MONDAY, the baby-sitter arrived early and Boyd left the house in a pantsuit and low-heeled shoes and drove to the medical building, near the university. She met Dr. Irene Resnikoff, who, true to Remington's description, watched the clock as Boyd chatted with her.

"Cut to the chase with patients," she advised Boyd. "Don't let them start talking. They'll never shut up. Then think where you'll be."

Boyd observed four pelvic examinations, two Pap smears, and an eighth-month exam of an uncomfortably pregnant patient—her baby's head was against her spine. She listened to a discussion of hormone replacement therapy, laparoscopy for endometriosis, and, finally, a session with a young woman who had come to talk about the results of her pregnancy test. The test was positive and the young woman was very upset. She was just seventeen, she had no money, she was the daughter of Remington's cleaning woman, and she didn't want to be pregnant. Remington and Resnikoff did not perform abortions, but they could recommend a clinic.

"You don't ever want to learn how to do those procedures," said Resnikoff outside the examination room. "Who wants to pin a bull's-eye on her back? Right-wing, rich donors are putting pressure on medical schools not to teach them as part of standard curriculum anyway. The clinics get more and more isolated. And look at those poor doctors—they have to wear bulletproof vests and check under their hoods every morning."

"It happened to me," said Boyd. "I learned the procedures."

"If I were you," said Resnikoff, glancing at her watch, "I'd forget them fast."

Sunny Red Tree Gunderson, the pregnant young woman, sat crying quietly on the examination table. Boyd stood next to Remington as she handed the girl a card listing phone numbers for Planned Parenthood clinics, including one in Highland Park, that offered abortions. Sunny continued to sob, the flowered cotton gown sliding off her shoulder. Remington loomed nervously over her like a police officer reading out her Miranda rights. Because of Sunny's age, Minnesota law required parental notification, though not consent. Nothing would be done for her until her mother acknowledged, in writing or by her presence, her awareness of her daughter's decision to abort.

"Are you surprised I haven't told my mother?" Sunny cried. "She'd run to the priest and drag me there, too. She wouldn't listen to me, but she'd listen to you."

Boyd had witnessed her arrival at the office, uncertain but hugely bold—like a child dressed for Halloween, with long Valentine-red and cobalt-blue dyed ringlets, nine jeweled earrings, a nose ring, and a black dress with a long fringed and beaded black scarf. But her disconcertingly blue eyes were deep-set and troubled, Northern eyes: snow-watching eyes. She was half–Santee Sioux and half-Swedish, according to Remington, who also told Boyd the father of the baby was an older man, married, who'd officially disappeared but had apparently resurfaced just often enough to confirm the flawed nature of his character. Sunny, after some fumbling, found her thick glasses and put them on. They made her look melancholy, sweetly frog-faced.

"A *situation*," Remington murmured. "And Marie Red Tree Gunderson will fall apart when she finds out about this."

Sunny looked at her. "Who can I go to for help if you won't help me?"

"You must tell your mother," said Remington. "That's all there is to it."

"That's not exactly all."

Remington sighed.

"Reservation Catholic," she whispered to Boyd. "Devout. Marie believes *she* got pregnant because a burning dove descended once when she talked to a Scandinavian—the late Mr. Gunderson."

Sunny pulled her backpack toward her, weeping silently. Then she stopped herself. "You stand there like statues! Really, man, like cigar-store white people! Tell me what I should do. My mother is never going to say yes to this, maybe not even if a doctor talks to her, is she?" she shouted, outraged by her own helplessness, her youth. A laminated bus pass fell out of her backpack, and she fumbled to retrieve it. Boyd watched her tears drop one by one on the tiled floor as she bent over and shook them off.

Dr. Remington cleared her throat, picked at the buttons of her coat. "Where is the father of the baby? Can he help in any way?"

Sunny made a sound like a laugh, flicking a last tear away.

"This is not a baby. This is a mistake. And the *father* told me he's already got a family to take care of. He mentioned this when I called the last time. *They are my first concern.* And I don't want nothing from him. I have enough money. I just need"— she looked at Boyd—"to get my own life back."

"I'm sorry," said Boyd as Sunny weighed her in her troubled gaze. "I'm sorry."

CHAPTER 18

THE DAY AFTER her observation of Remington and
Resnikoff, Boyd sits on the floor in Russell's study and
lines up his collection of snow globes. Transparent
moments of frozen life, like tiny discarded futures once seen and
read in crystal balls: *You will go over Niagara Falls in an inner
tube. You will dance around the maypole with people of many na-
tions!* Angels and trees, children with happy futures, with silver
glitter lapping at their feet, waiting for the world to be picked
up and jostled so that excited snow could fall again: spinning
upward, sparkling, resettling in drifts. His collections. What will
she do with the Ferris wheels and beaches and Washington
Monuments inside these glass bubbles? What will she do with
the rows of books, floor-to-ceiling, the standing lamp shaped
like a rocket ship, the Pop art, the red kilim on the polished
wood floor? The blown-up photograph of Frank O'Hara, the
broadsides of poems, the framed photograph of her, mugging

on the beach at White Bear Lake, the drawing by Freddy of a butterfly, the drawing of Keats by Severn? The first editions, the Gauguin mug filled with pencils and pens? The pile of clothes and objects, the Vulcan suit and mask in the bedroom closet?

She gets up, walks to the bookshelves, touches the rows of spines. In between volumes she finds Russell's poems, his random journal entries, tucked among these dignified volumes of verse and critical prose. He buried his words inside other writers' words, safe in the pages of literature. As if, like a coffin sinking deeper into the earth, into nature, his poems would grow richer, more surprising, somehow more capable of revealing what was in his heart. *Death is allowing him to be taken seriously,* she thinks, then regrets thinking it.

She slides Ovid's *Metamorphoses* from the shelf and shakes the heavy volume. Nothing. Then *The Aeneid,* then Juvenal, *The Satires.* Out tumbles one page, then another. Boyd exclaims, turns to the window, and pushes aside the curtains. Light storms the room.

Here is a poem by William Carlos Williams, "Queen-Anne's-Lace," written out carefully by hand. The next page is a scribbled journal note—or a note for something he'd been working on. Words were crossed out; words were written in the margin. He had struggled.

What happened to William Carlos Williams after all his years of philandering was that he had a stroke that activated some lobe in his brain that made him confess all his sins. He kept telling Flossie about all the affairs he'd had—he couldn't stop himself. He'd been cock of the walk, now he was this tattletale, on himself.

———

Picnic today at Como Park. We were all happy feeding the ducks with Freddy, and later, visiting the greenhouse conservatory. So. Haven't had a drink in days. Yet, though we walked together carrying the picnic basket and fold-up stroller, talking, I sensed Dr. Boyd still judging me. Those ducks made me nervous, I said as we stared at orchids and century plants and weird succulents. They have a better sex life than I do. She laughed. It has been a while. Since right after Freddy, I said, trying to gain ground. It was occurring to me that most cactuses have a better sex life than me. Since Freddy, she said, or is it since Tahiti?

Boyd closes the book. The curtain shudders. A few papers on the desk lift, and the hair on the back of her neck stands; she turns to look behind her. She understands suddenly, as clearly as if someone has spoken to her, that Russell has left these notes tucked away in his books for her. He'd known she would read them. It was a trail. To what? Other poems? An autobiography? She notices her old medical texts, her old *Physicians' Desk Reference*s lined up on a lower shelf. Why had he kept her med school books? She opens her huge red pediatrics textbook carefully. Some notes fall out, a few pages in his hand on old pharmacy letterhead stationery. There are doodles of women's breasts, flying fish, top hats. Then, written in headlong script:

Sometimes I think I worship two gods: cruelty and desperation to please.

She turns a page.

People are too durable, that's their main trouble. They can do too much to themselves, they last too long—Bertolt Brecht.

Nothing happens to any man that he is not formed by nature to bear—Marcus Aurelius.

She looks at the shelf and pulls out a stapled stack of pages, a journal. She pages through to a Minnesota entry: *Now instead of taking a drink, I write a poem. I put down the scotch bottle and sketch out the first lines of a sonnet. The cliché's true: Poetry is saving my life. Now I go out to see about other lives—here and there. Tonight I ran into a priest. Or, let's be honest, I went into the Cathedral, late, they were still open for business there. I found a confessional with its taxi light on and I got into the taxi, God's taxi, expecting to be driven—where? The priest told me I loved struggling—I was a "struggling soul." And guess what?—"a soul born to ease the suffering of others." I'm a regular Santa Claus—or what Auden called Rilke—"the Santa Claus of Loneliness."*

Boyd makes a face and pages back to passages headed by the words *New York: It's easy to love Boyd when she is facing adversity. I want her to need me and she does. She is not strong, this is what I've discovered about her—though she thinks she is. Me? I'm strong, I'm inventive—and I do everything in my power to cheer her up—I write 100 haikus, I dress her fat cat up as Thomas Jefferson . . ."*

She skips down the page. *She's depressed by the death, she blames herself when, in fact, it's not her fault, it never was . . . It's the hospital that allows residents to handle procedures that are beyond them without a trained, experienced physician present.*

Boyd jams Russell's comments back into the shelf of books. "Thanks for your faith in me. Is that what you have to say to me?"

As if in answer, the doorbell rings three times, the syncopated *bing-bong*s tumbling over each other.

On the doorstep stands the Pizza Boy.

"Oh, Kyle. Hi. Nobody ordered pizza."

Kyle smiles at her, a kind of grimace. She notices then that he is dressed up, in schoolboy fashion, wearing a blazer that appears too small for him, his shoulders pulling the shiny material in warring directions. He wears a necktie, awkwardly knotted, and his hair is slicked back, wet. He holds out a sealed white envelope, which she accepts slowly.

"I just, you know, wanted to stop by here and say I was real sorry about . . . Mr. Schaeffer, you know, dyin' like that."

It is a Hallmark sympathy card with a bouquet of posies in a basket on the front. Inside, it says, "Things will never be the same. Please accept our deepest sympathy." And Kyle's child-like signature.

"Please come in, Kyle."

"I'll just come in the entryway here for a minute, okay?"

They stand awkwardly for a second, facing each other. Kyle is a little taller, but he slumps into himself, his shoulders determinedly rounded like an old man's.

"Would you like some pop, a root beer?"

"No thanks. I wanted to just say . . . one thing."

Boyd waits. It is so quiet that she can hear the living-room clock ticking. Why had she answered the door? Why hadn't she had a cup of tea, put her self down for a late morning nap?

Kyle grimaces again. "I had a . . . problem with drugs."

"You had a problem?"

"You bet, and I finally got it all out of my system, you know. But . . . Mr. Schaeffer helped me."

"Are you sure you don't want to sit down?"

"I'm sure. I just wanted to say to you that he . . . talked to me one night. He followed me out there to the truck and he tapped me on the shoulder and real quick he says, 'Are you high? You are, aren't you?' And I told him all about it and he gave me the name of a place I could go to get straightened out. He stood right there on the curb and he talked to me. He told me he'd had some, you know, dependency problems in his life, too."

"Yes. But how did he know you were high?"

Kyle squints at her. "Mrs. Schaeffer? You didn't notice how I could never seem to find your house? I didn't even know what planet I was on most of the time. I once drove the wrong way on the freeway for about ten minutes before I noticed. Luckily it was four A.M., no other cars, but I sure scared a sanitation truck driver."

Boyd sees herself painstakingly drawing maps on pizza napkins.

"Anyway, I'm clean now. I went to Spirit, where he said to go. He paid for my time there. He took me there. He sat with me when I felt awful."

Kyle looks up at the skylight. In the midday radiance pouring down on him, he grows bright, brighter.

Two gods: cruelty and desperation to please.

"Well, that's about it." He smiles at her again. "Good-bye, Mrs. Schaeffer. I'm real sorry, you know."

"Good-bye, Kyle."

Kyle hurries down the steps toward his truck. He stands in the street, looking up and down. She wonders if she should call out some directions, but he doesn't seem to need her assistance. He spins on his heel suddenly, jumps into the cab of the truck, and is gone.

CHAPTER 19

O N MONDAY, Boyd's day at the doctors' office, Will
drove east on 94, the city freeway that had risen up
like a poured concrete wave and paved over the once-
thriving black neighborhood of Rondo. He remembered, as a
child, visiting St. Peter Claver, the church of the black saint,
with his father. He had liked to memorize street names then,
and he could still call them up: Rondo, Carroll, Arundel, Igle-
hart. Many things that happened to him now generated a longing to share his experiences with Boyd. Had she known Rondo?
Rondo had vanished whole—a whole black town swallowed by
a white freeway, blocks and blocks, houses, storefronts, yards,
barbershops, benches, pocket parks with old men playing check-
ers. Most of its former residents had resettled years ago on the
north side of the freeway, under the gold dome of the State
Capitol.

It was early in the evening and Will was on his way to Leland
Mortuary, a family enterprise that had tended to the deceased of

Rondo and the former Rondo for forty years. Will had gone to high school with the Leland "son," as they said, whose name was Roger. Roger had settled into the family business, unlike Will, right after college, but they had remained friends, writing to each other when Will was back east. Death was egalitarian, thought Will. Death was color-blind, oblivious to human prejudice. Nevertheless, it pained him to think that Death's employees cooperated with a polite, unacknowledged apartheid. Black mortuaries, white and Asian mortuaries, Hispanic and Indian mortuaries, all ministered to their dead with equanamity and implacability: There were rites, there was sitting all night with the body—and prayers, Kaddish—there were hymns—nobody crossed the community lines drawn around a shrouded body on its way across Lethe.

Will pulled up to the curb. Set back from the street stood a one-story stucco building with a blue neon sign: LELAND FU-NERAL HOME, a spot-lit dark-skinned plaster Good Shepherd in the parking lot, holding a black lamb in his arms. At the door, a heavyset middle-aged woman in a flowered chintz dress, a gardenia pinned to her shoulder next to a badge that read DR. VASHTI WRIGHT, nodded to him, then indicated the stairs leading down. Will heard organ scales in the background, a quick blast of trumpet, then silence. He thought of Boyd suddenly: Would she like this place?

"Roger? Step over here, honey—down there."

Roger Leland was Will's age but looked slightly older. He had stature and girth; at school he'd been a football player. Now he'd grown a mustache, and his close-cropped hair was graying at the temples, and round wire-rimmed glasses sat perched on his nose. He wore a pin-striped shirt and a muted-pattern tie and bright blue suspenders. He rose from behind a gleaming desk, grinning at Will in his office doorway. "Who the hell let *you* in here?"

They shook hands, embraced awkwardly, then Roger disappeared behind a screen into an adjoining room, emerged with two sweating cold beer bottles. They sat down in twin leather chairs whose design Will recognized from his own office— Weeping Chairs, with tissues and tumblers hard by.

Will toasted Roger, drank a long pull. They exchanged pleasantries, family questions, then he plunged in.

"Why are we doing this?"

"You talking about my livelihood? The work done by our fathers?"

"Big effing deal. *They* never had to contend with the bullshit we have to deal with. Some ignorant handler telling me he won't touch a body . . ."

Roger frowned over his bottle. "Go by me again?"

They talked about the embalmers' fears; they talked about AIDS. Roger said they'd had their share of the afflicted. But nothing would change the job. "Someone pass, we hand 'em along to the Lord." He opened his hands in an inclusive gesture, a touch of self-mockery. "Except, of course, when they don't want to go."

"Hello?"

"Sometimes they stay attached, they want to hang on. You can tell by their expressions."

"Trust me. It's only gas."

"No, well, that's another problem."

They pointed at each other and laughed, then slapped hands, high five. Will sat down, his face flushed.

"Then of course there's the knuckle-cracking."

"And the goddam late-night community sings."

"And the way they keep asking for room service!"

"Then they stiff you on the tip!"

Will doubled over, nearly falling out of his chair. Roger, more subdued, watched him closely, an expression of barely contained delight on his face.

Will took out a pocket handkerchief and wiped his eyes, gasping. "Could the jokes be worse? That's one thing about this profession, the humor stays *bad*. You can count on it. Unlike your employees. How do you get them to do what you say?"

"I don't have to say anything, Will. They work here. AIDS, no AIDS—they work here."

The idea of an embalmer turning away from a body personally offended him—Will could see it in his face. He picked up the standard. "I sacked these guys . . ."

"Who's gonna do your customers?"

"I still got Griggs."

Roger snorted, sat back, and lit a cigarette. "They used to call that guy the Hyena."

Will finished his beer. Roger, waving away protestations, picked up his cigarette, rose to get him a second bottle, shouting over his shoulder.

"Did I ever tell you once at a convention he got drunk and sang me a song about a black guy—he said, 'a Negro fellow'—named Pete? Pete had a big dick and died with a hard-on and kept it through eternal rigor mortis. The song was about how they kept trying to bury him and just couldn't keep Pete down."

"This is why we don't let him near anyone with a heartbeat."

Will swallowed beer, then coughed, laughing. "The guy has tact only for the dead. When he's working, he bumps up against a body and he keeps going, 'Excuse me,' and, 'Oh, I beg your pardon.' "

They sat back, drank, and listened. Above them, the music had organized into a steady organ bass with brass response.

Will cocked his head. "Somebody big died, huh?"

"Woman, ninety-seven. Five generations will be here today in a little bit to lay her to rest. Mrs. Euphrosyne Miller."

As if to underscore her name, a trumpet trilled, soared. Will heard the first muffled phrases of gospel: "Lift her up!"

"Bake and shake?"

"No way. The family's had her plot ready since Mr. Miller passed twenty or so years ago. We don't go much for the flames here."

Will shook his head, took a long swallow. "You got the touch."

Roger blew smoke through his nose. The rehearsal music shook the ceiling and he smiled upward.

Will followed his gaze, dizzy. "You know, I keep trying to read my dad's books, trying to get close to death, and all I've gotten is more sentimental about life. I see those billboards that say ABORTION STOPS A BEATING HEART in sky-high letters and I get weepy. And I can't take the baby coffins anymore. I cannot take the damn dead babies."

He accidently knocked over an empty. It rolled soundlessly away on the carpeted floor. He rose to get it and Roger waved him back in his seat.

"I'll get it later."

"Griggs works on babies, little kids. I can't watch that."

Roger waited. The music strengthened, a steady bass. Above them, feet began moving, clapping could be heard.

Roger said, "You want to *hold* the baby. We get the families to do this, just for a second. You got to put your hands on the baby before you can mourn."

"You remember my sister?"

"You always ask me that, Will. She's not put to rest in your mind. Is she?"

On the way up, they talked about Mega-Death, how it was swallowing everything. Upstairs, the front doors were opened; people dressed in solemn finery were beginning to arrive. Will glanced in to the chapel area. The bier was lily-covered, a hill of lilies. The organ kept up its steady beat, then an unearthly sound filled the air.

The woman who had opened the door for Will, Dr. Vashti Wright, stood at the front of the chapel, near the coffin, her mouth open, her chest swelling, as her extraordinary, deep soprano voice filled the air. Some people raised their hands and began to sway. Others began to clap.

"Crossin' now, crossin' the river."

In the pews, in the bright light and the blossom smell, the family of Euphrosyne Miller and all her friends began to sing and move as one.

Roger put his arm around Will's shoulders as they stood looking in.

"I don't know, Will. I'm sorry. Maybe it's true. We all just do death *better* than you!"

CHAPTER 20

ON WEDNESDAY, Boyd heard the phone ringing as she pulled in the driveway after dropping Freddy at preschool. It was Dr. Remington, calling to tell Boyd that she was hired. Could she come in sometime this week, fill out tax forms, other documents, start next week? Boyd stared at her hands, doctor's hands, trained and sensitive hands, her stock-in-trade. They were shaking.

She looked out the kitchen window at the yard where Russell had lain as the paramedics worked on him. They wouldn't let her near him. And Gerda had taken her arm, led her away. How had Gerda known to come over that morning? And why hadn't she, Boyd, identified herself as a doctor to the paramedics? Why hadn't she knelt at her husband's side, helped adjust the oxygen flow in the clear nose tube, talked to him, taken his pulse? Why hadn't she massaged his extremities, slipped a tab of nitroglycerin under his tongue, helped them shock his heart? Why hadn't she touched his body? *Why hadn't she touched his body?*

She walked upstairs and down the hall to the master bedroom, opened a closet, and lifted out her crisp white lab coat, newly purchased from the medical uniforms and supplies store. She walked to the triptych mirror, stared at herself in her costume, then held up her hands, watched them tremble as if they were being shocked, the way the brain is shocked with electrodes: swift jolts, lightning, forking, uncurling the clenched fingers of reason.

She folded her shaking hands behind her back and smiled at her reflection. "Good morning, Doctor." She smiled, nodding. "Good morning!" But the tremors did not stop. She picked up the phone near the bed and dialed.

Her mother answered almost immediately. Boyd could picture her sitting on the deck of the condo where she and Boyd's father had retired, reading, the phone and her small, senile Yorkshire terrier beside her.

"I'm going back to work, Mom," Boyd said. "As a doc."

"Well that's good, honey. But isn't it a little *soon?*"

"I need to work, Mom."

There was a rustling sound as her mother lowered the phone to talk to her father.

"It's to the *right* of the refrigerator! No, no, not *there,* there! And Boyd's on the phone!"

"Mom?"

"Can't you see straight? It's right in front of you—to the right!!"

The Yorkie began to yap.

"Mom?"

"That man is blind as blank dice, not to mention deaf. What, honey?"

"Mom, do you remember that story you told me about the Woman with the Wooden Leg, the one who had all the adventures with her false leg? You'd always say, ' *"Aha," she cried and shook her wooden leg!'* before she solved a mystery?"

"Those dumb stories I made up?" She sounded pleased.

"They weren't dumb, Mom. She had a wooden leg, but she *danced*. She had a wooden leg, but she flew in a balloon, right?"

"Well . . ."

"Do you remember the one when she's cold and lost in the woods and she makes a fire and burns her leg to keep warm?"

"Oh sure. She found a stick and hopped home. I remember that one."

"The wooden leg was a *good* thing. I just realized that. I can go back, Mom. I can do it. But I wanted to ask you where the wooden-legged woman *came* from."

"How should I know! Maybe I dreamed it or maybe my mother told me a story that had that line in it. I've forgotten. But the point is, honey, it was a wooden leg. And she *shook* it."

Boyd's mother talked on and Boyd listened, but not closely. Her hands had stopped shaking. She listened to the dog barking hello into the receiver, she greeted her father, but her mind was on other things. *Let me start the fire, Lord, with my wooden leg.*

A few days later, early on a balmy autumn evening, Will was halfheartedly listening to Samuel Barber and watching the basketball game in his spectacularly messy apartment when the buzzer rang downstairs. When he pressed the switch that activated the speaker, no one answered, but the buzzer kept ringing. Will was dressed in an old basketball jersey and paint-spattered jeans. He was tired. He sighed and buzzed open the door, assuming it was a resident who'd forgotten a key.

Will had worked out at the gym, come home late, and lain on his bed, thinking about Boyd. Now he stood in the middle of the living room floor, remembering the day Russell's body came in. Gerda's physician had called about it, and Will had sent the van, the death ambulance, to pick him up. He had arrived: a young middle-aged man, roughly Will's age. He was rolled from the wrapped stretcher onto a steel worktable with a steel gutter surrounding it. He had soft brown hair, which fell in his eyes. He was dressed in tennis clothes—not whites, but pale Levi's cutoffs, a Stones T-shirt (ripped by the paramedics in their revival efforts), a wristband with a cobra logo stenciled on it, size 10½ Adidases. Eyes shut, but not completely, so that he appeared to be watching Will surreptitiously. His mouth open, tongue slightly protruding and stiffening now that the initial grip of rigor mortis was clamping down his muscles as the lactic acid surged through him. Will knew that after sixteen hours or so, the body would release its grip on itself, relax again.

Will watched Griggs float over to the table on a wheeze of the pneumatic door. Griggs looked like a deranged astronaut in his Plexiglas eye shield. He smiled politely at Will and waved, indicating the body. He put his gloved hand in Russell's mouth and gently forced the tongue back into the mouth. One of his assistants, Lila Knoblauch, tiptoed in with the Polaroid camera, scuttled about, taking a few "before" shots.

After she left, Griggs began to remove Russell's clothing. He said nothing to Will, though his eyes, through the transparent eye shield, occasionally flickered up and caught Will's. Russell looked bluish, Will remembered, which was typical, especially after sudden death. The blood had begun to settle in his body. Will moved closer and noticed the red *X*'s fading across Russell's brow where the elastic band of his sun visor had pressed against his skin. There were a few bruises on his left leg, darkening; he had fallen on the court. One hand was scraped in a couple of places: impact abrasion.

Griggs cut away the T-shirt, ripped and dirt-stained, and pulled off the shoes and socks. Will stared at Russell's large, bare, vulnerable blue feet, his clipped toenails. Griggs unsnapped the beltless cutoffs, pulled them down. Russell's body, stripped to his fitted underwear. A jock strap, filled. He had long, strong legs, brushed with brown hairs, just a little thickening at the waist. Blue veins everywhere, darkening like striations in marble.

Griggs stood thinking a moment, slid his eye shield back on his head, then approached the body with purpose. He moved behind Russell, clasped his arms around the torso, and pulled up. A moan, long, low, then growing higher, filled the room. Will jumped back, exclaiming. Griggs readjusted the body's position, lifted his mask.

"Leftover air in the lungs," he said, smiling. "Never fails to surprise. But I shouldn't have to tell you about this stuff, Will. You learned all this in undertaker school, no?"

Will, chastened, watched Griggs cutting away the underwear, feeling behind him for another implement. Next he would make incisions, drain Russell's blood. Will left the room.

His doorbell rang three times in quick succession. He opened it, without thinking, then started, stepping backward. It was Priscilla. She was dressed in a very tight, very short black dress and little black heels. Her glossy black hair was loosely piled at the back of her head in a chignon held by two black lacquered chopsticks. She wore large dangling earrings that resembled chunks of lava. Her expression was terrifying. She smiled the smile of an avenging goddess; she bared her teeth at him. The black slash of her lipstick rode up over the natural line of her lips.

"I want my painting," she cried, pushing past him.

Will tried to smile, backing up. "Priscilla. I should have called you."

"Oh no. You? Call me? Why? Why would you call me?" She strode to the center of the living room, then whirled around to face him. "I have a date tonight. You notice I'm dressed up? I've found someone who really likes me, who likes being with me, who appreciates my art. I'm going to show him the painting."

She spotted it on the desk in the corner. Will sent up a sudden grateful prayer that he had not left it on the floor, thrown it on a pile of magazines or in the wastebasket.

She snatched it up and held it close to her heart. "Now, if you'll excuse me—"

"Priscilla, how about if you listen to me for a minute? I just need a second of your time. I want to say I'm sorry."

Priscilla held the painting away from her, glanced at it, pressed it back against her heart. Then she began, slowly, to cry. She stood rigid in the center of the floor, her arms crossed over the painting, with only her head moving. She shook it back and forth, so that it looked like she was repeating a no over and over again, her lava earrings swinging dangerously as tears flew in all directions.

Will put his arm around her waist carefully, leaving distance between them, and walked backward, towing her. He reached behind and down to the messy couch, pushing aside some newspapers, a box of pretzels, and a hockey stick. Then he let himself and Priscilla fall backward gently onto the sofa.

Priscilla's hair had fallen free of the chopsticks, which hung, tangled, in her hair. She smelled like gardenias.

Will gently took the painting from her hands, placed it reverently on the hassock. "Priscilla, I didn't dislike the painting. It just went past me."

She began to sob again; her shoulders shook. Will, staring at her hair, smelling the tropical perfume, the smell of her agitation, began to feel aroused, then, abruptly, did not. He slid forward awkwardly on the couch as Priscilla leaned slowly toward him. His arm, as he pulled away, accidentally brushed her breast.

"Damn," she said. "That's perfect. You say you want to apologize when all you want is sex." She plucked up a tissue from a box on an end table. She pressed it to her eyes, her smudged mascara, and sighed melodramatically. "Let's be honest here. Why did you hire me? No, really. Not to promote me. To keep me as a handy fuck?"

Will put his elbows on his knees, his head in his hands. The oboe cried out in despair from the speakers. "You weren't *that* handy."

"Fuck you."

Priscilla jumped up suddenly, grabbing the painting as she rose. She jerked her dress down, adjusted her hose, looking over her left shoulder and down, straightening the seams that bisected her legs. Will looked away, confused. He *had* wanted her as a handy fuck. But he didn't want her now. He saw Boyd's face before him. He coughed, embarrassed.

"Look at how you live. You're going to be forty soon and you live like a graduate student. Do you think of this as charming? Listen to me. I ran your office and never got credit."

"Priscilla," he cried desperately. "I eventually saw what you wrote on the back of your painting. I just didn't see it right away."

She paused at the door and looked at him. "It's what's on the front that matters: Downstream and no oars—that's you all over."

She slammed the door.

Will sighed, a sigh of relief. He kicked a pillow into the air, like a football, and it bounced off the wall. "I'm sorry, okay?"

He shook himself and looked back at the door.

"What the hell do you know?" he shouted. "Why don't *you* take over the goddam business if you know so goddam much?"

He kicked aside a soccer ball and a litter of newspapers, some blueprints he'd been working on for an imaginary project, "Intergalactic Gas Stations." He went on shouting, his tone altering slightly. Now he was enjoying himself.

"Okay, so I didn't get your painting. Ex-cuuuse me! So sue me, okay? I'm a goddam undertaker. And you, hey, nobody would ever mistake you for Picasso, sweetheart!"

There was a knock at the door. Will glanced at it with fear, then crossed the room and opened it.

Priscilla stood there, holding her painting. "I heard you yelling."

"Oh, sorry."

"Hey, if you want me to help run your business, offer me a better job."

Will stared at her.

"I heard you saying that I should run your business for you," she said.

"Would you like to come back inside?"

"No. I want you to do the right thing by me. I'm a good worker. I'm an even better organizer. You know that."

"There's an opening in management at the Anoka office— you want that job?"

"Okay. I'll take it."

"Okay, it's yours."

She transferred her painting to her left hand and shook his with her right. "Good-bye, Will," she said. "Thank you."

He waved as she trotted down the hall in her small heels.

"Good-bye, Priscilla."

He waited, listening, till he heard the elevator creak up the shaft, the doors open, close, then the sounds of the car's descent.

When he was sure that she was gone, he yelled at the top of his lungs. "Fine. You want the job? Take the job with my compliments! Just don't ever show anybody your paintings, okay? Okay?"

He pointed at the door. "And I'll tell you something else, Priscilla Soukpun . . ."

Then he stopped—he'd run out of wind. He scratched his head, and a knot of images unraveled before him. He saw his father in the hospital bed, reaching out a weak arm to touch him, smiling at him, his eyes filled with mild light as Will sat down to read him the newspaper. His father turned into Griggs, hanging silently over the faces of the dead, returning them to the illusion that the self perpetuated of itself. The dignity of resemblance. Looking closer, he saw that Griggs was working on Russell Schaeffer, dead man, simulacrum of the once-animated face and form—that strong body thrown to the ground by an inhuman force.

Then Russell floated to the ceiling, out over water, became a ship carrying a little girl in black pajamas squatting next to her mother on the deck. The ship slid and rolled in the waves. He heard the singing tones filling the little girl's throat as she ran to the rail suddenly, gesturing to her mother. What was it she wanted her to see? He heard the mother answer, calling her back in the singing language. But the little girl did not run back to her side. She was brave, eager to see what lay ahead. Later, she would remember these waves, the wide wake, this hopeful ship, the light in the sky. Later, he understood, at last, dimly, that she would paint this scene for him. She would place him in it. But blind as he was, he would not see what gift she was offering him, how it resembled a history.

CHAPTER 21

A WEEK LATER, on a warm September day, Boyd slipped into the offices of Lindegaard, Skoglund, and Kiefer, on Nicollet Mall, ten minutes late for the reading of Russell's will. Through the open door of Bud Skoglund's office, she glimpsed Gerda sitting in a leather armchair, dressed in a cranberry silk suit. Boyd wore a denim skirt and blue suede clogs and twisted her hair into a messy figure eight against the nape of her neck as she hurried past the reception area.

A secretary waved her into the large office. As she entered, Bud Skoglund, the Schaeffer family attorney, leaped up and took her hand. Boyd, apologizing for her tardiness, nodded toward her mother-in-law, but Gerda pulled at her skirt and drew her into a perfunctory embrace. As Boyd brushed her cheek, they looked into each other's eyes, then Boyd stood up, pulled away, took a chair near Gerda's, facing the desk.

Bud smiled benignly at the two women before him. He was a

portly man in red suspenders and bow tie, with droopy eyelids. This sleepy-eyed expression was deceptive; his eagle eyes under the hanging brows missed nothing. Gerda raised her eyebrows back at him, nodding for him to begin.

"Gerda dear. Boyd. The absence of Russell's siblings, Marta, Stephen, or Clare, or any other family members, serves to emphasize that what I have to relate to you is a highly sensitive . . . situation in the matter of Russell's will."

He paused, glancing at a sheaf of documents before him on the polished desktop.

"Well. Bear with me as I say a few things you already know. Since Thaddeus's death, our Gerda has been controlling stockholder and chair of the board of Schaeffer Enterprises and its subsidiaries. The subsidiaries, as well as associated stocks, holding companies, and other assets, were divided equally among the four Schaeffer children, who share executive responsibilities with Gerda and who themselves are a corporation formed to protect against prohibitive inheritance taxes. With the"— he paused and looked at Gerda, then Boyd "tragic death of Russell, all his shares in the corporations, as well as stocks, annuities, insurance—of which his spouse is the sole beneficiary— properties, et cetera—indeed, his position in the Schaeffer sibling corporation"—another pause, a longer stare at Boyd— "as per his wishes, would normally pass to you, his wife, Boyd Maris Schaeffer, with the exception of certain monies to be held in trust for their daughter, Frederica Janine, till her majority."

He looked up at Boyd, to see how she'd reacted to his words so far. "However. We have some complications here."

Boyd smiled at Bud Skoglund and caught Gerda's eye. In the

split second before she spoke, she realized that Gerda knew what she was going to say. "Actually it's not complicated at all, Mr. Skoglund. I don't want any money."

The attorney glanced in Gerda's direction, as if she could explain what her daughter-in-law had cooked up. But Gerda was staring at her daughter-in-law's face.

"I don't want Russell's money. Having said that, I would like to ask Gerda if I may keep the house, which she so generously gave us as a wedding present. And Freddy's trust should remain. But that's it. You can have the rest."

Gerda reached over tentatively and touched her hand. "Boyd. Can I tell you—"

Boyd pulled her hand away, excited. "I got a job offer, Gerda. In my field. Ob/gyn." She flashed a snide smile at Bud Skoglund. "Women's health."

Boyd stood up. "But I want you both to know that even if I hadn't been offered this job, I'd do the same thing. I just don't want the money."

Bud Skoglund mopped his brow with a handkerchief, his eyelids actually lifting as he peered at Boyd. "Sit down, sit down, dear. I know how you feel. This has been a terrible, terrible tragedy. A shock for everyone, but most especially for you. My God. Now, we can easily reschedule all this."

"There's no point in rescheduling, Mr. Skoglund. I've made up my mind."

He nodded sagely, dramatically, leaned back wearily against his great desk, closed his eyes, then he opened them again, lizard-slow, and looked conspiratorially at Gerda. He spoke very slowly, as if he were speaking to two slightly retarded children.

It was his fault, he said—he'd scheduled this meeting too soon, way too soon after the tragedy.

Boyd shrugged, then glanced at her watch. She nodded to Gerda, then brushed close to her as she bent to pick up her bag. "I've thought this through very carefully. I was afraid to walk out while he was alive. I can still walk out now."

"Boyd, this is ridiculous. This is melodrama."

"Well, Gerda, people have to find a way to live."

Gerda shook her hand in a dismissive gesture, her face twisted.

Bud Skoglund glanced at her, an inquiring expression on his usually masked face.

"Good-bye, folks. I'm going to work now."

"Boyd. All of this . . . all it means is that you are still arguing with him."

Boyd slipped a clog off and on her foot nervously as she paused in the doorway. She bowed her head, smiling coquettishly. She waved cheerily to Gerda and Bud Skoglund, two people thwarted in their desire, as she saw it, to give her a fortune. "You know, that may be true. But now I'm winning."

CHAPTER 22

A FEW DAYS LATER, late at night, Boyd sips wine in the kitchen and talks to her dead husband. Stacked on the kitchen table, near her elbow, are some of Russell's favorite books. Through the door leading to the dining room, she can see the half-lit expanse of polished parquet, a corner of blood-colored kilim. She can also see the shadow of her dead husband on the floor, holding still, then flickering like a fire.

"I know you're there," she calls out, her voice raised but not loud enough to wake Freddy. Her voice sounds polite but firm, the voice a mother might use calling to a wayward child.

"I want to tell you something. You've left only confusing messages, pal. Couldn't you act the way ghosts act traditionally and *make a point* eventually? Like Hamlet's father or Miss Jessel? Concentrate. Isn't there some kind of ghost self-actualization support group that can help you *focus?*"

She pours herself a third glass.

"Ask me if I like my new job. I like my new job, Russell! But how can I manage this work if you . . . can't figure out what you want? If you want to scare me—hey, bring out the chains and the flying objects, moan a little, okay? If you want to *tell* me something, float a lighted candle and I'll follow it down the hall. Just *get to it!*"

The shadow figure remains still.

"Looking through the passages you've underlined here and there, Russ. *King John,* where Constance longs to be mad, with 'her tongue in the thunder's mouth'—because if she had the excuse of madness, she could forget her grief. She says, 'grief fills up the room of my absent child, lies in his bed, walks up and down with me.' "

Russell steps slowly out of the shadows to face her. She stands up, holding a book over her heart like a shield. They stare at each other, gazes high, sniffing the wind like two animals facing each other in a wood.

"Let's face it—you were always a ghost."

Russell raises a hand and slowly touches it to his heart. She takes a step toward him and he floats back into the shadows.

"Why did we stop making love? Because you were a ghost?"

She glances back at the table.

"Let's see what your journal says. Better than a Ouija board!"

She picks up the stapled notebook pages, skimming though.

"Where was I last time? New York? Tahiti?" She moves toward the shadow. "Bingo!" she shouts, then reads aloud:

" 'December second. *It's as if Freddy is some kind of expiation, some kind of offering to the Gods of Go-Wrong. We have her now and that's everything. There is nothing more for the two of us to say to each other, to do for each other.*' "

"Gods of Go-Wrong," Boyd repeats aloud, impressed.

She turns to a page that is dog-eared, sentences written over and crossed out again and again. She recognizes the dates. She reads aloud again:

" *'Her endless suffering over this death is making it impossible for her to work or, more important, to think about me. She sits and stares at the wall or she does* The New York Times *crossword puzzle endlessly. What is a five-letter word for* paralysis? Guilt?' "

There are many words crossed out after this.

" *'I called the* Post *and the* News *today, trying to help, but somehow blundering, creating the opposite effect. I wanted to tell her story, I mean the story of how hard she tried to save the patient. They listened closely to me. They'd gotten a call from a protester already. They seemed eager to hear the other side. They asked a lot of questions. I thought I'd done a heroic thing, and then they took what I told them and betrayed me. They published something that made her look like a murderer, and I saw what a fool I'd been.' "*

Boyd rereads the sentences aloud, then again to herself. Then she points at the shadow. "You're the one? You brought all that down on me?"

She stands paralyzed, deep in thought for a few minutes, mumbling to herself. Then she crosses the room toward him, stretching out her hand. This time he does not withdraw. His lidded eyes, lion-green, look into hers. Her fingers, extended, begin shaking—just a quarter inch from his face. Trembling, they trace the air above his eyes, his mouth, then abruptly close the distance. Boyd brushes with her fingertips, at last, the face, the ungiving cheekbone, the hard, smooth plane. As she makes contact, she utters a sound, a strangled cry, and yanks back her hand as if she'd put it in fire. It is undeniable: She has felt resistance. She has felt flesh, bone, substance, something solid. And *there*.

She cries out, and Russell fades into shadows.

She covers her face with her hands. She will not look at the place where Russell has been standing. She walks carefully, holding herself erect inside, like someone badly burned, to the red wall phone. Runs her shaking finger down a column of scribbled names and numbers on the flowered wall-pad.

Will jolts upright in bed at the telephone's shrill alarm. He fumbles for the receiver and the lamp switch simultaneously. Knocks the lamp over, but pulls the phone receiver to his mouth in the dark, croaking out a half-conscious sound.

Boyd, without identifying herself, begins talking into his ear. "You were the only person I could think of to call . . . who might understand what's happening here. Could you come over and talk? Just for a minute or two? I'll make coffee."

"Boyd? Do you know what time it is?" He coughs, his heart pounding, feeling on the floor for the fallen lamp.

"Late. It's late, right?"

He abandons his search for the lamp, sits up in bed. "What's the matter? You sound . . . Boyd? I'll be right over."

She let him in, pushing back her hair with one hand, waving a cigarette with the other, directing him to the kitchen, where lights blazed. She stayed in constant motion, making a series of repetitive gestures, dressed in leggings and a thin sweat-top torn from an old sweatshirt, over which she had thrown a battered hacking jacket, her hair straggling behind her ears, where she nervously pushed it.

Will caught his own reflection in a standing mirror in the hall. He looked exhausted but alert. He was going to see this through, his set jaw said, despite his thrown on jeans and rumpled hair; he was awake, clearheaded, a man who knew his business.

"There. He stood right there. I was talking to him about . . . something he did a long time ago." She looked at Will, a look that mingled absolute doubt and absolute certainty.

He pointed toward the table and they sat down. He glanced at her wineglass and the half-empty bottle. "You said you had coffee?"

She got up and went to the stove, the steaming Melitta urn. She poured two cups into flame-colored glazed mugs, keeping her hands steady.

"What are all these books?"

"His. There's a trail here, a trail he's left . . ." she began to explain, but the sentences broke over each other, jagged waves. She stopped, struggling to reorder her words.

"He wants me to find him, find his thinking in these pages. You know—messages. He left messages for me."

She picked up one of the volumes, paging quickly through it, talking to herself. She dropped the book and lifted another; notes fluttered to the floor. She buried her face in it, then held out the book to him.

He took it from her, then gently closed it. "Boyd. These are not messages. Or not exactly. Okay, you saw him tonight. People see things. People wake up and see the one they've lost in the bed next to them, or on the bus, or standing in line ahead of them at the bank. It's not uncommon—in fact, they're natural, these kinds of visitations."

"Why?"

"Why? Because the dead, you know—they still need us." He looked at her, surprised at himself. "I've never said that before."

"What do you usually say, Dr. Death?"

"I say things the other way around. 'We need the dead,' I tell people. 'You'll have dreams of the person, you'll see people in the street who look just like her or him. Because you are having trouble, naturally, letting go.' People will do anything to hang on for a while. It's denial, it's consolation, it's wish fulfillment."

She smiled at him distractedly, then stared into her coffee cup.

Will looked hungrily at the top of her head, gleaming red-gold in the bright overhead light. She wasn't really listening. Her senses, her antennae, were tuned to some invisible wave, something in the air. He tried to regain her attention.

"But I've never said what I just said before. I wanted to convince you of the opposite."

She tapped a cigarette out of a pack on the table, offering him one. He shook his head and watched her stare at the cigarette, then crumple it into a ball, flick it away from her. "But do you believe it? That the dead need us?"

He sipped his coffee slowly, then nodded. "I suppose I do."

"Then why, do you think, if the dead need us, they wouldn't send us messages?"

Will watched the agitation rise in her. He decided to get the truth over with quickly. "Because these are messages Russell left for you when he was alive. You just didn't tune in on them then."

Boyd continued to stare at him. Then she got up and stood in front of him. "He was in this room. I touched him."

"What do you mean, you touched him?"

She pulled him up, awkwardly, from his chair, stood him in the middle of the room. "I put my hand out like this. He was right in front of me as I reached out."

She frowned at him, extending her hand, reliving it. "I'd just discovered something in his journal—you know, something I hadn't . . . expected. And I pointed at him like this. I reached out to him and then . . ."

Boyd pointed at Will, then touched his cheek lightly, pulled away. He stood, his eyes half closed, lids fluttering.

"I felt flesh, bone. Something living, Will."

He opened his eyes, reached for her hand, which had fallen to her side. He lifted her hand to his cheek.

She felt the rough stubble of his beard, and, as he moved her hand down to his neck, near his ear, where the blood throbbed, his pulse.

They stood quietly, her fingers held to his face. Then he placed his hand on her cheek, a mirror gesture from which she at first seemed to withdraw. Then she closed her eyes as they stood together quietly and, after a while, let her cheek fall into his palm.

Just then the refrigerator's ice maker dropped a load of cubes into its plastic bay: a hollow, rattling sound. They jumped and moved apart.

"A living person feels different—you see?" he said. "What

you felt was a phantom. Like a phantom limb. C'mon, *you* know
about that stuff!"

"Tell me something. Why is it that on practically the first day
of my job I'm confronted with a young woman who brings back
every ghost from my past. Is that a phantom limb, too?"

Will sighed. "I don't have an answer to that one."

"Will you stay with me? I mean, just till it's light? This is the
hardest time for me, this time of night." She blinked at him as
she shrugged out of her jacket.

"I don't mean anything like . . . you know. I just want . . .
company."

In the living room, they sat stiffly on the couch together, a few
inches apart. Boyd's quilt covered them. Then Will pulled her
to him.

"Look. Just put your head down. Sleep. You don't have to
worry now."

"Jesus. What a basket case you must think me."

"Just let it go."

"Everyone keeps saying that to me. I'd just like to know what
to let go."

He touched her neck, the hard tension there, pressed his
hand against it. "Let this go."

His hand slid down her spine a little, massaging her back
muscles. "Let this go."

Boyd made a sound, shaking off his hand. "I hate massages."

"Let this go."

He took her shoulders in his hands and tilted her upper body
back so that her spine arched slightly and her head lay back
against the cushions. Despite her mild protests, he put his hand

flat on her face, sculpting it, gently outlining her mouth, closing her eyelids with his fingers, smoothing her forehead. Her eyes, as she relaxed, stayed shut, the lids fluttering as he touched her.

"And this." His hand moved carefully, diffidently, down her exposed neck, hovered above her chest, the torn sweat-top, paused at her sternum, then covered it: a warm palm against the bone. "This is where so much grief collects."

She made an attempt to push his hand away, then felt the warmth emanating from his palm and let the hand stay against the small shield of her breastbone. She was conscious of his hand, the splayed fingers pressing against her breasts, but she was neither angry nor aroused. A great surge of exhaustion and warmth swept over her, like a breaker, the wide bath of a wave.

Will closed his eyes as well, his hand steady against what he knew to be the hard store of her grief. He was acutely conscious of her breasts and the beauty of her face in repose as she let her head fall against his shoulder. But he held her pinned to him, his hand chaste inside her shirt, feeling each swell of her breath, letting everything he knew about the body and the body's sadness concentrate in his hand.

She was sound asleep suddenly, drawing each breath with exhausted gravity, her mouth slightly open, her body's heat against him. He floated, awake, for hours in a kind of ecstatic restraint, his hand radiating. Then, after a while, he relaxed slightly. With her body against his, with his hand over her heart, Will too fell asleep.

CHAPTER 23

THE NEXT DAY, Boyd, on her lunch hour, hurries up the brick preschool walk, lined by neon-bright green and yellow and red plastic tulips, and shakes hands with Freddy's teacher. The teacher has asked her to come in and observe Freddy at play. She is worried that Freddy may be sleeping too much, taking too many naps. She also talks, disturbingly, all day long in fact, about an underground beanstalk. The teacher, Laurie Lou, as she is known by everyone, waves Boyd into the glassed-in one-way observation room and offers her juice and cookies. She asks Boyd if she thinks it wise that she has gone back to work so soon. She asks her if Freddy is okay at home. Laurie Lou is young and earnest, with washed-out, worried blue eyes and a master's degree in education.

"I don't go to work every day," Boyd replies curtly, then relents. She is home on Tuesday and Thursday, and she has hired a nanny for the other days, but Freddy wants to go to school every day. Freddy *has* been sleeping a lot, but she does not seem depressed. She is eating fine; she is busy . . . doing what? Planning her trip down the beanstalk, Boyd admits—it's true. But it seems to help her . . . adjust to the enormous change in their lives. Laurie Lou nods and smiles, looking unconvinced, then slips away to make sure her assistant has put out the snacks. She'll be right back.

It happens that on this day, the day of Boyd's visit, Freddy is very busy. Freddy is scrupulously arranging a handful of brightly colored plastic letters on the large red rug, coaxing them into a syntax only she can decipher, spelling out a world in her own language. *A* has nothing to do with the boring *apple* that always seems to accompany it in alphabet books. It has to do with long legs and folded wings. *A* is a projectile or standing bird, like a stork, and *B* is a sideways, vertical camel that climbs into the sky, but never the smiling insipid *bee* in the book. Freddy has no trouble understanding representation. *A* and *B* are themselves but turn quickly into other things. She can recite the whole alphabet, but she resists going further into transactive language. These letters before her are her own, her secret tribe. In the sunlight, against the unvarying background of red weave, they change shape. Here is the *X*, a beautiful mouth that opens, talking to her, and here, against the horizon, is the strange glacial forest of *W* and *M* spied on by the balloon, *Q*. Freddy moves the plastic letters close together, then apart. The mouth immediately lifts into air, buoyed up by *Q*. They are on their way to *W* and *M*, despite the terrible *R*, who comes winging with its relative, greedy *K*, who dines on smaller letters, who live a life of fear. Clouds made of *P*'s gather, rain made of *H*'s falls. A convocation of the letters ends in dispersion across the great red veldt. Some collapse near a waterfall made of *O*'s and *L*'s; some enter a small herd of *Z*'s, who have always grazed peacefully, never bothering anybody.

A picture book, lying open on the rug next to her, catches her eye. In the same instant, superimposed over the book's illustration, she sees a striped rolled shirt sleeve, a large flat gold wristwatch, a wrist brushed with dark hairs; she recognizes this disembodied part. It is her daddy's arm, reaching down, moving the letters into a special sequence, a pattern that she admires but never chooses to imitate. He had been trying to teach her something about the letters. Where is he now? She immediately feels sad, wondering about this. Then, too, there is the matter of the last time she saw him—she doesn't like thinking about that day. She has heard her mother and grandmother discussing how her father left her in the park alone, and she understands that this was not a good thing for him to have done. In fact, to Freddy, being left behind was a matter of some indifference at that point, since her father had told her already, loudly and in a clear voice, that he was leaving her. She understood then that leaving her behind in a park playground was only a beginning, an introduction to his real disappearance.

"I'm going away, honey. Daddy's going away."

He'd walked in circles, his eyes moving quickly over everything around him, his car keys jingling in his hand as she perched on the edge of the sandpit and stared up at him. Then he put his car keys back in his pocket.

"Let's play hide-and-seek, okay, Fred?"

He'd started her off counting. She went up to ten, started over again twice, as per their arrangement, then shrieked, "Come out, come out, wherever you are!" and began looking for him. That's all. That's all there was to remember.

By the time Ashley's mother came up and shouted questions to her as she pumped her legs, rising higher and higher on the swing, there was nothing to tell, either. She'd looked for a long time and he was gone.

Freddy stares at the book, open to a picture of a tree—bright green leaves, trunk, branches laden with apples. Beneath the tree, she sees a few letters she recognizes—the terrible *R*, the great kindly *E*'s, and one of her favorites, *T*, the happy *T*, with its tail draped on top of its head. She compares the plastic letter *T* and the illustration, sighing to herself, listening to the sound of the roses talking to each other in the teacher's vase.

Approaching her now is the dread Brandon, banging discordantly on a set of multicolored chime bars—red, blue, yellow, green—with a balled wand. He waddles over to her, holding out the wand, smiles hugely, and strikes her on the arm with it.

"Go away, Brandon. You stink!" she cries, a more or less accurate observation.

"I went pee-pee on Brianna's mat," he confides thoughtfully, scratching his buttocks with the wand. He displays a large, crusted scab on his knee. When these intimate revelations elicit no response, he regroups, smiling at her again. Then he sighs. "I will kill you now."

He drops the wand and wearily lifts the xylophone, propping it against his shoulder like a machine gun, then he mimes discharging several rounds at her head.

"No." Freddy speaks loudly and calmly over his sound effects. "No, you won't. You're just a small boy."

Brandon instantly drops his weapon and runs off, shouting for a teacher.

"I'm not a small boy!" he throws back, furious, over his shoulder. "She said I was a small boy!"

Freddy returns to her consideration of the tree and her letters, safe in her milieu. To her right, near the aquarium, grim, asthmatic Felicia batters pegs into holes, wheezing and grunting. They are all in place around her, all the categories, the predictable social types that she will meet and remeet throughout her life. The Aggressor throwing blocks, the Whiner sobbing in his wet plastic pants, the Seducers, he and she, tossing their curls, the Good Citizen preparing to report to the Teacher.

One spring day they had planted seeds together. She sees his arm again, then sees him beside her, digging seed furrows, showing her how to hollow out soil with the bent teaspoon.

Later, he showed her the green shoots of the flowers as they pushed out of the ground. "Freddy, look," he said. "Sunflowers."

She looks at the tree, then the *T*, the *R*, the two *E*'s. She picks these letters out of the formation and lines them up just as they are lined up in the book. She feels something, a movement of air at her elbow. She is distracted by this invisible urgency, then turns back and sees it, simply sees it for the first time: tree. Tree, the great leafy one, with its roots spreading below the earth's surface, birds and fruit in its branches. TREE. She laughs aloud, tracing the letters with her fingers. T-R-E-E. She sees it now, that these letters mean the tree in the book, the tree outside the window, the trees in her yard. T-R-E-E. Now it is no longer unique, her own, it is all trees, but now TREE becomes her sign, her saving sign—like the beanstalk spiraling below the earth—

and TREE is his face. It will mean, always, a flicker of the lost one.

She reads aloud, a newly learned voice in an ancient world planted with these great breathers, makers of green, some planted with teaspoons and spades, little furrows for the seeds dropped patiently, one by one. *We put Daddy in the ground.*

"TREE!" she shouts, jubilant, but the teacher is lining up the other children for juice and cookies, and no one hears her. She looks back at the other letters, the sly bird, the speaking mouth, the forest, the waterfall, the terrible *R*. She looks down at them as if she is ascending into a new, rarefied atmosphere. Everything has changed. The teacher calls to her, but she does not get up. She sits, looking at the letters that will spell, for the rest of her life, the same triumphant word, with its twin, the branching image, leaves rustling above what is disappearing: the kingdom of joy, the red veldt, momentous, preliterate.

" 'Tree,' " she reads quietly, to herself. " 'Tree.' " And the sun, in its crown of fire, burns silently through a passing cloud. And he disappears, with his arm held out to her, holding the seeds in his palm—sunflowers—gone so gradually, into that same light.

Laurie Lou steps back into the observation room with a blue plastic cup of orange juice for Boyd.

"She seems much happier today—a little distracted, but really happy," she says, but Boyd does not turn to look at her. Boyd is watching hungrily through the glass, watching Freddy stand up in the sunlight and smile all around her, looking straight at the glass wall but not seeing her, seeing instead the letters that spell the words that spell the world everywhere around her.

❦

CHAPTER 24

"I USED TO KNOW," said Boyd to Resnikoff, "a joke about a hysterectomy and a lobotomy, but I forget the punch line. Must be my lobotomy."

Resnikoff stared blankly at her, smiled patiently, then looked up at the clock. She was filling a syringe with dye. Boyd had been looking at files. The offices had expanded over the years into a mini-hospital, with X-ray units and "procedure rooms"—like small O.R.s, with oxygen, anesthetics (and even a quasi–resident anesthesiologist), computers, monitors, and scans.

Resnikoff was preparing to do a hysterosalpingography—from the Greek: *hystero,* womb; and tubes, *salpingies.* The procedure involved injecting demarcation dye (Boyd reminds herself) through a cervical cannula into a patient's Fallopian tubes, to determine if there was a blockage, which might prevent conception. The spread of the dye was then tracked via fluoroscope. This, Boyd knew, was a conservative procedure, neither radical nor invasive, and Resnikoff was proceeding conservatively, facing the wall clock.

The patient, who was prepped and in the stirrups, was a woman in her late thirties who was having trouble conceiving. She had asked for a sedative, but Resnikoff had not thought it necessary.

Boyd talked to the woman, Candace, as Resnikoff answered the intercom, then prepared to inject the dye, checking her watch. Candace untensed a little as Boyd held her hand. Boyd watched her close her eyes and try to control her breath.

"Relax!" Resnikoff barked suddenly over her shoulder, and Candace jerked back into fearful watchfulness.

"That's *my* problem, too," whispered Boyd. "As soon as someone says, *'Relax,'* I get tense as hell."

Candace glanced at her and smiled and nodded too eagerly, as if Boyd were some kind of pre-op comic. Boyd heard herself paged, squeezed Candace's hand, then backed out of the room, waving. "I'll be right back."

The receptionist met her in the hall, frightened, and pointed out an examination room. "Emergency," she said. "Dr. Remington's at lunch."

Boyd walked in on Sunny, who was crouched on the floor, grimacing in pain, something bloody hanging from between her legs. There was a gleaming trail of blood across the tiles.

"Sunny? I'm going to try and get someone else to see you."

The girl looked up, her thick glasses glittering. "No," she cried. *"You."*

Boyd came closer, took a quick glance at the blood, then asked Sunny if she could stand.

"I think so."

The door opened and Ronnie, the nurse-practitioner, entered. They each took an arm and then half lifted Sunny to a step stool and from there to the gurney.

"Let's clean this up," said Boyd, and the nurse turned to the sink.

Boyd and the girl looked at each other. What had always seemed possible, even natural, to Boyd—the act of putting her hands inside another woman's body—seemed a violation here, a forced entry. Sunny's short skirt was soaked and her unlikely white athletic socks were stained. The center of her body, between her legs, radiated a nearly visible pain. The inadequate sanitary napkin was crumpled and saturated inside a torn pair of underpants. The nurse cut them both away, then she lifted the bloody legs into the stirrups.

Sunny's face was full of defiance. She fixed Boyd with a burning gaze, her clumsy glasses slipped down on her nose.

Boyd washed her hands and snapped on the transparent examination gloves. Ronnie stood by her side.

"Sunny," Boyd said. "Forgive me. I have to see what's happening here."

There was nothing wrong—or, rather, everything still was. With her gloved hand, Boyd felt the pregnancy still in place. Sunny had managed to chop around inside the vagina with a razor blade but hadn't come close to aborting the fetus. She was still bleeding a little, but not profusely. It was not a life-threatening amount of blood, though the gloves came out dripping.

Boyd consulted with Ronnie, then gently swabbed the vaginal area with an anti-infectant as the nurse injected a syringeful of antibiotic into the girl's hip. The blood flow had almost completely stopped now.

Sunny's eyes stayed on Boyd, the question unasked.

"You're still pregnant, Sunny. I'm sorry. But you can't—"

Sunny began to cry, abruptly sobbing. There was no buildup, just great heaving gasps that shook the metal table.

"I can't say I'm surprised," said Boyd. "I thought you might try this."

But Sunny was not listening. She was trying to pull her legs out of the stirrups as Ronnie appeared near her head, murmuring to her, holding her arms down.

As Remington entered, Sunny nodded at Boyd.

"You're *afraid*, Doctor."

Boyd shook her head and hastily pulled off the examination gloves. "Would you mind taking over, Doctor? I'm sorry, I have to get some air. Ronnie will fill you in on Sunny's condition and what's been done."

Remington stared at her, surprised, and Ronnie nodded, then turned away.

The terrible sobs started again.

"I'll be back, I promise. I just need air."

S HE CAME BACK a half hour later and stood in the doorway of the examination room. Sunny had been cleaned up and wrapped in a cotton robe, her bare feet crossed. Ronnie had set up an IV line running into the girl's left arm. Boyd could see that they'd administered a sedative. She rummaged in a cabinet and pulled out a blanket, shook it out, and drew it over the girl, who opened one eye, looking at her just the way Freddy did.

Boyd pulled up a chair and Sunny laughed at her. "I wanted you to take care of me because you look really alone to me. I thought you'd understand how I feel."

"I look alone?"

"Yeah. Like you've been thinking about something—no, *one* thing all by yourself for a long time."

"You're right. You know what that thing is?"

Sunny shook her head; fear crossed her face. "I know it's definitely the reason why you can't help me."

"You're right. Here's the one thing: The last time I performed an abortion, the woman died."

"For real?"

"She was supposed to have been healthy, she was supposed to have had no physical problems, but she had problems that no one knew about, not even her. Her heart was weak. And it stopped."

"Did you do something wrong?"

"No, I didn't do anything wrong. I've been over and over it in my mind. But her heart stopped all the same." Boyd stopped talking and stared beyond the girl.

"And so now you don't believe in doing abortions."

"That's right, I don't believe in it anymore. I can't take what's growing inside of you and *stop* it. I shouldn't have that power."

Sunny shook her head slowly; she appeared to be getting sleepy. "I don't see why what happened to you didn't give you *strength*. You know—make you tough. You're a *doctor*. That's your job—being tough. Isn't it?"

Boyd stood up, rearranging the blanket around the girl. "A doctor's job is, according to the Oath, to do no harm."

"But you didn't harm her on purpose. You tried to help her, didn't you?"

Boyd nodded.

"And you should help me. Shouldn't you? Because next time, Doctor, I might do *myself* harm."

Boyd turned on her before she realized what she was saying. "Look at what you tried to get here—a quick D-and-C, right? You moved that razor blade around, but you didn't cut yourself nearly enough to warrant a scrape of the uterus. In order to get *that,* you have to *really* do it. You have to cut yourself wide and deep, sweetheart. You have to lean on the blade. You have to risk *dying*. You have to get the cervix. You have to sever connections. You have to *hemorrhage*."

Sunny laughed. Tears began to run down her face again.

"After my patient died, I left the hospital, went outside. Snow was falling, and every single flake I saw had a drop of bright red blood in its center."

"I see blood in snow. I see blood in the toilet. I see blood filling my bed, Doctor."

"Should I feel guilty because you're a nice girl who got herself in a pickle? You want to kill yourself? I can't stop you. I can't stop *anyone*."

She felt her heart startle up, or was her heart *cringing*. Was she going to say it again? Was she going to invite the Gods of Go-Wrong in one more time? How easy it would be to say it: *"Die, leave me alone."* How easy it had been to say it to Russell!

"Yeah, I'm a nice girl, even with my weird hair. I play basketball—did I tell you that? I was All-State, but I got tired of hearing the jock guys call me *squaw*. I beat up one of those white guys in the parking lot. I'm *strong*, you see, but I'm a nice girl. Nothing special, but I've worked at McDonald's and the skating rink to get money to go to school. To help my mom. And some older dude talked me into sex without a safe—and now he needs to be a family man again. This has all *upset* him *quite a bit,* he said."

She pulled herself up to a sitting position. "You're not lookin' at one of those *incest* victims. And I'm not raped. I'm not carrying some armless freak inside of me, either. No sob story to me, is there, Doctor? Like you said, *a nice girl who got herself in a pickle*—that's me."

"I can't get involved, Sunny."

"It's all right, Doctor. I understand. You take care of yourself, now! And your family!"

Boyd closed the door softly.

CHAPTER 25

H E TUCKS THE PHONE under his chin. He is looking over new coffin orders for October. The salesman, who had just left, had flashed a huge ruby pinkie ring at Will.

"Took a lot of teeth to get this baby," he'd said, winking. Then, "Just kidding, son. Just kidding."

The new coffins, illustrated in the brochure, look exactly like the old coffins. A coffin is a coffin is a coffin. Or it is a casket. The two are virtually the same. A coffin has eight sides and screws, some decorative, some actually holding it together. A casket is rectangular and the lids are hinged. Otherwise, in terms of function, they are identical. But one coffin, Will notices, has a delicate, long-stemmed rose carved into its polished mahogany lid. Across the stem, lovely calligraphy carved into the wood: *A Rose for Remembrance.*

"When you get a chance," he murmurs into the receiver, "give me a call."

———

She phones him back toward the end of the day. Will is tired, impatient. His day has been long and complicated. He is trying to hire someone to replace Sechman and Robideaux. It's nearing the end of September and he has to hire someone soon. Roger is sending a handpicked candidate over tomorrow, because the people Will interviewed today were hopeless— graduates of funeral academies who are "motivated big-time" to "increase their assets."

There is nothing wrong with this cheerful, commonplace, profit-margin rhetoric, Will realizes. He knows he will never find another Griggs, but he had been hoping for a smile, a gesture, a speech, a spark of humor—something beyond these stamped-tin graduates of the corporate crypt. Coffins and caskets, all the same. A fifty crushed into the organist's palm. His father made money on the dead; so does he. The gilded stink of lilies, the business card surreptitiously palmed. But, in interviews, he searches for some human reaction to death—thoughts on sorrow, grief, loss. He'd like to hear a joke or two, maybe even the coffin salesman's brand of terrible humor. Anything but that sleazy, commodified trade-school sympathy, he thinks— lubricated, tight-fitting, inhibitive as a condom. Death, he knows, can be funny, even hysterically so—always, after suffering, it is a relief to laugh. As if to prove his point, the charcoal minivan cruises by, crunching gravel, circling the drive outside his windows. His in-house mechanic and handyman, Nils Larson, lies flat on top of the van, his profile rigid, holding a wilted sunflower perpendicular to his chest. Will hears end-of-the-day laughter, banter. When it comes to death, in fact, almost everybody is scared, so almost everybody is a comedian.

———

"I'm a friend," he says to Boyd. "I want you to know that. I'm not a poet and I'm not rich. I'm not mercurial or charming or constantly quotable. I have other qualities. For example, I'm alive. I'm not a ghost, Boyd. I'm alive."

He has practiced this little speech, sitting at his desk. He's spoken it to Roger. He realizes it sounds a bit self-conscious, even as he hears himself speaking the words.

"Well," she says. "That clears up *that* confusion, then."

"*You're* still alive."

"I'm a little of both right now."

Will glances out the window again. Nils and three others are standing on the gravel by the van, telling jokes. Soon they'll leave for Tollson's Lounge.

"It's such a beautiful day, and I've hardly had a chance to look outside, Boyd. Why don't I pick you up and we'll get a bite to eat, go for a drive? I can leave here in a few minutes."

"Sorry," she says. "I have an appointment."

CHAPTER 26

✦

RIGGS, IN HIS PURE-WHITE death suit, in clear plastic goggles, humming a little tune, stepped into the gleaming expanse of his operating theater. The scent of blossoms had been recently overwhelmed by other, stronger, smells: formaldehyde, alcohol, phenol, acetone. Griggs sniffed the air appreciatively, then checked his watch. There were covered bodies at stations along the wall, all of them requiring attention, requiring that Griggs continue his work till late into the night. It had been a busy week for Death.

The three worktables that resembled operating stations were overgrown with a jungle of equipment: hanging plastic tubing, artery pumps, gallon jugs of embalming fluid, trocars—three-foot-long probes hooked up to vacuum aspirators—blood drain-canals, siphons, an ozone machine for removal of odors, steel hampers marked BIO-HAZARD, wall posters outlining safety procedures. Portable tape and CD players filled niches above the tables. Griggs lifted off his protective goggles, set them aside. He didn't like doing his work feeling obstructed. He had never believed that the danger of disease was as great as his need to closely observe. He checked his watch again: seven-thirty.

He heard a footstep behind the door, but he was not alarmed. Lila Knoblauch, his assistant, often worked till eight o'clock, as did Will. The pneumatic door behind him opened, hissed closed. Griggs turned and beheld Boyd Schaeffer, looking frightened but determined. Griggs stared at her, then nodded once and turned away.

"Mr. Griggs, I'm Boyd Schaeffer," she said in a loud, clear voice. "I believe that you worked on my husband not too long ago."

"Mrs. Schaeffer," said Griggs, nodding again, rolling his slow, intimate gaze over her. "This area is off-limits to the public. You can turn around and go back up those stairs there on the right to get out."

He inclined his head one last time, dismissively, and turned back to his work, but Boyd held her ground.

"Mr. Griggs, I have a right to ask a couple of questions."

Griggs faced her again. "Now, Mrs. Schaeffer, that's true, you do, and I'm not trying to stand in the way of that. But I'm oc-cupied right now. Someone here urgently needs my attentions. You and I can meet at another time."

This last comment was delivered with an ominous arching of eyebrows, a shrouded smile. Then he returned to the sheeted form. Boyd became acutely aware, suddenly, of the surgical brightness of the overhead lights illuminating the other dead bodies in the room, stretched out alongside the machines, qui-etly waiting. For what? She kept her eyes trained straight ahead.

Griggs glanced over his shoulder at her reprovingly. "Things are exactly what they appear to be here. And they are exactly not what they appear to be. Either way, the deceased need privacy, okay? You cannot look at them and know them. They're not meant to be looked at and understood. Time is running out for me here. I've asked you to leave. If you don't go now, I can't help what you see."

Still looking over his shoulder at her, he pulled the sheet from the body in front of them. It lay on a gurney-like table ringed with a stainless steel gutter. The naked body, which belonged to a woman of eighty or so, was propped up by Styrofoam blocks strategically tucked under the neck, spine, and upper arms, which thrust the torso forward and up—an awkward posture. She wore, on her left hand, a diamond ring and a gold wedding band, stuck tight to her bony finger with wrapped tape.

The woman looked as if she had suffered from a wasting disease, most likely cancer. Her white hair had thinned to pink scalp in spots. Her cheeks were sunken in, her mouth puckered as if she'd tasted something sour. Boyd spotted a flesh-colored plug under the woman's heart. She was not intimidated.

"I'm a doctor," she said loudly. "There's nothing here that will shock me."

She stared at the body: It *did* look different from the cadavers she'd worked on in med school—or the dying or newly dead that she'd encountered in hospitals. This body's flesh seemed to change color before her eyes. The lower parts were concussion-blue; bruise-like discolorations formed rapidly on the extremities and at the little well of the collarbone.

Griggs, holding her eyes again with his, raised himself up on his toes, stretched his left arm over his head like a ballerina, and felt for the activation button on the CD player mounted on the wall above his worktable.

"Well, Doctor," he said. "Then you'll be right at home here. You won't mind if I hear my music?"

Strains of the musical *Evita* seeped into the air: "Don't Cry for Me, Argentina." Griggs began to execute a sort of in-place tango, still keeping his eyes on Boyd. He barely moved his feet, but he honored the rhythm, quietly, impeccably, swaying and dipping. He was a bulky man but graceful. He murmured to himself as he rolled his shoulders and slowly rippled, head to heels. " 'The truth is I never left you.' " He turned, bobbed, and crooned to his dead listeners, his strange flame-colored eyes glowing.

"You're trying to upset me," said Boyd, "but it's not working."

"Dr. Schaeffer, this is how I go about my work. If what you see now offends you, you have only yourself to blame. I've asked you to leave." He stopped undulating and seemed to soften a little toward her; he threw her a brief sheepish smile. "Do you want me to turn up the air?"

Boyd shook her head.

Griggs reached up and turned the volume down, just enough to move the voices from center stage to steady background.

"Embalming is a remarkable thing. It can hold 'em for two weeks, y'know," he said to her. "Like putting cheese in the refrigerator—it kills bacteria, retards that spoilage."

He waited. He seemed uncertain that she would appreciate

the importance of what he said. Boyd in fact could think of no conventional way to respond, so she smiled politely at him. They stood, sizing each other up. The voice of Evita—herself a miracle of embalming—fell to one knee, breathless, picked itself up, and staggered, accusing, reckless with love and grief. The propped-up woman stared into proximate infinity; the companion bodies, lifeless, stared also.

Boyd looked closely at the other corpses. Each was partly covered by a sheet, each reclined on Styrofoam blocks. All were nearly naked. Some sported bobby-pinned curls, some appeared made up. While the unembalmed woman was blue, the embalmed drifted to a cool shade of alabaster. All the embalmed sported a flesh-colored plug under the breastbone. Someone had carefully drawn a pair of polyester airplane slipper-socks over an old man's feet. He was going first-class, wearing a golf cap, a pacemaker, and a half smile. Next to him and nearest the wall, lying on her side, was an exotic-looking dark-haired woman, very fat, wearing Cleopatra eye makeup. On the gurney next to her was a young man who had met with some sort of accident. He'd been expertly patched up, but Boyd could make out fissures under the smoothed out veneer of flesh. A jigsaw puzzle effect. He must have traveled through glass at high speed, she thought. His hair was black and very neatly wetcombed, slicked back, and he wore a gold crucifix on a chain around his neck. There was the wink of a gold earring at his right lobe, a half note, a gold comma. Against the white skin of his chest, the black hair curled, vibrantly alive despite the contrasting stitched gash from nipple to navel. Whatever wrenching, disfiguring violence and whatever terror he'd suffered was over now—he presided, reconstructed, over his own carefully groomed emptiness. Boyd became gradually aware that emptiness filled this room and made it whole.

The four dead bodies formed a kind of soundless backup chorus for the unfortunate Evita. Griggs began his trance-like tango again, humming, stolid, seemingly beyond thought yet watching her.

She couldn't help herself. She laughed at last, a little wildly.

Griggs shook his head, gently, reprovingly. "Dr. Schaeffer, we are not here for your amusement."

Boyd struggled not to laugh again. It was difficult—not because anything was *funny*, but because of the enormous feeling of portentousness in this room. Boyd looked closer at the bodies. What did they remind her of? Then it came to her— they all looked like the just born, they had the same aura of the other world, the wrapped-in-light, washed-up-on-the-shore aura. They were on the other side, the side she touched when she pulled a baby from a womb.

"I would very much like to know," she said, "what you do here."

Griggs nodded, reached out, and patted the right hand of the woman who lay before them. He reached up and flicked off the music, then picked up the dead woman's hand again. He gently set the hand on her chest and began to ready a tray of instruments near the gleaming sink to his left.

"People tend to die ugly—it's a sad fact. But people are beautiful, y'see, one-of-a-kind beautiful. Okay, so. Granted, it is, this thing I do, done for someone who ends up lyin' in a coffin, lyin' in the ground, but that doesn't matter. If the look is restored— if that one exact look is brought back for just a little peek—

that's enough. I admit that it's done for the living, too. For just as long as it takes for the ones left behind to see and remember. Because what they see lasts forever."

As he chatted, he opened a large bottle of liquid. He pursed his lips and blew into metal tubes that Boyd recognized as cannula tubes, the kind used to instill dye or fluid into the uterus. She watched him, transfixed.

"Anyway, I can do those things," he said. "I have that gift."

He looked at the dead woman with tenderness.

"In front of you is Mrs. Lillian Stirzl. She died in her kitchen of a cerebral aneurysm—a brain hemorrhage, as you know."

Boyd found her voice. "She looks like she . . ."

"Yeah, she looks like she was sick a long time, don't she, but she wasn't. She was just old a long time. She only wanted cherry Popsicles at the end. Mrs. Stirzl, Lillian, was a little senile, y'see. Her daughter told me that she was living way back in her childhood, when she ate ice cream on sticks all summer. Lillian was a widow a long time. Arthur Stirzl passed through my hands too." He turned and placed a smaller tray of instruments on the table to his left.

"What are you doing?"

He looked into her eyes—a steep, unfathomable look. "I'm sorry. I have to proceed with my work now."

She watched him carefully reposition Lillian's body so that her arms hung over the sides of the table and her legs were stretched out. He began to press his fingers around her neck and arms, patting the tissue emphatically. Boyd watched him closely and inhaled sharply. All at once she got it: He was selecting arteries and veins.

"Yes," said Griggs. "I see you understand. I am going to

use the right and left common carotid, here in the neck, and here, the right axillary in the upper arm and the right femoral in the groin."

She watched him lift a glittering surgical dissecting knife from the tray and use it—fast, almost faster than her eye could follow—to sever the arteries, left carotid, then the other. He removed a bit of tissue from each vessel so that he could insert—swiftly, as the blood now poured over his transparent gloves in dark rivulets—the hollow cannulae he'd earlier filled with his breath.

"You know what these are," he murmured. "They're going to force embalming fluid into the arteries as the veins drain. It's like the 'cut-down' you all do in hospitals to start an IV catheter when you can't get it in any other way. Sometimes I have to inject fluid through both neck vessels and drain it from the right jugular, but that's if the body's fat. We'll use the femoral for Lillian, because she's so thin."

There was a sound, an indescribable sound. Boyd closed, then opened her eyes as the bruises began to move under Lillian's skin, traveling as her blood traveled—as Griggs tenderly massaged her extremities—through the tubes into the gutter around the edges of the table, then from the gutter into a wall waste sink, down to a drain in the floor and out into the underground pipes. Lillian's body shook. The bruises flowed. She seemed strangely aware of what was happening, as Griggs had noted, connected to some extraordinary new shape of animation.

Then Griggs folded her hands, the diamond ring flashing, over her heart and touched each finger joint with a spot of superglue, urging the hands together at the middle knuckle. He elevated Lillian's head—"So the blood will not go north," he said, "and discolor her face. They call that embalmer's gray, y'know." He tilted her face slightly to the right—"facing the viewers"—and lifted her chest above the abdomen by readjusting the soft blocks—"Makes her look restful in the casket.

"I have to continue setting her features now. I usually do that before starting the embalming fluid, but you . . ." He paused. He had been rummaging through a stainless steel drawer and straightened up to look at her. "You changed the order." He said this without rancor. He glanced at the gutter and the drains. Lillian's blood had disappeared, and her body held its liters of fluid. He removed the cannula tubes from the incision sites.

"I've cleaned her already," he said, "and closed up the windpipe. I've massaged her. I've used a trocar to . . . puncture the internal organs, and I've vacuumed that fluid out."

In the silence that followed, he hummed a little.

"You know, we use a solution with bleach in it on the skin, just like you do, to kill HIV or hepatitis. Now I have a beauty question: Do you think her hair looks all right, or should I put some pincurls in?"

Boyd had trouble finding her voice. She said she didn't know. Then she said she thought Lillian's hair was okay.

Griggs bent over the drawer again and found what he'd been searching for. A manila envelope appeared in his hands, encased now in a fresh pair of transparent gloves. He shook the contents of the envelope out onto the steel table. Boyd came closer: three photographs, two black-and-white, one color. The first, a faded sepia square with curling, perforated edges, showed a dreamy, chubby little girl, her face cast down but with an upward gaze, shy but laughing, touching the *V* of her middy blouse. She was seated on a porch swing in bright sunlight, a long-ago summer afternoon. Boyd could just make out, on the blistered wooden arm of the porch swing, a row of sun-bleached ice cream sticks. The next photograph was of a young woman: a chignon, a striped blouse with padded shoulders, a seed-pearl brooch. It had been a hot day when the photograph was taken. Boyd noticed that tiny, damp curls sprang out along her hairline; her lips were wreathed in beads of perspiration. There was an inscription: "To Artie, with all my kisses forever. Your Lill." The third was in color: a couple in their fifties or sixties in front of a large hewn-stone fireplace. Her gaze amused, her husband bald but still youngish-looking; he balanced a half-full drink in his hand. They wore bulky ski sweaters. Reindeer pranced across their chests; snow fell, unmoving, outside the windows.

Boyd swallowed. "Lillian."

Griggs, poring over the photographs, said nothing. He was preoccupied again, humming as he measured the distance from Lillian's brow to her chin with his thumb and little finger held apart. Cotton balls and forceps appeared in his gloved hands. He retouched her features, inside and out.

"I'm lookin' for warm color areas," he muttered. "I'm lookin' for prominent eminences."

Then Boyd thought she heard Griggs murmur, "I can bring her back."

He stopped to mop his brow, then opened more drawers, produced a Lucite palette of bright and dull colors, brushes, sponges. He stirred spots on the palette, mixed a flesh color with a flat-ended stick, added white, mixed again. He looked up once and followed Boyd's gaze to the sewed up young man.

"What happened to the man who looks sort of patched up?"

"You mean the one who has the flawlessly reconstructed complexion? That one?"

She laughed, but Griggs remained serious.

"He was on the roof of his apartment building, cutting through a dead tree branch that hung over the roof with his chain saw, and he stepped backward through the skylight with the saw still running. Well. Everyone went with that version of the story, but I'm not so sure."

Boyd watched Griggs's face. "What do you think?"

"I think he may have gone through that skylight on purpose."

Boyd moved closer. "Why?"

"He came in looking as if he had been waiting."

"Waiting?"

"For release from pain. Suicides usually look like that— hungry to get out! When I worked on the guy, I felt his desire for relief. And he'd done it. He'd stepped through—do ya know what I mean here? He escaped. Maybe from AIDS, maybe from a lonely life, financial trouble. I don't know. I don't care what the law says, or religion. I touch each person and they tell me what I need to know."

"He had AIDS?"

"Dr. Schaeffer, I don't know. I didn't test him for it. I only felt the war that had been goin' on inside him."

As he talked, he peeled back one of Lillian's eyelids, slipped a thin curved disk of plastic, like a half eggshell pimpled with tiny spikes, under the lid to hold the eye shut. He closed one eye in this manner, then the other. Then he opened a drawer, flipped open a plastic case, and took out a set of white false teeth with very pink gums. He opened Lillian's mouth with his fingers and inserted the teeth. Then he injected something—"a mastic compound"—into the soft tissue of Lillian's cheeks. Then, holding her mouth open with one hand, he reached inside with the other and expertly crossed and looped wire around the teeth till he could pull the jaw shut. "Don't want your eyes poppin' open or jaw saggin', do we, Lillian?"

He glanced at Boyd as he worked. "The dead's eyes stay open. They have to be closed so that the living won't be disturbed by their stares. And the jaw—after rigor mortis wears off, it hangs slack. Gotta assist in its closure. But you must know about closin' the dead's eyes, no?"

Boyd didn't answer. She had never closed the dead's eyes. *I did not touch his body.*

As Griggs hunted through an array of theatrical cosmetics, tubes, jars, and vials, Boyd tapped his shoulder. "You said you felt a war going on inside that young man over there. And my husband? What did you sense about Russell when he . . . passed through your hands?"

"Look at her," murmured Griggs. "Look at her. She's coming up."

Boyd looked. Lillian's mottled, inky-blue color was gone; she was pale, but she had acquired a burnish. Her thin lips were fuller. She did not look painted but rather retouched with intent, with tenderness.

Something was heightening in her face, an expression connected to the faces in the photographs. Something not only of the middle-aged Lillian or the twenty-five-year-old Lillian. Here was the shyly askew half smile from the child's mouth, that unexpected smile that had grown up with her and now reappeared intact on her eighty-year-old dead lips.

Boyd reached out and touched Lillian's hand dreamily, her face strange. "He had a scar on his left knee—from a bike accident when he was nine. He wouldn't let them stitch it up, so it healed oddly. It looked like a lightning bolt. It was here, right here, on his kneecap."

She bent down, touching the knee of her linen trousers. She didn't wait for an answer. "And do you remember the lines around his mouth, ones that came from this expression?"

She drew her lips into an ironic line, curling the top one slightly, but then her mouth began trembling and Russell's characteristic look crumbled.

"He was very brown, you know. From playing tennis. He had starbursts around his eyes—did you notice? You see, his skin was sensitive, he often burned . . ."

Griggs turned to look at her. Great tears had welled up in her eyes and were spilling down her face, a sudden hot flood. She didn't seem to notice the tears. She went on talking through them, like a person behind a waterfall, calling out.

"You had no photographs of him to work from, did you? You wouldn't have known, then, how he looked as a little kid, or even a young man. Not that he was old. He was so young. I mean, he was quite young."

Griggs excused himself, speaking to Lillian. He put down his palette and touched Boyd's arm. "My dear. There was no need for photographs. I could see right away, y'know, who he was. His whole history was there in his face."

She folded her arms across her chest, trying to breathe normally, struggling to stop the tears. "And did you sense a war inside, the way you did with the other . . . person?"

"Yes," said Griggs. "I felt it. But I also felt his acceptance. He'd made his peace with it, his death."

She took a step forward, blinded by tears, her hands lifted in front of her as if she were feeling her way in the dark. She groped her way unsteadily sideways, leaned against a metal cabinet, which rattled as her body began to shake. The tears soaked her blouse, her hair, and still kept flowing. Before her eyes were two faces—the face of Tina Coburn right before the anesthetic took hold, kissing a photo of her children. And she saw Russell's face looking back at her, his last second on earth, on the grass, the paramedic bending over him.

She tried to stand straight, regain her composure, but instead the façade collapsed from within and she staggered a little as another wave of grief struck, and she slid downward.

"Look at me," she cried in disgust. "Look at me."

Griggs took her arm.

"I don't care. I didn't really know either of them."

"Yes," said Griggs. "I can see that."

He asked Lillian's permission to leave for a minute, and when she gave it, he escorted Boyd, sobbing, through the pneumatic doors into a hallway, then guided her into a small consultation room with stained-glass windows that gleamed like phony gems when he switched on the light.

The room held cremation urns of every size and description, and stacks of leather-bound albums filled with color photos of hundreds of other urns and their prices. Griggs urged her into a deep leather chair, then sat down in a chair opposite her. She waited, gasping, holding her handkerchief to her mouth. She felt Russell in the room suddenly—like a chord, struck, reverberating. How he would have laughed at all this, she thought. For the first time since Russell's death, she thought of him with love. He was in this room, but it did not feel like his other visits. She found Griggs's eyes. She took a careful breath.

"Can you leave Lillian now? What's supposed to happen next?"

He adjusted a snap on his white suit, shrugged. He was clearly not used to this role as comforter of the living. "I need to dress her and I have to pack her body, y'see. But that won't take long."

Boyd looked around the room, locked and unlocked her hands, shaking her head. The tears started again. She stopped them. "Could you tell me—what is all this?"

She'd just noticed the low table, shiny with urns. Most were conventional in style, but there was one shaped like a golf bag. There was a cowboy boot, and a guitar. A perky chef's hat stood next to a laminated price sheet.

"I've told you," said Griggs. "There is so much room for misunderstanding between the living and the dead."

He picked up a burnished brass Coors beer cooler urn, sighed. "Those about to die are filled with longing. Very specific longing, y'see, Doctor."

She began to cry again and Griggs took her hand. "I wonder if you could tell me anything about . . . what he looked like. You were the last one to touch him."

"I will," said Griggs. "You know, I was thinking we're bound to have snow early this year. You can feel it outside in the air. Don't you think, Doctor?"

CHAPTER 27

T HAT SAME NIGHT, Will stood outside his mother's
house, listening, his head cocked. He heard a sound
within, an oddly pitched cry. The sound repeated
twice before he finally swung into action, jamming his key in the
lock and shouldering the door inward in one gesture. Then he
was in the hallway.

The front of the house was dark, but in the rear, in the direction of the sunroom off the kitchen, where she kept the piano,
there was a hint of a reflection: lamplight, coincident with the
strange sound rising again. Images flickered before him: his
mother fallen, crawling toward a telephone, her legs useless,
eyes white with terror. He flew through the dark house, touching the walls for reassurance, every step, every turn familiar to
him even in the blackness. He ran, too frightened to call, then
froze in the doorway of the sunroom.

There was a single illumination: an old goose-pimpled milk-
glass lamp set on the piano. It cast a circle of light over the dim

and bright ivory keys and the paisley shawl sliding from the piano bench. And there, beside the piano, was the erect figure of his mother. She stood facing the window, her hands stretched out before her, head raised. She hadn't heard him.

She was singing. Her wavering, age-changed voice rose and fell on notes as unfamiliar to Will as her dramatic posture. The emotion in her straining voice made him want to turn away. He felt he had violated an extreme privacy, as if he had come upon her naked.

He tried to back up, brushed the wall and jumped, startling himself. She whirled toward him, her face confused but still bright. She was under her own rapt spell.

"Mom?"

Her head bobbed disconnectedly. She pointed to the yellowed printed score opened on the piano top. "I'm singing."

Will waited.

She looked defensive. "Schumann."

He continued to stare at her.

"I just wanted to get an idea of how rusty I am." She seemed to be spiraling down from a very great height. She let her hands fall to her sides, looked at him, and laughed. "I'm rusty."

Then she began finally to see the expression of concern on his face. "What's the matter?"

"I was worried. I was coming up the steps, I heard this strange sound . . ."

"It wasn't a strange sound. It was me singing."

"But I didn't mean . . ."

"I can sing the old show tunes too, kiddo. I still have it in me."

"Mom, sit down. You look funny."

"I look like a person singing. What's the big deal? I feel good—does that bother you?"

"Not really. I was just . . ."

She sat down at the piano, defiant.

Will leaned back against the wall and looked at her. She held herself upright like a furious little girl practicing her scales. The lamplight shone on her veined hands. She began to play violently, loud crashing chords.

Her anger at him, at the world, was a habit, he reminded himself. He knew she was reassured by this way of keeping him at bay. She played recklessly, pumping and echoing the volume with the pedals.

At one point she turned halfway around to look at him. "You see? I'm just fine! So don't stick your tongue out at me, kid. You can take off!"

Will turned to go, obedient. Then came back, suddenly furious. "I wanted to ask you, Mother, just one thing . . ."

She stopped playing and turned around to face him. Her face was emptied of anger. "Will? Sweetheart? You were born first. You were six minutes apart. You both came out with the same expression on your face. The one that's on yours right now."

HOURS LATER, Will moved slowly down the hall of his apartment building. After he'd talked to his mother for hours, he'd gone to Tollson's, then out to sit on the edge of Dayton's Bluff. He'd driven home in a dream, then parked the car and come upstairs. In the hallway, he'd heard the phone ringing behind his door. He sprinted, key in hand, to the door, then sprinted across the dark living room, reached wildly, and grasped the receiver to his heart, panting, then lifted it to his ear. A voice was already speaking to him, saying his name.

"Will? This is Boyd. Are you, by any chance, free tomorrow?"

Will was having trouble focusing. He nodded emphatically, bobbing his head as if she could see him.

"Tomorrow?" he said finally. "Saturday? Yeah, I'm free."

"The cave we went to the other night? Carver's Cave?"

He nodded again, stupidly.

"I want to go back."

"Okay, sure."

"Why don't you come by my house in the morning? About ten?"

"Sure," croaked Will again, feeling around for the tiny chain that turned on the lamp. "Absolutely."

They hung up, and just as Will lit the lamp and staggered back from it, the phone rang again.

"Will? It's me again. I'd like to bring my little girl, Freddy. Will it be safe?"

Will swallowed, looking into the middle distance. "Don't worry. I promise I'll take care of you both."

B OYD HUNG UP THE PHONE on the wall outside the hospital delivery room. She stopped herself as she came back through the door, pausing to look at the woman on the table whose baby she'd just delivered. A nurse was carefully extricating the newborn from her arms and the mother was protesting gently, "Please let me hold her just one more second."

Boyd was sweating, her scrub cap stuck to her forehead, her eyes bleary. It had not been an easy labor or delivery, but there was the infant, raising its voice now, crying for its mother as the nurse lifted it and wrapped it tighter in the yellow cotton bunting. The room smelled of disinfectant and sweat and blood and great happiness.

Boyd pushed out through the door again and lifted the wall phone receiver a second time. She fished in the pocket of her slacks under the surgical gown and pulled out a crumpled piece of paper. Squinting at the scribbled phone number, she leaned against the wall and dialed. Voices floated in the hall, intercom pages for doctors and hospital administrators, laughter from the nurses' station.

Someone answered at the other end. Boyd took a deep breath.

"Mrs. Gunderson?" She spoke over the squawk of the intercom. "This is Dr. Schaeffer—I work with Dr. Remington? I'd like to talk to you about your daughter, Sunny."

CHAPTER 28

S O THE DOCTOR COMES IN *with my file and he gives me that you-poor-fucker look, shakes my hand, sits down behind the desk.*

"Russell," he says. "It's not a positive report."

Well, Christ. Of course it's not a positive report. When is it ever a positive report? The worst thing you can get is the so-called clean bill of health—that just about guarantees sudden death. The body's a joke, and death is the punch line. So what else is new?

He told me what else was new.

"Well, from what we've determined here, I'd say you have your father's heart," he says, "but with a few extra and, I'm afraid, alarming complications thrown in. Let me explain."

All the while he explains, my mind's turning up the volume—I can barely hear him over the roar. I do hear him recommend a by-pass, and even with that, my prognosis is "uncertain."

I must not exert myself. No strenuous exercise, no workouts, no tennis. No booze, no coffee, no cigarettes, no salt, no sex (well, that's not a worry anyway!). No drugs. No prescription drugs but the ones he gives me.

So it's my ticker that betrays me. I think of Boyd, how to tell her it's my heart that's going to do me in. Would she laugh? Would she like to hear it amplified as I am hearing it now—the doctor kindly playing a recording of its stuttering and gasping for me as I watch it on a monitor, poor articulate muscle, struggling within the superimposed graphs and tallies, the digital colors of its doom.

And Gerda: How will she take this? Her ruined son. Her prodigal. I know she loves me best. And I was on the road back. I'd planned to start over clean.

The doctor drones on. This does not have to be looked at as a sentence of death. *And I think, hopefully:* I'm clean, off drink—or as off drink as I get. I don't believe in miracles (leave that to the real cynics), but I think I can swing a stay of execution. If I could feel welcome in my life again.

Which is the rub. No booze, no drugs. But that's not the point. What kills the heart is no forgiveness.

CHAPTER 29

WILL THINKS ABOUT how there are no miracles, no resurrections. But in St. Paul, there are caves beneath the seven hills, beneath the snow piled on the Indian mounds, beneath Seven Corners, just beyond the Wabasha Bridge, beneath the hurrying feet of office workers and shoppers, beneath the Pioneer Building, beneath Fort Snelling and beyond. He sees them as a chain of dark dreaming rooms beneath the lit and busy chambers at street level. He's read about the linked caves. He knows they're part of buried river valleys, lost as the glacial meltwater passageway pushed through rock. Acids dissolved the limestone and sandstone and further sculpted the rock along joints and cracks of weakness in the strata. And into these empty rooms, in the present, in the cold, unrelenting days of winter, like the Indians before them, a few silent people creep. Transients, homeless people who would die of exposure on the streets in dead winter. The temperature inside the caves stays constant, approximately like a cool spring day, and if the human body is wrapped up sufficiently, it can survive comfortably. A kind of housekeeping can be set up, small dangerous fires banked and water boiled in tin cans. In the Wabasha caves, in the St. Peter caves and others, there have been mushroom growers, bootleggers, beer- and boat-storage companies, a restaurant, a ballroom. The homeless can sometimes tap into the electricity or plumbing built into the cavern's front rooms; then remote parts of the back, the dim recesses, sputter eerily into light. The wet, carved rock appears, the shadow-lit walls. Liquid runs out of a pipe into a cup. Then sometimes the cops are called and they come, make arrests. In other caves, the homeless lie in darkness, sleeping, maybe making love. Their eyes become accustomed to the dark. One or two who are sick or old die quietly. But the caves welcome them, the spirit welcomes them, Will thought as he lay in bed. They have a place from which to consider resurrection.

He tried to cough, to clear his throat, but his windpipe was so dry he made a rasping sound. He was hungover and feeling oddly sentimental about the caves. He didn't want to hear Boyd making fun of them again. He wanted Boyd to love the caves as he did. He wanted Freddy to love them. He coughed, wretchedly, and thought of a hot shower and coffee. But he didn't move for a while, and he drifted off back to sleep.

The reservoir sat on a high hill, a built up embankment accessible on three sides by nearly perpendicular ascents. It glowed overhead, double-lit under its pale yellow arc lights. The moon had risen directly overhead, and its sheer radiance seemed momentous: The hooded figure plodded toward the looming tank, resting on its spindly legs like a just landed spacecraft.

A second figure, stumbling and covered with snow, caught up now and the two of them climbed the hill dragging the toboggan, slipping, digging in, stopping occasionally to look up.

When they reached the summit, they stood, staring down, gold-lit under the tank lights. The wind had picked up, and the big balsams around the legs of the reservoir groaned and shook snow and pine needles on their heads.

Will threw down the sled rope, flipped back his fur-edged hood, and dropped on one knee, pulling off a leather mitten, feeling the icy guide ropes that ran parallel down the inside length of the toboggan.

"It's too slippery," he said, blowing on his hand, pulling the mitten back on. "It's like glare ice out there. I told ya."

Signe turned in her cat-eared hat to look carefully at him, then smiled and stared down at the icy trails scored like runnels in the hillside. Her profile in the pale light stunned him: She looked complete, emphatic, and finished, the lines of her mouth decisive as a grown-up's, decisive as Mother's.

She's just fourteen, *he thought.* She can't look like that. Then the inevitable: That's the way I look, too.

"Chicken," she called out cheerfully. That precise cadence. "Chick-chick-chick-en." She laughed. What a stupid laugh she'd acquired, he thought. He smelled the Doublemint on her breath and, just under it, the bourbon she'd nipped from the liquor cabinet, and then a waft of her Christmas perfume: light green smoke.

He said nothing. The wind picked up again and sawed the branches, one by one. Clumps of snow fell near them and the trees started their low grieving sound.

She laughed again, making a stupid face. Freezing wind flut-

*tered the layer of fur around her head. She closed her eyes and fum-
bled forward, her mittened hands stuck out like a blind person's.
She staggered, her tongue lolling grotesquely. "Hey, spaz. I'll go
down alone if you're scared."*

*He snorted, stood up, and kicked the toboggan close to the edge
of the slope with the toe of his boot. Then he knelt in the front by the
curved prow, doubling the frozen rope around his right fist.*

*"Come on," he shouted over his shoulder, into the wind. "Get on,
stupid."*

*He felt her clear voice in his ear, her arms around him, the lay-
ers between them. "I remember this one. This is what they call The
Baby Run."*

*The slope plunged before them, wide open, a few hairpin sled
tracks, then just blinding white space, snow drifting.*

*He stuck his left foot out, launching them with a heel-and-toe
maneuver like a motorcycle kick-start, then retracted the foot as
the sled began to shudder and move; he sat down as they took off.
Seconds later, they were hurtling around curves, over rises. Signe
made a humming sound in his ear. They hit a big bump and flew
high in the air, bouncing hard. Will shouted and Signe kept humming, higher and higher. At last the sled slowed, then stalled in the
track, and they slid off lazily, one by one, lying on their backs, gen-
tled, looking up at the moon.*

*Twenty minutes earlier, they'd been in the living room at home, a
fire leaping in the big stone fireplace, the air spicy with the smell of
cooking. There'd been a discussion with Mom and Dad: Signe had
painted her face—too much lipstick and eye shadow. Signe shouted,
then went upstairs and washed it all off. When she came back*

down, she was wearing a sweatshirt with a large peace symbol on the front and the Black Panthers' raised fist on the back. Her face shone vindictively. She looked just beyond everyone, almost crying, but not quite.

Will stared at the television. He knew she was circling him. He knew that she wanted him to stick up for her, but he wouldn't do it. He stayed out of it, tuning them all out. She'd changed in the last year, and it alarmed him, almost as much as his own sudden spurt of growth, his roller-coastering voice. She'd stood just under his lower lip, looking up. "Stop growing," she said. "Do you hear me?"

Sometimes she wore his old Levi's and a sweaty jersey for days. She kicked the cat. Or she crashed about the back entrance hall, cursing dramatically, staggering in her black, heavily scarred hockey skates and shin guards, slicing up the linoleum. Then, with no warning, she'd appear at the dinner table in a neon-colored sweater over a push-up bra, tight pants, ratted hair, painted wings around her eyes. She drank filched shot glasses of Jack Daniel's and Wild Turkey—"Straight up, straight down," she'd say. She had the smartest mouth he'd ever heard on a kid, and she was fearless. That was their deepest secret, their most intimate shared pact as twins: She'd acquired her courage to cover his fear.

She'd stood before him, her scrubbed face belligerent. "C'mon, Slow Start. Let's go haul the toboggan up to the water tower."

He'd stared at the TV. Fred MacMurray had just discovered Flubber.

"Not a chance," he'd said, not looking at her. "It's too cold."

Will's hood had fallen off again, but he didn't miss it. He was sweating and exhilarated, burning up. But he knew enough not to take off his long wine-colored wool scarf or his mittens or the hockey sweatband around his skull. That was how people froze to death, drifting in this false warmth and well-being—hypothermia—a word he'd recently learned. He wanted to go home now, but he knew she'd laugh at him if he said so. He felt something wrong in the wind.

They struggled back up the hill. Signe would run lightly, then stop, complaining. She shook her hair out from under the squat fur hat and it shone down her back, flash-cube white.

"Shut up," said Will. "Quit complaining. Pull."

At the top, Signe shook herself again and stood straight as a sentinel, looking out over the snowy links. "Ah, Nature!" she cried, throwing out her arms. "I hate it!"

They went down three more times, each time faster. The wind was turned up high now; snow blew everywhere.

"It's time to go," Will yelled over the wind. "Last run!"

As he moved toward the front, Signe pushed him away. "I'm steerin'."

"You don't know how to steer, Signe. Come on."

But she was already on the edge of the precipice, doubling the rope, her foot cocked, a brake, skidding in the snow. He leaped on behind her and she turned, leaning back, and put her head against his. Through a layer of fur, he felt the pulse jump in her temple.

Her voice, precise, quiet, perverse, carried clearly over the scream inside the wind. "You're really scared, Will, aren't you?"

As she spoke, she swung the toboggan prow, her foot scrabbling crab-like, around to the north side of the hill. No one ever went down this side. It was a sheer, unequivocal drop, clumps of trees at dangerous intervals.

"What are you doing?"

"I'll stop, Will. You just say it to me: Stop. Okay?"

"You trying to get us killed?"

"Maybe. Then they'd have to put makeup on me. Whaddya think?"

"Signe. Let me steer."

"No. Wait, Will. Do you want to fly?"

She turned and looked at him, pure dare, pure terror. The wind blew her hair across her face.

He laughed. It struck him funny. But then they were over the edge, bouncing once, twice—they were moving too fast for him to react, and suddenly they were airborne. The sled hung in the air, in the blowing white light for a second or two, then struck earth with enormous force. No tracks. They were on sheer ice, splitting drifts where they'd fallen and frozen, spinning wildly to the left and right. Snow shot up into their faces. Will tried to lean into a curve, but they were moving too fast for any control of the sled, free-falling, ninety degrees, straight down.

"Signe," he screamed into her ear, tugging at her as they dropped. "Lean this way!"

She laughed and laughed. He could feel her body shaking through all the padding.

"Get ready to die!" she cried.

They hit another bump and careered sideways, spun around again. Then the trees were straight ahead.

He pulled hard at her, trying to drag her off.

"Signe. Jump!"

He used all his strength, but she refused to budge. He was leaning hard to the left, pulling with his full weight, but as they came up on the trees, he felt himself letting go of her jacket. At the very last second, she turned, looked at him, and reached out to him, *grasping, her face terrible, but he couldn't take her hand. He was blowing away. He hit the snow rolling, and she flew away from him.*

He rolled a long way, over and over, till he stopped, facedown, snow and pine needles in his mouth. He lay quiet for a few minutes, listening. He could hear the trees overhead in the wind, and then it all began to die down. He thought he heard a sound, her, but he couldn't be sure.

After a while, he pulled himself up on all fours and staggered to his feet. His mouth was crusted with needled ice, and he spit. When he stepped down on his right foot, pain shot through the ankle, and he limped, moving downhill toward the trees. He could see the toboggan up-ended near the clump of pines.

She was lying next to the sled, right up against the trunk of a tree, her hair spread out on the snow, the hat flung a few feet away. One of her legs was bent under her.

*He called her name, but she didn't answer him. When he knelt beside her, he saw that she was looking directly at him, exactly the way she had before she'd shifted their course, laughing at him, her eyes boring through him. He started to speak—*Cripes, what kind of nut are you anyway?*—but as he put out his hand to help her up, he saw for the first time what had happened, how the blood had stained the snow dark behind her head.*

CHAPTER 30

WILL PICKED UP BOYD and Freddy at ten o'clock. He'd folded an annotated map from the Minnesota Historical Society into his back pocket, and when Freddy asked him questions about where they were going, he consulted it with the air of a tour guide. He'd also bought some sandwiches and fruit juice packets and chips at a convenience store on the way and popped them into his backpack, along with a small white first-aid kit. He'd even thought to buy a toy for Freddy, a plastic Looney Tunes character, which he would give her later if she got bored.

Boyd looked subdued, dressed in jeans and a dark plaid shirt, a leather bomber jacket, her hair pulled back. Will was feeling subdued himself. The rough edges of his hangover had been sanded down with aspirin and coffee, but the morning light hurt his eyes and he wore roundish dark glasses. He and Boyd looked just past each other, embarrassed. In the driver's seat, he rubbed his hand over his chin. He felt unshaven; his hair had grown in the last weeks, and it curled over his jacket collar.

"You have long hair," observed Freddy, staring at his neck from the seat behind, where Boyd was fastening her seat belt. "It's very pretty."

He thanked her, with a bowing nod, then glanced in the dash mirror, made a mental note to get a haircut. Boyd closed the back door, got in the front passenger seat, and, as Will jumped out to run around and close her door, waved him away through the glass, then pulled the door shut. She sat Sphinx-like as he started the car. It was warm, though it was an October Saturday. She buzzed down the window and crooked her elbow over the lowered glass.

"I hope we dressed right for this," she said, looking straight ahead.

He glanced at her profile. "We have to crawl on our hands and knees a bit. That's about it. No fashion statement required."

She remained silent.

"You're both dressed fine," he said. "Don't worry."

They drove past downtown on Kellogg Boulevard to Mounds Parkway and they parked as before near the entrance to the Indian Mounds area. There were a few people in the park, walking dogs, jogging. The sun had climbed higher, but it was still a little cool. Will parked, opened the trunk, and pulled out his backpack and flashlights.

He shouldered the pack, flashed Boyd and Freddy a thumbs-up sign, then started down the path, feeling like an idiot.

Freddy ran into the park ahead of them, chattering. She asked

Will about the Mounds and the cave below, and he told her the original name of the cave.

"Wauken Tebee," he said.

She looked down shyly at her new hiking boots, unable to pronounce it. He kept himself from patting her bright, bowed head.

Will glanced at Boyd, who stood with her arms folded, staring at the Mounds.

"You know," he said, "we're doing something kind of like trespassing here."

She cocked a rueful eye at him. "Why? Who cares if we crawl into a cave?"

"There've been a few accidents, even a couple of deaths. I think one or two people drowned in the lake down there. They get small landslides inside, dirt-fall caused by transients' fires. I think I told you that's why they sealed up the original entrance. I know I can get us in and out okay. I just want you to know that it's considered off-limits."

He opened the map and held it in front of his face. She set her jaw.

"It doesn't matter," she said. "We're going in."

Will nodded, then struck out alone, looking back to be sure they were following. Freddy caught up immediately, trotting at his side, asking questions. He told her, after consulting the map, a long story of the ancient people who'd built the Mounds. He told her about Jonathan Carver, whom the Indians trusted.

"Now is the cave his cave?"

"Well, it's named for him, and he had the Indians sign their names—make their special signs—on a piece of paper, saying that they gave the cave to him, but the president said no, he couldn't have it."

"What person owns the cave now?"

They paused at the edge of the Bluff. Will looked down at Freddy. Her red hair was neatly braided. He noted again her tiny hiking boots, the smallest he'd ever seen.

"I don't know. The state of Minnesota wanted to make the cave part of the park, but the Indians say it is a holy place and that it still belongs to them. You know. It's Wauken Tebee, House of the Great Spirit."

"Is there a beanstalk, do you think?"

"A beanstalk?"

Boyd approached silently, brushing at her jacket sleeve, too nonchalant. "She believes that there is a huge beanstalk somewhere, like in the fairy tale, only it grows down instead of up." She paused. "She wants to climb down this beanstalk under the earth."

"And find my dad." Freddy pulled at Will's sleeve. "He died. My daddy died. We had to put him in the ground. I can climb down the beanstalk and I can get him back."

Great, thought Will. *I get it. Not too much pressure on me or anything.* For a second, he felt resentful, and then he smiled down at Freddy. Then he looked up. For the first time that day, his eyes met Boyd's, then veered away.

He knelt down slowly before Freddy. "I don't know if there's a beanstalk, but there's a lake."

"A lake? Under the ground?"

"Come on, I'll show you." Will stood up, then bent to take

her hand. He glanced, just a little smugly, at Boyd. She nodded, her mouth twisted down. Then, at last, she smiled.

"Come on," he repeated, storing that smile inside, waving them forward toward the grassy edge of the Bluff.

It was hot and dusty going down. Freddy's new hiking boots slipped, and brambles scratched her bare arms, but she didn't complain. Rocks seemed to leap up and bounce ahead of them, which made her laugh. She chattered about a big spider that scrambled across a rock in front of them. She seemed perfectly content to make her way down holding Will's hand, Boyd following closely behind.

Every so often, she would turn slightly, look over her shoulder, and shout, "Isn't this neat, Mom?" or, "Are you coming, Mom?"

"Don't know if you remember," Will threw back, "but the entrance is really narrow."

Will loved the fact that he could use the word *remember* with Boyd—that they had a history, brief but real, to which he could refer. She remained silent for a while as they marched. Then he heard her murmur: "I remember."

"There's a wider entrance at the base of the Bluff, but the city cemented it over to prevent kids getting in. So we have to squeeze in that small one." He paused. "The one my sister found way back when."

In the daylight, he found the opening almost immediately. He knelt down, rattled stones, tore away shrubbery. He shrugged off his pack, unzipped a pocket, and took out two power-beam flashlights.

"I'll slide in first. Then you can hand me Freddy, then follow us in. We'll have to crawl a few yards after we first get in. Here. Take this flashlight."

Boyd nodded and looked doubtfully at the opening, then at the flashlight.

Freddy glanced up at her, picking up on her uncertainty. "Is there a monster in there? I saw spiders, and I didn't even count how many!"

"No," mumbled Will, still kneeling. "No monsters and no spiders—or at least not any spider that would hurt you."

Freddy stood solemnly at his side as he cleared debris from the opening. When he was ready, Boyd took Freddy's hand and Will flipped over and shimmied on his back through the narrow mouth. As his feet disappeared, he called out, a muffled voice.

"Okay! Hand me Freddy."

"Watch me!" cried Freddy, and, in a flash of colors, spun onto her back and wriggled into the opening. Her tiny hiking boots kicked and were gone.

Inside, the cave was cool and damp. The coolness washed over Boyd as she slid in after Freddy. It was the sense of dark— what? saturation, stillness, stasis—and the smell of dank chill that had frightened her the other night when she had leaned back into the void. Now she was determined, for Freddy's sake, to ignore her fears.

She inched in backward, then flipped over as she pulled her whole body in. Freddy had wiggled ahead of her. Up ahead in the narrow passage, Will was shining his light back on them. The beam lit up a face, a leg, a patch of streaked red sandstone wall. Then her beam illuminated a wide path ahead of them. They were crawling under a lowering ceiling of moist, occasionally dripping rock, knocking aside sticks and pebbles.

Freddy shrieked, and the sound echoed and echoed, unstopping. "Something with spider legs came right over my hand!"

"It's okay!" Two voices, Boyd's and Will's, swam into her echo, then separated.

"I'm fine, Mother!" Freddy called back to her, self-important.

Will's voice floated back, cautioning them to keep down, to slide slowly forward. The floor was slanting downward.

Boyd's skin moved on her bones and a spike of claustrophobia rose in her throat. "Can't keep up with you guys!"

Her voice repeated itself, and she jumped. The flashlight beam wavered. She found it awkward to crawl forward holding the light in one hand. She tried to rig it around her neck, but it fell, so she held it in her teeth for a while, her jaw aching.

She could just make out the beam of Will's flashlight circling below, and she launched herself toward it. The smell of closed dampness and mold, the airless, fetid breath of the passage, grew as she crawled forward, the white beam blazing from her mouth. Freddy was far ahead of her, almost caught up to Will. A cobweb brushed across Boyd's eyes and she slapped at it. Her light wobbled, the beam leaping in the tunnel. The sharp and smooth pebbles under her hands and knees were changing to sand, a coldish, sinking sand, as she crawled downward faster and faster. She looked down at her hands, the light bouncing, and saw that the sand beneath her had grown luminous; it was becoming white.

Up ahead, she heard Freddy and Will laughing and she came into the sphere of his beam—it was traveling over the same eerily white sand—and suddenly she noticed how the low ceiling had risen. She could stand up, hold the flashlight in her

hand, look up at the twenty-foot-high dome above her. Freddy
and Will stood on a rock a few feet away, looking up.

"My God," Boyd cried, her voice repeating into the cavern:
"God, God, God . . ."

The cavern seemed enormous, momentous, but her initial
shock came from seeing Will and Freddy so casually and inti-
mately arranged. Freddy clung to Will's leg. He'd rigged a sort
of miner's lamp, the flashlight stuck in his bandanna-headband,
and he bent down solicitously, like a fireman comforting a kid in
a news photo. He looked up suddenly, and his light shone at
hers. She could just make out his eyes; he looked different to
her.

He flung out an arm, indicating something beyond them in
the dimness. Boyd followed his gaze. A few yards beyond them,
placid and depthless in the darkness, was the source of the
sound of trickling water. It was a lake—a huge lake, with a white
sandy shore, utterly incongruous, as if it had dropped down
from aboveground, as if swimmers might surface suddenly
and wade in, waving. The lake gave off light, a phosphorescent,
green-white radiance that played on the walls.

"My God," Boyd cried again. Then, stupidly, "Is it real?"

"It's real, Mom."

Freddy drew herself from Will's side and hurried to Boyd,
pulling at her sleeve. "This is the lake! Now we can find where
Daddy's beanstalk goes down!"

Boyd looked around, desperate. She was still struggling to see
clearly in the dimness, in the strange, sourceless light that fell
from unseen breaks in the rock above them, as if the cave had its
own cracked sky. She was still trying to grasp the reality of the

body of water before her, the ancient graffiti, what looked like petroglyphs on the walls. All this had been illuminated by random passes of her flashlight. Now Freddy's importunings left her speechless. She looked out across the lake, which drifted into darkness. Then she looked down, kept the flashlight beam just over Freddy's head, her little upturned face.

"Daddy probably just crossed this lake," she offered weakly. "That must be it."

Freddy made a disgusted noise and kicked a stone. "Crossed? Mom—he climbed down on a stalk, remember?"

Her voice rose and "stalk" echoed. She tore away from Boyd and began climbing around on the bigger rocks, stumbling a little, Will's beam trailing her.

Boyd walked across the sand to stand next to him. "I thought you were . . . exaggerating. This is beyond anything I could ever have imagined. Why don't people know about it?"

Will spread his arms, encompassing the great sweep of Carver's Cave as if he owned it. "Mid–nineteenth century, they were going to open a park here, make it a tourist attraction. But they couldn't agree how to do it, so they closed it up again till the thirties, when it came out that bootleggers were using it to stash illegal booze, and they tried to excavate again. At one point, the railroad came along and sheared off the natural opening of the cave, which was right at that point down there. A stream used to come out there . . . but the Indians were against any development—and that's it. So all that there is aboveground to announce it is that brass plaque you saw at the top of the Bluff. Here's where the Indians used to take torches and float their canoes back there on the lake into the other caverns. Divers have found ancient arrowheads and pots deep under water, and look—there's two centuries of wall writing here."

He moved the beam along the rock wall facing the lake. It was a tangle of old names and dates scratched into the surface. The beam froze at one set of names. SIGNE YOUNGREN & WILL YOUNGREN. They stared at the names silently, till Freddy's shout split into echoes.

"Mommy, Mommy! This is Daddy's beanstalk!"

They trained their flashlights on her. She was scrambling around on a small boulder. Embedded in the rock wall near her was a twisted, knuckled root system, gleaming in relief as it appeared and vanished in the sandstone.

Boyd shook her head. "Freddy? Come here, honey. That's not a beanstalk." Freddy ran up to Boyd, waving her arms.

"You don't know, Mommy! Grandma and me were gonna plant a sunflower, but now I finded this root."

She began to cry when Boyd reached out to put her arms around her, then pulled away. She ran back to the rock she'd been standing on and ran her fingers over the roots in the surface. "This is where Daddy went down, Mommy."

"Wait," said Will. "Wait."

He walked to Freddy's side, training his light on the roots. He glanced back at Boyd, her face half in shadow, though he could see the half-grateful, half-cynical look she threw him. *God,* he thought. *I can't stand men who make cute with kids.* But here he was, on his knees, mugging, trying to help.

Freddy looked at him suspiciously. He'd set the flashlight on a rock ledge, and it shone out in a triangle, spotlighting the two of them. She pointed defiantly. "This is Daddy's. I *know*."

"You're pretty much right. When people die, they climb down a beanstalk that looks like this."

She turned her back on him, her small shoulders quaking, and he gently turned her back around to face him. She'd stopped the tears, just as Boyd had done once before. Her mouth was set.

"Listen. The person who . . . dies . . . climbs down a stalk like this, and he goes down into the earth, step by step. With each step, the stalk above him disappears. Like this . . ." He picked up a small chalk stone and, in the flashlight glow, scratched the rough shape of a stalk on the boulder. He placed a pebble on it and told Freddy the pebble was the Climber, traveling down its length, then erased the stalk above the pebble as it moved down. He rubbed out the whole stalk finally, as the soul descended . . . to where? At the bottom of the stalk he drew a question mark and placed the pebble next to it.

"Then this Climber," he said, "goes on alone to the Secret Place."

Freddy stared at him. "He never climbs back up?"

"No."

"Daddy won't climb back up?"

Boyd knelt beside her. "Fred, no. Dad's not coming back."

Freddy pulled away, stood up very straight, and looked searchingly into their faces.

"I dream my own ways of Daddy," she said. "My own ways."

She walked away, found a smooth rock with a bowl-shaped niche just her size, curled up into a ball, and fell abruptly, deeply asleep.

"Is she okay?"

"Yes. She does that when things are just too much for her."

Will looked at the small, sad form, asleep in her loneliness, and felt the familiar sense of failure that attended, always, his talk about death. Signe's face rose before him, then evaporated.

"Thanks for the beanstalk."

"Afraid it didn't help much."

"I hate to tell you this, Dr. Death, but nothing helps much. You haven't noticed that in your many dealings with the Bereaved?"

"Don't call me that."

Boyd glanced at him.

"Let's sit down," he said, motioning at a table-like rock. They sat gingerly, then relaxed, leaning back against the stone wall, sighing companionably. Boyd shot her light beam up at the ceiling. A vibrating shape leaped in the air near their heads. They ducked, and it swung away into the darkness.

"Bat." Will shot his light into the deep veils of black. Nothing.

Boyd set down her light and pulled a pack of cigarettes from her back pocket, offered him one.

He shook his head. "You're still smoking?"

"Not really. Just off and on since Russell died. It seems to fit the drama of the situation."

She puffed in silence and shivered a little. "I went to see Griggs."

"I know."

"He told you? What we talked about?"

"No, of course not. He just mentioned that you'd . . . come by."

"He talked to me about Russell."

She talked quietly, smoking, about the morning Russell had

died. She repeated the story as if it were courtroom testimony—how Gerda had arrived at the house just a few minutes after she herself had come up the drive. Gerda had seemed indomitable: She'd commanded Boyd to go inside, lie down, and had then dismissed the paramedics.

"While I was inside," Boyd said, "she must have called the physician who'd been treating Russell, and when he arrived, she informed the paramedics that Russell was his patient and they packed up. The jerk failed to mention any of this when I called him.

"That was that." Boyd stared at the tip of her burning cigarette. "And then you filed the death certificate and sent it to that doctor to sign."

"Well, sure," Will murmured defensively. "I did what was expected of me."

"And so did I."

He looked at her. Her face was streaked with dirt and her eyes looked like bruises in the reflected light.

"Gerda somehow knew that morning. By intuition or logic, knowing his heart condition, as she did, she figured out that he was going to do . . . something."

Will reached over and touched her hand, a request for a puff of her cigarette. It was a gesture so intimate that he froze as he realized what he was doing as he held out his hand.

Boyd handed over the cigarette without noticing his expression. "Griggs said he'd taken digitalis. There was a little left in his pocket. He didn't think it was suicide, just a challenge to fate. He doesn't consider suicide a crime, in any case. He considers it a choice."

"Griggs doesn't recognize any law but the dead's law."

"That's right. He saw that Russell had made a choice. Revved up his heart, took the gamble. Then took the consequences."

He handed the cigarette back. Boyd glanced at him. He looked at his watch. "We should go back soon. It's getting late."

They didn't move. Freddy stirred in her niche, then went back to sleep.

"Does it get a lot colder at night in here?"

"The temperature stays constant—fifty-three degrees."

Boyd hugged herself and shivered again. "It's like living in the city's lost memory."

"Yeah, you go down here, people forget you."

"The thing is," she said, "I can't forget him."

"Nobody can forget him. People loved him."

"People are stupid."

"You do remind me of my sister."

She got up, walked over to check on Freddy, turned back. "I'm not your dead sister, Will."

"I didn't say that, did I?"

"You don't have to."

Will laughed. The laugh echoed, a cackling and recackling, like a fake ghoul's laugh. "She wasn't old enough to have been anyone. I wouldn't know her if she was alive and walked up to me now."

"Of course you would. She was like me—a smart-ass, huh?"

"It's uncanny. You do say things that she actually did say."

He didn't finish. He seemed distracted suddenly. He stood up and retrieved his pack from a little distance away on the ground. He patted the pockets, looking for something. Then he stopped and looked at Boyd.

"It isn't just Signe," he said. "It's everything. A goddam baby casket reduces me to tears. An *anti-abortion sign*."

"I don't want to hear this."

"How do you know what I . . ."

"You were going to say how abortion now takes away the great respect for life that people used to have. Like the respect they once had for the dead—you know, back in the days when they popped their stiffs on the dinner table and sewed the shroud around them, if you'll pardon me. But it's not the same. With the dying you watch, watch how they disappear. But the unborn are climbing up the same stalk. They're climbing up and sometimes they only get so far. The living have power over that beanstalk, women have power over it, because that beanstalk is *the mother's body*."

She felt tears starting. "The mother's body, the woman's body. Same thing, Will."

She wiped her eyes and put out the cigarette. "Russell lied to me. He lied to me about everything. He fucked up, he complicated my life. But he understood about the beanstalk."

"You know, I do nothing but lie to people. *Yes, your drunken, abusive, son-of-a-bitch father was the best old man on earth; yes, your cancer-riddled kid is an angel in heaven; yes, yes, your sunken shell of a mother looks beautiful.* Yes. To all of it. But I can't lie about dead babies. It gets to me. *That's* death that shouldn't have happened. And I have had enough death. You know? Do you know what I mean?"

Boyd stood up. "I was performing an abortion procedure a long time ago, when I was a resident in New York, and it all went wrong and the patient died. Her heart. That was how I knew I couldn't make it as a doc. After she died, I couldn't continue treating people."

"*You* performed abortions?"

She nodded in his direction. "Yeah, I *did*. See these hands? They're trained in life and death."

Will shook his head back and forth, slowly. "You did *that* for a living?"

"And what about *you*? You clean out the pockets of the dead, pal."

"It's what I *do*."

"So was my job. Giving women—"

"A choice? Right. Explain what choice the unborn child has."

"It's not a child, is it? It's an intention."

"What do you do with the bodies? Of the intentions?"

"Bodies? Oh. We don't embalm them. We give them back to the God of Intentions."

They stared at each other, but they'd stopped hearing each other. How long could they go on, singing their different and parallel sorrows?

Then Will bowed his head. She saw the tears, though he brushed them quickly away. "Listen to me. What's on my mind is just this: *wrong* choices. I couldn't leave my sister there in the snow. She was dying, but there was a chance that if I'd gone for help, she'd have lived. But I stayed with her. She asked me to. Still, I keep thinking—every day of my life—why didn't I *do* more?"

"Maybe you should have gotten medical assistance. Maybe human intervention in *fate* would have saved her, Dr. Death."

Then his face broke her heart.

"No. You did the right thing. It was below freezing. She had a head wound. She was *gone*, Will."

Will rubbed his eyes. "The Lakota came down here and talked to the Spirit."

"And now you're talking to me."

"Yeah," he said, and smiled sadly. "I'm talking to *you*. And not getting anywhere."

"You're getting somewhere. Could you please hand me one of those—what are they? Fig Newtons? If you don't mind?"

He pulled the cookies out of one of the pack pockets and opened the cellophane.

Boyd sat down again and they each ate one without speaking.

"I'd been thinking all this time that you were in the wrong job, Will. But, you know, I see it now, I see how you . . ." She lifted her shoulder to her cheek, hunched it as if it were a wing, brushed away a tear with it. ". . . you have a gift."

Suddenly Freddy stood before them. "I will see this beanstalk then when I die—right, Will?"

They sprang apart. Will, dazed, acting his part, reached down quickly into the pack, pulled out a wrapped chicken sandwich, and held it out to her. Freddy hesitated, then accepted it slowly, sniffing delicately.

"That's right, Freddy."

"That day, when I die, I will climb down and I will see Daddy again, right?"

Will looked at Boyd, who was gazing at Freddy.

"Yes," said Boyd. "When that time comes, a long time from now, a hundred years from now, for you to climb down the beanstalk—you'll see him again."

"I will see my daddy."

"Yes, Freddy," said Boyd, brushing the damp hair from her brow. "Then you will see Daddy again."

"And, Mom, when you climb down, you'll see Daddy again too?"

Boyd's hand stilled, then it resumed its tender shaping of her face. "We'll all see Daddy again, Freddy. There's no doubt in my mind."

They ate quickly, cleared up, and began gathering up the pack and the flashlights. No one glanced back at the niche where Freddy had been napping. Norman, the plastic doll, a refugee from the dollhouse, lay there on his back, where Freddy had carefully placed him. He wore an expression of surprise, perhaps joy, on his face. His arms were outstretched, flying at last toward the great descending root as it twisted deeper into the rock and downward.

Climbing out of the cave, Boyd thought of herself in the cremation urn room with Griggs, saw herself weeping, hunched into herself, after reading his notes on Russell—how Griggs had found the digitalis in his clothes, the heart speed in evidence throughout his body.

Griggs had put his hand on her shoulder; he'd wanted to tell her a story. He'd thought it might interest a medical person like herself—familiar as she was with the disposal of bodies, body parts. Hospital lab storage and incineration. Boyd had wiped her eyes and stared up at him, incredulous. A woman had once come to him with an aborted fetus and asked him to embalm it.

Boyd's tears stopped. "You turned her away. You sent her off, right?"

Griggs smiled. "Oh no. I embalmed the little body. I did what she asked. She had bought a white baby casket. She put the remains in it and buried it. I don't know where. She weeps over that grave, wherever it is."

He had lifted his hand from her shoulder. She recalled his touch and lifted her shoulder now, brushed her cheek.

"It's all done for the living," he'd said. "And don't you see? The living are *blind*. My motto has always been: Let those who understand the dead bury the dead."

CHAPTER 31

B OYD HAD EXPECTED SCREAMING, but they were silent. The members of Operation Rescue and assorted other right-to-life groups stood quietly behind yellow police tape and stared. Their signs bobbed up and down, some fluttering in the breeze, their ghastly accusations oddly muted: MURDERER!! PLEASE, MOTHER, LET ME LIVE! HOW WILL YOU FEEL AFTER THIS, MOMMY DEAREST??

The silence maintained itself until the other side's ranks began to swell. Boyd stood in the parking lot, watching as women from Fight Back, a feminist group, began lining the sidewalks on either side of the clinic door, a peaceful method of obstructing the view of the opposition. They lined up, with their white armbands, like MPs, not looking at one another, chins out, arms at their sides. They were mostly college girls, but there were others—a few older women, one in a nurse's uniform. One woman had brought her two daughters, who waited, alert, at her side, in kneesocks and plaid skirts. Three policemen stood with crossed arms at strategic points, indicating the distance that had to be maintained, by law, between the two groups.

Boyd looked around the parking lot. She was waiting for a particular car, a particular driver. A turquoise sedan pulled up, parked quickly, and a tired-looking woman in a print skirt and blazer stepped out, straightened her shoulders, and began walking toward the clinic. As she neared the walkway, Boyd realized that the demonstrators had only been lying low, conserving energy for the outburst that followed. As the woman neared, they pushed forward all at once against the police tape with a rising cacophony, like a flock of hungry seabirds. They chopped the air with their signs, and Boyd heard their catcalls and entreaties clearly: *"Come on, Mommy, don't do it! Don't kill me! Don't kill me! Hey, lady, wake up! They're going to kill your baby in there! There's blood on their hands! Turn around! Choose life!"* they shouted. Some raised lurid color photos of tiny body parts— arms and legs and heads—labeled as products of vacuum curettage. A fat man with a ring in his ear rattled a glass jar, the inevitable pickled occupant curled inside.

The policemen raised their nightsticks in a pantomime of intent. They pointed to unruly individuals and made them step out of the walkway. They scrutinized all hand gestures, each sudden move—earlier, they'd searched everyone for sophisticated weapons, as well as brickbats, rocks, and broken glass. There was a bomb-sniffing dog, a cheerful German shepherd, which now sat on the sidelines, smiling and panting.

Then Boyd saw the car she'd been looking for pull into the lot—an old white Honda, with Sunny at the wheel. It was her mother's car. She waved at Boyd, then got out slowly, brushing off her clothes—a heroic effort to appear collected, Boyd thought. She wore an anonymous outfit: jeans and a peacoat, her red-and-blue hair pulled back and clipped, her ear bangles and nose ring gone, her glasses held in place with an elastic band, her sweet, froggy face grave.

She took Boyd's arm, her grasp tightening as they walked past the parking lot entrance and across the street. The right-to-lifers' heads turned as one. Boyd felt their unified scrutiny.

It was still fairly silent as they stepped from the curb and started up the walk to the door. Then a low, almost melodious woman's voice crooned: "Baby killer."

Sunny gripped her arm; Boyd stared straight ahead.

The cries started, rising. Someone threw a bruised-looking rubber doll, dripping bright red poster paint, in front of them. The doll landed faceup in front of them and stared, then one eye closed.

The police moved in quickly, isolating the man who'd thrown the doll. Clinic workers, some in street dress, some in white lab coats, opened the doors and called to them, hands outstretched.

"Please move quickly," they cried. "Keep your head down. Don't speak to them. Don't let them upset you. Move quickly."

Boyd scanned the contorted faces on either side. Toward the edge of the right-to-life crowd, a thin woman stood by herself, passionately weeping. The tears poured down her face, ran down her neck into her clothes. She did not look up; she didn't notice anyone around her. Her grief was entirely private, even in the midst of this public display. As Sunny and Boyd passed, she looked up: a fleeting tortured glance into Boyd's eyes.

"It's okay," Boyd called to her softly. "Cry. It's okay."

Sunny shot her a betrayed look. In her nervousness, she'd

loosened the restraining band and her glasses sat askew again on her nose. "You talked to her?"

"Because I think tears are the one thing we have in common."

Just as they neared the doors, a man shouted, "God is watching you, you killer!" And then: "Go in there and I'll blow your brains out."

"A gun?" asked Boyd, turning around, giving in to a terrible impulse. "To help preserve life?"

The man opened his mouth just as the attendants unlatched the security gate, but no sound came out. He ducked under the yellow tape suddenly, swiveling himself down and under, and stood before them. He was broad-shouldered but stooped in his faded plaid shirt and he stank of sweat. He was breathing quickly, and Boyd glimpsed pieces of him—his badly chapped lips, a shaving scar near the lips, the damp sweat stains at the armpits of his shirt, his belly—as he lunged toward Sunny and pushed his face into hers.

"Get away!" Boyd shouted. She grabbed his arm and pulled him halfway around, but he swung back mechanically, hinge-like, to Sunny's side, lowering his mouth to the girl's ear, baring his teeth as if to bite her.

Boyd came at him again, pounding him as she heard him say in a calm, dead voice to Sunny, even as he flinched at each blow, "You go in there and have that abortion, you little bitch—I'll tear your cunt right out of you."

Boyd pushed him with all her strength, and he turned, snarling, and swung at her. He snapped her head back with his fist, stopped her cold. Boyd looked at Sunny, stunned. She felt warm blood moving over her lip. She tried to speak but could not.

Sunny had been hunched over all this time—Boyd had thought she was sobbing. Now she lifted her face and Boyd saw that it was distorted with an indescribable emotion. She rose up on her toes with a kind of balletic grace, moved toward the man as if to strike him, then faked him out by shifting sideways, throwing him off balance, then she lifted her knee fast and hard to his groin.

He grabbed himself and bent over, roaring, but he reached out and grabbed Boyd's leg as he swayed down. *Come on,* thought Boyd. *Come on, you scumbag.* She kicked her leg free of his grasp. She saw the protesters outside Columbia, she saw the daggers and skull and crossbones, the spit on her arm. She kicked the man in the side, hard, with her wooden leg. She was yelling something, her heart pounding so hard she didn't hear or see the two police officers who exploded through the screaming crowd at last. They surrounded the man, pinned his arms behind him, and shoved him back, still bent over, through the tape.

He shouted back over his shoulder: "You're on our list! You're *next*!"

A panting Hispanic officer, a woman, asked Boyd if she was okay and if she wanted to press charges, but Boyd shook her head, putting her hand to her nose, where the blood had already dried. She spotted Sunny at last, slumped against her car in the parking lot.

Boyd ran, bumping into people, struggling to hold her emotions in check. She'd wanted to hurt the man in the plaid shirt. She'd wanted to kill him. The extraordinary release she'd felt striking him stayed with her, clarified her vision, and made her blood pump faster in her veins.

Sunny waited for her, silent, leaning her head against the car door. "Cripes," she said. "You've got blood on your face. The guy was trying to kill you." She stared at the man who'd attacked them, now handcuffed and stepping up into a police van, three officers around him.

"What's the matter with him?" she asked.

Boyd, panting, followed her gaze, wiping blood from her nose with a wadded handkerchief. "I don't know," she said. "I don't know what's the matter with him."

Sunny closed her eyes, reached into her bag, and pulled out her mother's car keys. "I've fought a lot of fights, but I can't walk past those people again right now. Isn't there some way to just fly overhead and drop in?"

"It's okay," said Boyd, and touched her arm. "Don't worry. We'll work it out."

CHAPTER 32

THE BABY HAD TURNED AROUND as if it wanted to start back up the birth canal—as if it had gotten a glimpse of this world and decided to renege on the contract—and gotten stuck tight. When Boyd reached into the canal, she felt its tiny, slippery haunches: a classic breech presentation.

"You've got to come out, little one," she murmured, bent over, and the mother groaned above her.

Carey Anderson had been in labor for a few hours before coming to the hospital. Her regular doctor was Remington, who was out of town at an early-October conference—the baby hadn't been expected for three days. Carey, the prima gravida, had been given imprudent advice by the receptionist in the office when she'd called to say she was in labor. The receptionist had determined that the patient was not in labor. ("First babies take a long time," she'd said, laughing, echoing what she'd heard around the office.)

This first baby had decided not to take a long time. The day-long "winces" Carey Anderson said she'd felt turned out to be real labor contractions. Following the receptionist's advice, she'd waited through the pains, then suddenly everything happened at once. The "bloody show" appeared, her water broke, and the contractions dropped to five, then three, minutes apart. The light dinner she'd had with her husband—who stood by now, his eyes, over the surgical mask, frightened and dark—a meal eaten on the receptionist's blithe advice—reappeared dramatically in the form of projectile vomiting.

Her husband, frantic, had phoned the office and reached the doctor on call—Boyd—who told him to get his wife to the hospital immediately. She'd meet them.

Boyd called home and asked the baby-sitter from St. Catherine's to stay late.

"There's a baby that wants to come into our world," she whispered to Freddy, using their familiar description. "She's in a hurry."

The baby had been in such a hurry that after being "held back" and squeezed up and down in the birth canal—"Ask her to try not to push," Boyd had instructed the terrified husband—for a few hours, it was now stuck.

It was stuck tight in breech position—Boyd could not move it up or down with her gloved hands. Though the nurse indicated the lubricated Piper forceps on the tray, she shook her head.

"Come on, Mom," she said to Carey, who was weeping in pain and frustration. "Let's push."

"I can't do it." Carey's hair was soaked with sweat and her arms waved helplessly above the fetal monitor belt, an electronic cummerbund cinched just under her breasts.

Jess, the nurse, patted her hands back down.

"Okay," said Jess. "We're set up for a section. Let's take her."

Carey wanted to have a vaginal birth. At the mention of a C-section, she pursed her lips, her lower teeth biting in, tensed her body, and bore down.

Boyd felt the canal walls ripple, and the baby shuddered a little in her hands. Then the fetal monitor spiked up: The heartbeat was accelerating, indicating possible fetal distress. Jess cleared her throat and put her hand on the forceps again, her eyes on the delivery room clock. As soon as the heartbeat slowed, they would be on their way to the C-section. There was another contraction and, amazingly, the fetal heartbeat slowed to normal.

Carey pushed suddenly and the baby began to move. Boyd could feel its crossed feet, its bent knees, and its thighs. She tried flexion and abduction of the right thigh to free one of the legs. But the little body was still stuck, and the fetal monitor shrilled again. This time the heartbeat did not come down as quickly, and Jess and the daddy looked at her over their masks.

"Just *this* and then we'll go," Boyd murmured. She'd learned a commonsense breech-extraction technique in med school: put pressure on the thigh, then pressure in the popliteal fossa, the furrow of the knee, causing the knee to flex, then extend. When the baby stuck out its leg, delivery could be accomplished leg first by traction on the foot.

She pressed on the fossa of the knee and rotated the baby slightly as the leg popped out, then tugged on the foot with her

other hand, pulled carefully, steadily, on the foot, kept pulling. Slowly, slowly, as the mother pushed, the baby came out
of the womb, feet first, with a sucking noise, as Carey gasped
and the new dad staggered back, then forward, exulting, shouting. He had a large camera and several lenses slung around his
neck but had forgotten all that.

After the shoulders and arms appeared, Boyd rotated the
body until the spine was beneath and the head in the occiput
anterior position. Jess moved in, helping to turn and extract the
head.

As soon as the face presented itself, she was ready with the aspirator, cleaning mucus out of the nose and mouth as Boyd
lifted the baby free on its pulsing umbilical line.

Carey tried to sit up and hold out her arms.

Boyd patted the tiny bloody posterior, and the mouth
opened, sound came out, the legs and arms began to wave.

Boyd looked into the eyes, dark and nervous as the daddy's.
"Welcome to the world, kiddo. Glad you decided to come out."

B OYD STEPPED OUT of the elevator, sipping coffee from a
paper cup, and glanced at the clock in the lobby. There was
still time. She turned to a bank of telephones and punched in a
number, then spoke quickly, looking at her watch again.

Twenty minutes later, she opened the offices of Remington and
Resnikoff with her key, stopped the beeping of the security system with a swift series of numbers fed into the wall panel. She
flipped on the lights, then strode down the hall to one of the
procedure rooms. As she paused in the doorway, there was a

quick knock at the front door. She retraced her steps, opened the door, and Sunny, dressed in a dark raincoat and a Mickey Mouse scarf, came into the reception area.

"Come in, kiddo," she said, reaching out and pushing her glasses gently back up on her nose. "This way."

In the room where she'd examined pregnant women, infertile women, and menopausal women, Boyd washed her hands, pulled on gloves and scrubs, examined and prepped Sunny on the table, and set up an IV line to administer a little Versed—and in order to have an open intravenous line in case anything went wrong.

The girl watched Boyd move about the room—at the sink washing her hands again, setting up the IV bottle, arranging her speculum, cannulae, dilators; as she prepared the tray of instruments, as she injected the sedative into the IV line.

Boyd explained suction curettage to her.

Sunny listened, a dark expression on her face.

"I don't want to forget this," she said. "I want to remember this."

"Well, the drug might erase a bit, but you'll still remember what you need to."

After a few seconds, Sunny began to relax a little, then relaxed completely.

Boyd checked her breathing, then began to dilate the cervix with instruments, checking over her shoulder, looking for a suction cannula of the right diameter to enter the uterine cavity. She found the cannula, hooked up the aspirator, and began the suction pressure inside the uterus.

"Products of conception," Boyd murmured to herself as the aspirator began pulling away tissue from the lining of the uterus. "Products of conception," as the pregnancy broke apart, tissue and cartilage and bone bits and placental tissue.

She kept her mind on her work. She let no thought enter her mind other than what she knew about the size and position of the uterus, the volume of its contents, what she knew about the integrity of the internal os, the decrease in uterine size at evacuation. Though Sunny was almost at twelve weeks, the procedure was safe—Boyd had examined her carefully.

"The procedure is safe," she said to herself, then checked her hands. They were shaking only a little.

Sunny half woke, stirred, spoke to Boyd about her mother, then drifted away again.

Boyd continued until she was certain the uterus was fully evacuated, then performed a quick instrumental curettage of the uterine cavity. Then she lifted the girl's legs from the stirrups, slipped a sanitary pad between her thighs, and clipped it to a thin elastic belt that she drew up and under her waist. She began sponging up blood from the steel table, threw away the soaked absorbent paper cloths, stopped to check Sunny's vital signs, her pulse and breathing. She disconnected the IV.

As she shifted the IV pole, she accidentally bumped up against the light switch. The room went dark, except for the lit panel of the phone, the green ciphers of the digital clock, and pale light reflected from the courtyard lamps below.

Boyd stood in the darkness facing the window, then turned suddenly, intuitively. She felt someone in the room.

He stood quietly, perfectly still, looking at her.

"Well," said Boyd. "I knew you'd be here."

He moved closer and Boyd nodded at him.

———

Sunny groaned, slowly waking up.

"I figured it out. I was the ghost, not you."

There was, far away, the sound of car horns in the street, the sound of the wind picking up.

"I should have touched you."

Suddenly, her breath would not come. She gasped and tears came to her eyes. "I'd like to touch you now."

He moved his hand from his heart and held it out to her.

"Then you can go."

He hesitated, then she felt the conscious summoning of energy drawing close to her. She held out her hands to him, still in surgical gloves, trembling. Now he was here: a humming silhouette at her side, though she could no longer see him, his body, *him*, Russell, his eyes, his mouth. She pulled off a glove and put her hand to her face. Then she felt another touch, *his* touch, on her brow, light as a kiss. Then, on her cheek, she felt his finger drawn along the declivities of her familiar lines of expression. *Like the intelligent fingers of the blind.* Like Tina Coburn's fingers touching her face delicately as she visited her in pre-op. *I have faith in you, Doc. You're my lucky charm.*

I'm a smoke-and-mirrors kind of guy.

Then, as Sunny moaned again and called out, Boyd thrust both hands out in front of her and he took them. She felt something close quickly around them, one of her hands still gloved, one not. She felt the steady pressure on her fingers—he was stopping them from shaking. She bent her head over her hands, his invisible grasp, and placed her lips on that grasp—across the line between life and death. He was holding her hands in his, still.

They'd stopped shaking; they were at rest. She kissed the air where he stood. She pressed her lips to the solid fact of this longing.

Then he was gone—like what? Like a fire in a mirror, gone out. She lifted her hands, but he had vanished, and she felt, for the first time, the absolute finality of his absence. She backed up to the wall, flicked the lights back on, reaching awkwardly behind her.

Then Sunny woke up, coming back into consciousness sobbing, cursing in Swedish. Grateful, free, *the products of conception gone, the presence of the dead gone*—her young, answerable life back in her own hands.

CHAPTER 33

ERDA SAT IN A LARGE, slatted wooden chair outside near the bird feeder. She was hunched over a white steaming cup. When Boyd first called her name from the patio doorway, she did not look up. The pressure of Boyd's hand on her shoulder startled her. She sat up straight, nearly spilling her coffee.

"Gerda, I'm sorry. Were you asleep?"

Gerda stared into space, moving her head dazedly to and fro, rubbing her eyes with her free hand. Boyd hadn't seen her since their meeting in Bud Skoglund's office a month earlier, but Gerda seemed unaware of lapsed time. "Oh. *Boyd.* I'm so glad you're here. I have something for you."

She looked altered, Boyd thought. Her radiant confidence, her white-haired athletic grace, seemed vanished; Gerda looked as if she had aged years. The hand she put out to Boyd trembled and the cup rattled in her lap.

Boyd set aside the cup, accepted the shaking hand.

Gerda stood up with her support, looking about, distracted. "I have it here somewhere. I put it . . ."

"Gerda, it's all right. We'll find it later."

"No. I have it right here, somewhere."

Her unsteadiness began to alarm Boyd. She watched Gerda totter uncertainly from her chair to the garden wall to the brick walkway, where she swayed in place, then hurried past a bank of wildly blooming blue bachelor's buttons to a stone prie-dieu, upon which a large album rested. The album was plucked up with a bird-like alacrity, and Gerda turned to her, hunched, triumphant, clutching her prize.

"Is that what you were after?"

"It's his baby book. I finally found it, after years! It had fallen behind a panel in the old chifforobe. It's uncanny—Freddy was the image of him at birth!"

She grew animated, waving the book, her eyes steady on Boyd, who took it from her, smiling. Then she guided Gerda back to her chair. "How about if we sit for a minute?"

"Don't you want to look at it?"

"Of course. Just give me a second."

They sat quietly. Gerda took Boyd's hand possessively and held it, looking away from her, her eyes shut. After a while, Boyd gently freed her hand, lifted the heavy baby book from her lap, and glanced at the cover. *Russell* was written in gilt script across the front. A breeze rippled the sycamores; leaves scattered over the wooden Adirondack furniture and the glass-topped wrought-iron table and littered Gerda's neglected breakfast tray: blood-orange sections, a bright yellow ceramic dish of plum jam, two slices of pale toast.

Boyd paused as a leaf floated down, settling on the sugar bowl. They sniffed the air tentatively.

"Winter," said Boyd, shivering. "Already. You can smell it."

Gerda looked up at the moving treetops. "Early this year."

Boyd watched Gerda drift away again. She turned pages. Here was Russell, newborn, the resemblance to Freddy predictable but mildly disturbing: the same gaze, the same fringe of hair, the same perfect mouth. Then Russell in a long, flowing white christening gown dandled by his poppa, an abstracted-looking Thaddeus, then relatives raising champagne glasses, and Gerda, a youngish Gerda, in high heels and a short-veiled cloche, her hair still dark, with delicate streaks of white, standing with Russell's siblings, her arm around the oldest. They had all moved far enough away, thought Boyd, except for Russell. Then Russell in his pram, his stroller—what Boyd's family had called a Taylor Tot—Russell in his high chair gumming rusks—what Boyd's family had called zwieback—Russell's sandbox, Russell's first step. He was laughing into the camera, his father behind him, holding out his hands like a magician releasing a dove. Boyd noticed that Gerda did not appear in many of the photographs—she wondered if Gerda had been behind the lens or if she had been off with the other children. Some of the holiday and school pictures were posed studio shots; they showed smiling, denatured faces.

She flipped through the pages: Russell at four and five and six, in a growing-out crew cut and too-big striped swimming trunks, Gerda, slim, at his side; behind them, the glittering pool, a towel on the ground next to a puddle transfigured by sun. Boyd noticed a change in him. He had grown from a fearless, pudgy toddler to a thoughtful, dreamy, pensive little boy. His eyes were cast down in most of these later photographs, his smile tentative. He was already thinking hard. Like Freddy.

Boyd looked up. Gerda was watching her with a greedy expression, barely breathing. Boyd smiled at her.

"I came over," she said, "because I want to apologize."

She closed the heavy book, nudged the tray aside, and leaned across the table.

"You were right. I should have just let it go. Russell was who he was—what does it matter finally what caused his death? It doesn't help me to know, for instance . . . what I know. Mr. Griggs, the embalmer, told me he'd taken digitalis to make his heart beat faster. And then he overstrained his heart."

Gerda seemed not to have heard her. Boyd got to her feet, putting out her hand to touch the bark of a huge sycamore. Once, years ago, Russell had shown her his name carved in the bark there, but now she couldn't find it. She ran her hands over the tree's rough armature. It must have been another tree, she thought. The wind picked up again. Leaves stood up on the branches, then dropped and settled, fell into her hair, on her shoulders. She shook them off.

"You told me that he didn't want me to know about his heart. I thought he was trying to punish me . . . by not talking to me, but I think now he didn't tell me because he had some hope— that he could start over. That *we* could."

She did not say what she was thinking—that even as she made this claim on his behalf, it seemed unlikely. *He was a liar, one of the best liars ever: a storyteller, a mirror, a fire.*

She began to pace up and down, her arms crossed over her chest, shivering. She was cold. She could sense the cold air already entering the atmosphere, the first delicate stream, a freshet, from the north. From Canada, from across the Bering Straits. They called that winter wind, bearing snow, the Siberian Clipper.

When Boyd was a child, she'd been forced to bundle up in leggings and scarves. When she went to high school, she and her friends had dressed oddly, rebelliously—the style they culti-vated made them look like Khrushchev and his Politburo on top and bottom: tall fake-fur Siberian hats and ankle-height fur-lined galoshes, called Kickereenos, which winged back at the an-kles. But they rolled their uniform skirts up high and kept their legs, blue with cold, bare all winter. It had something to do with their concept of femininity—the big tall hats, their glum expres-sions, the pale, vulnerable legs. As if one part of the body lan-guished in the tropics, a promise of sexual paradox. Boyd had never gotten completely warm again.

"Gerda?" Boyd sat down again. She picked up an orange sec-tion and nibbled at it unconsciously, twisting the rind in her fingers. "You wanted to talk. I'm trying now."

She realized, glancing up, that Gerda had heard nothing of what she'd said. Boyd watched her nod repeatedly, her eyes bleached as a blind person's.

"He was embezzling."

"What do you mean?"

Gerda nodded again. "He was embezzling money. From himself, from the corporation. Large amounts of money. Not enough to sink anything, but *lots* of money. Principal."

Boyd asked what he was doing with it, and Gerda laughed, then sighed.

"He was giving it away. Just writing checks to . . . delivery-truck drivers and poetry magazines—oh, *especially* poetry magazines, and many poets and people on the street. Beggars, bag ladies. And Cherry, his secretary, and an old Norwegian fellow who sells torsk to the markets."

Boyd sat back in her chair, twisted the orange rind through her fingers. She felt like laughing, but she was afraid of hurting Gerda. "So *that's* what you and Bud Skoglund were trying to tell me that day. All that stuff about—"

"He spent a lot of your family money, though he left Freddy's trust intact. He wouldn't touch that."

"Aren't you glad I have a job now?"

"I have something else to tell you. I saw him the last time he was alive. Early morning of the day he died."

Boyd sat very still. The wind lifted the leaves again and scattered them over the patio. She waited.

"I saw him . . . after you."

"You mean after I told him to die?"

"He rang my doorbell. My God, it was late. Two-thirty or later. I was terrified. He burst in—the dog was barking. I thought there might be an emergency—you or Freddy. Then I realized that he was the one who was in trouble."

"He came over to see you that night?"

"Yes."

They looked at each other, then Boyd laughed. "Go on."

"He was talking, you know, about dying. The worst thing about death, he said to me, very emphatic, was the clichés. He said he couldn't stand all that tedious stuff about tunnels and flashing lights. He told me that he saw people who looked like extras from an Ingmar Bergman film everywhere he looked: bug-eyed trolls and weird Scandinavians."

"Well, that would be kind of routine here in Minnesota."

Gerda nodded. She wasn't listening. "The morning of the day . . . he left Freddy in the park, he'd visited the doctor again. I didn't know this till he came over that night. The doctor told him that the prognosis was much worse than they originally thought. They didn't even want to operate. They thought it was hopeless. And that his heart was too delicate for him to make it through surgery."

Boyd sat forward in her chair. "Are you telling me that before hearing that second diagnosis he was not that bad?"

"His condition was operable. Then it wasn't."

Gerda pulled herself up from her chair and stood slowly. She put a shaking hand on Boyd's shoulder, and Boyd slid from her grasp.

She straightened up, then walked back to the sycamore tree. This time she saw his name. It leaped right out at her—RUSSELL, carved in rough letters. How had she missed it before?

"That last night he came over, he kept talking about how cold he was, how he couldn't get warm, and I told him how he got that way. I confessed."

Boyd nodded. "You mean the high-fever story."

"Yes, but there's more to it than I've ever told you. I had a kind of romantic involvement, and I was with the . . . man the night Russell . . . got so sick. I waited too long before taking him to the hospital, and, my God, his fever went so high! I told him about the hotel room and his tears, about my terrible failure to tend to him till it was almost too late."

"What did he say?"

Gerda put her arms around her waist, holding herself, swaying to and fro. "He told me that he remembered it all. He remembered the hotel room, the scratchy blue blanket on the daybed where I'd left him, how hot he was, how he called for water and no one gave it to him. He said he could see, very clearly, the tin ice bucket, the puddle of melted ice, and the bottles on the bedside table. He said he could almost taste the cold water, the ice, but no one listened to him. Then he looked straight at me and asked me what lesson I thought a child would learn if the one person he expected to always be there for him refused to come to his aid? What kind of sense would the world make to a kid whose mother sat on a bed right across the floor from him as he burned up before her eyes?"

Gerda laughed to herself a little.

"I broke down. Then he pointed a finger at me and laughed. *'Gotcha,'* he said. 'I don't remember a goddam thing about that room. I made it all up—everything. You've gone through your life, Gerda, thinking you ruined me, and I don't even recall one single thing about that night. What a silly fabrication. And you've built your life around it.' "

Gerda sat down heavily in her chair. "He was so strange, Boyd. I don't know how he got to be the way he was."

She paused. "Boyd? I didn't tell you about Russell's heart, because I was being selfish. I wanted to be his mother again. I'd let him go once, you know? He could have been a criminal, he could have been a saint. He grew up wild—he had no rules. He was a creature of impulse. You see, I didn't want him. Of course when I had him, I loved him. But not *carefully*."

The patio door banged open, and Freddy and Towser galloped together across the grass. Freddy waved two chocolate chip cookies, one in each hand, which Towser was attempting to intercept.

"Sweetheart! I didn't know you were here! Come and give Grandma a kiss."

Boyd tried to catch Freddy by the arm, but she danced away with Towser. She blew Gerda a kiss, then disappeared into the house with the dog.

Boyd shook her head. "She was supposed to stay back there with Mrs. Nelson, give us a minute to talk."

"He said that remembering and imagining are the same thing. He said, 'If I die, I'll die the way I want to. It's my choice.' "

Boyd sat down across from her, where she'd started. The wind had picked up. A napkin blew across the table and leaves flew everywhere. Boyd picked up Russell's baby book and held it to her heart. "Time to go inside, Gerda."

"I did what he told me to do. I did it all—the doctor, the death certificate. He wanted no autopsy. He died the way he wanted to."

Boyd fought back each ironic remark that rose to her lips. "You let him go then, Gerda."

"Yes. And so will you."

Freddy's voice rose over the wind. She stood in the doorway. "Momma and Grandma, come now! It's too cold out there!"

*S*AY YOU WERE RICH *and gave away all your money to fools and crazies and so-so poets and arts agencies and poetry societies and bad lit mags living only to perpetuate themselves. Out of*

this gesture might come one good poem—no, one GREAT poem—
about codfish. One good sonnet about a lost Swede town.

And you, wounded by your profession—say you screw up again,
which you will, as any doctor does. You have blood on your hands
and you weep for the dead and even for the cells of the person-to-be,
but this is your work. Blood on your hands. Your work: the living
and the dead.

I know I can't write poems. But what can I do but write poems?

> *Then*
> *all the words signifying history*
> *fell from the sky—*
> > *then the symbols*
> *of science and mathematics,*
> *followed by the words of the great poems.*
>
> Passion *fell and* Property,
> Greek Pi *and* Tao *and* Duende.
>
> *People gathered all the words*
> > *trying to order them,*
> kaddish, suschnost, lilac
> > *in their hands.*
> *Then money fell, with its death's head emblem.*
> *The lilac bush covered with snow.*
> *Then moon, snow, money swirling.*
> > *No wind.*

The absolute silence of my sleeping house. I wave my hat. I like
hurricanes. I like you. I loved you with all my heart, but my heart
wasn't whole. I like the truth: how we never, our whole lives, under-
stand another human being.

THE SCHAEFFER MONUMENT was being installed at the grave site. It had arrived, a gleaming slab of white, un-shadowed Carrara marble, inscribed with a single-line epitaph in the swirling imprimatur of calligraphy—LET BE BE FI-NALE OF SEEM—along with Russell Schaeffer's name and dates. Will had agreed to meet the stonemason and his delivery men at the cemetery, but now he was delayed.

Roger Leland had dropped in on him, carrying a bottle of champagne and a box of musical condoms. It was Will's fortieth birthday. He'd told no one, but somehow word had gotten out. The Pre-Need counselors surprised him with a hat, a classic black bowler. "You can tuck your ponytail under the band," one said, and then, embarrassed, handed him a gift from Priscilla, who was now managing the Anoka branch: a cremation urn that played selections from the Grateful Dead. It was wrapped in Japanese handmade paper.

Griggs sidled in, dressed informally, a party hat on his head. He carried an aftershave scent in a stoppered glass bottle, an elixir of ylang-ylang and embalming fluids, whipped up by the members of the mortuary staff. EAU DE FINALE, the label read. Griggs reappeared later with a copy of his "favorite book" for Will—a volume of empty pages, entitled *The Book of Scandinavian Humor.*

Will had just popped his new bowler on his head—the weather had changed; it was autumn; people were starting to dress more defensively—and was winding a new silk white-and-gray paisley scarf around his neck, a gift from his mother, when Roger appeared.

Will raised his bowler and saluted him with the gift bottle. "I'd offer you a glass, but I have to run out and check on a stone delivery."

"Don't fret. I gotta get back for a night of nonstop tears and recriminations. Baby wake: seven-month-old drowned. The eight-year-old who was minding her left her for a second crawling around next to the wading pool. Just three inches of water and brown leaves, left over from summer. I don't wanna face that one."

They sat quietly for a second, trying not to think about the three inches of water, the eight-year-old's shout.

The phone rang and Will didn't answer.

After a while, he and Roger lit up and smoked some terrible-smelling cigars Will had fished out from the back of his desk drawer.

Roger nodded at him, puffing. "What did you do about Mega-Death?"

"I turned them down. I sat here and listened to all the things they were offering me and I just couldn't do it. Griggs would be forcibly retired, and I'd have to go through that firing scene I had with Sechman and Robideaux a few times over—without due cause, like the AIDS refusal. But as CEO, man, I'd be made for life."

"You should always wear that damn hat—it gives you gravity. Like right now, you need gravity to justify such a wrongheaded stupid-ass nonprogressive decision. Look what you gave up!" He blew a smoke ring and laughed.

"So you gave in and said yes?"

"No, man—I'm with you. I turned them down again last week."

They looked over their propped up feet at each other and whispered, "Shit."

"We're gonna be crushed," Roger said cheerfully, and relit his cigar, squinting through the drift of smoke.

"No damn doubt," said Will. "They're gonna bury us, if you'll pardon the expression."

"Some days, Will? I don't think I want to do this anymore. Life is one big open casket."

"What happened the other night when I couldn't make it to the wake?"

"What wake?"

"The parents who died in the car crash. One of the daughters was going to sing."

"She did sing, beautifully. Except the last hymn—'Soul Don't Tarry,' her mother's favorite. She sang half, then just sobbed through the other half."

"But she sang."

"Yeah, she did. She sang."

"I gotta go to the cemetery," cried Will, swinging his feet down.

"Are you celebrating your birthday tonight?"

"It depends."

He rode his motorcycle through the cemetery gates, leaning into the gentle turns of pavement, past stone angels and Christs, flowerpots and wreaths, past official-looking oaks and clumps of poplar and birch near the carved mausoleums, and into the parking lot. He decelerated, so that the noise of his engine wouldn't offend grieving visitors. He parked the bike near the edge of the lot, where a manicured stretch of grass unfolded to a newer-looking, unplotted area. The "realistic" statue of a deer he'd noticed at the periphery of his vision straightened suddenly and light-footed away.

He could see the new gravestone from where he stood, the fold of freshly dug soil, the rather bald look to its placement on the rise. The wind picked up suddenly and blew a green plastic wreath, dark ribbon flapping, across a raked-gravel walkway.

Then he saw the two figures, a woman and a little girl, approaching the grave. They were carrying flowers. The little girl, who was hurrying, dropped her bouquet and bent to pick it up. The woman stooped to help her. Then they moved again, more slowly, more carefully, glancing at the headstones, the flowers, and the handful of brightly colored, spinning pinwheels, which were forbidden but which popped up anyway.

Will watched, leaning against a car, his new bowler on his head, his musical condoms in his pocket, along with the form on which Boyd had boldly printed *Let be be finale of seem.* He assumed the inscription was correct. Boyd and Freddy stood staring at it, and lay their flowers down before it. He watched as Freddy knelt on the newly sodded grass of the grave and, putting her hands around her mouth like a megaphone, spoke loudly and at some length to the earth. Boyd sat down on the grass next to her and every so often touched her hair.

Will thought he felt what Russell would be feeling if he could feel. He wanted to join the two of them, he wanted to talk with them and put his hand on their faces. He wanted to listen to Freddy's high-pitched running commentary and Boyd's clear-amber throat sounds, her laughter. He wanted to guide Freddy's finger in and out of the runnels of stone, spelling out the letters of the epitaph, reading its message by touch. But he did not do these things. He stayed apart, an observer.

Later, in another place, he might offer Boyd a glass of champagne, tell her it was his birthday, without once mentioning that it was his dead sister's as well. The dead, the living. *It's all stories,* he thought: *all resemblances out of which we make other resemblances.* He wanted to walk briskly to them, to wave. *I'm too good at this now,* he thought—*too good at standing by the grave, expressionless, watching the coffin descending.*

"Wait," he murmured, "wait"—a faint sound in his throat—and then he straightened up and began striding toward them, covering the distance quickly, then gently let his voice out over the stones and flowers as he drew closer.

As the choir's last note faded, Reverend Marshall nodded three times somberly—first to the choir, then to the flower-covered casket, then to the sizable crowd of mourners before him. He grasped the pulpit and quietly exhorted the assemblage to remember their own mortality just as they were here today remembering the mortal life of Sister June Sarah Planke.

Roger Leland, standing at the back of the church, signaled to his funeral-service staff and parish ushers to begin passing out the heart-shaped, basket-weave hand fans. It was hot in the church, even though it was late October—they were in the middle of Indian summer. He studied the mourners in their great flowered hats, African prints, and patent-leather shoes and purses as they passed the fans, chattering a little. A little wind began to circulate through the nave almost immediately as people drew back and gestured at themselves.

Roger had known Sister June, as she was called. She wasn't as old as Euphrosyne Miller, but everyone was familiar with her. She had been around since the old neighborhood, since Rondo, where they had come to her for everything.

She had been a midwife—she used the old remedies, herbs and elixirs and poultices. Many in the church of St. Peter Claver, whose stone likeness stared into the crowd, had had reason to seek her out. There were people who feared her. And to be fair, she had been a bit forbidding—her high brow and ginger hair wrapped in a head rag, her mouth set. Swift and unflinching was her severing of the throbbing umbilical, her recovery of the placenta; unexpected was her sudden breaking into song—old hymns, scat—as she performed her duties. She put up mixtures in stoppered vials to ease childbed fever and to "call blood" when a period was late. And more. She cursed and laughed immoderately. She was not exactly loved, but she was respected—and she would be missed. Roger, who had once had occasion, long ago, to stand trembling with a trembling companion on her doorstep, would miss her too.

Now, the Bereaved—a niece and a very old cousin and a woman who had been June's friend for fifty years—took turns speaking. The friend raised her hands and cried out occasionally. People shouted "A-men!" back to her. And then the choir hummed again and settled on a note.

They sang "We Are Climbing the Ladder." A girl, a young woman for whom the community had high hopes, stepped forward. She had a beautiful voice, and she sang a solo made up of clear blue notes that rose high above the altar crucifix, up to the painted ceiling and beyond. Her gaze was radiant, fixed. Roger forgot his duties for a moment and stared at her. Suddenly, he thought of his friend Will and the woman with whom he'd spent his birthday. Death had made Will a longtime loner, and Roger fervently hoped that now his life would change.

He closed his eyes, listening to the lovely voice, thinking of his old friend, and then jumped, startling himself. He'd remembered that he had to confer with Reverend Marshall. He moved quietly up the side aisle, and as he drew closer to the sacristy, he saw the soloist's face more clearly. She was weeping as she sang, tears rolling down her cheeks. Why was the young girl crying? he wondered. Could she have known the dead woman? Had she stood on her doorstep, too? How could someone so young sing so thrillingly, and with such control, in the grip of such sorrow?

But that was it, he thought as he smiled at the solemn reverend and shook his hand—that was it. We sing, amazingly, at the same moment in which we suffer. He kept this thought for himself as he moved on to his next task, which was assembling the family, the closest relatives, then the friends, so that they might pass by and offer their farewells to the body of the deceased, one by one.

ACKNOWLEDGMENTS

I thank my sister, Michele Mueller, indefatigable laborer for love. I am deeply grateful to my dear friend Michelle Latiolais, who in a time of grief and confusion helped me by reading and proofing galleys tirelessly, with her amazing discerning eye.

This book would be nothing at all without Daniel Menaker: one-of-a-kind editor, writer, and lover of words. I thank him for being who he is and doing what he does. I also want to thank Lisa Zeidner, for encouraging me to make that "leap of faith," and Molly Friedrich, for being the best agent around. I am also indebted to Olivia Crooke, M.D., for all her help and suggestions. Also, thanks to Pamela Schaff, M.D.

Thanks, too, to Mueller Mortuaries of St. Paul, Minnesota—in particular, Scott Mueller, for his invaluable assistance and advice during my research for this novel. Thanks to the University of Southern California and the Ahmanson Fund for continued support and encouragement. I also wish to acknowledge my friends at Washington University in St. Louis—and the Fanny Hurst Visiting Professorship that allowed me to finish this book.

My thank-you list includes the following friends, who read this novel in manuscript and offered advice and support: Molly

Bendall, Robert Pinsky, Mark Doty, Jill Ciment, Sara Davidson, Louise Glück, Susan Dubs, Erik Jackson, Pam Macintosh. Thanks to Christen Kidd, Veronica Windholz, Diane Melkonian, and Jason Shinder, and to Marie de Vaure of Small World Books for patient and unflagging assistance. Thanks to Kelsey Muske, my niece, for the "small boy" anecdote. And to my mother and father, who remembered Rondo and first introduced me to the woman with the wooden leg.

And to my daughter, Annie—who, with her father, helped read and print out copies of this manuscript, and who has kept me going these last weeks—all my love forever.

ABOUT THE AUTHOR

CAROL MUSKE-DUKES (Carol Muske as a poet) is the author of two previous novels, *Dear Digby* (Viking, 1989) and *New York Times* Notable Book *Saving St. Germ* (Penguin, 1993). She has also published six books of poems—the most recent, *An Octave Above Thunder, New & Selected Poems* (Penguin, 1997), was a finalist for the *Los Angeles Times* Book Prize and a *New York Times* Notable Book. She is professor of English and Creative Writing and Director of the Ph.D. Program in Literature and Creative Writing at the University of Southern California. She has received a Guggenheim Fellowship, a National Endowment for the Arts Fellowship, and an Ingram-Merrill Award, among many other honors. She lives in Los Angeles with her daughter, Annie.

ABOUT THE TYPE

This book was set in Galliard, a typeface designed by Matthew Carter for the Merganthaler Linotype Company in 1978. Galliard is based on the sixteenth-century typefaces of Robert Granjon.